OGILVIE AT WAR

OGILVIE AT WAR

Philip McCutchan

Chivers Press • Thorndike Press
Bath, England   Thorndike, Maine USA

This Large Print edition is published by Chivers Press, England, and by Thorndike Press, USA.

Published in 2000 in the U.K. by arrangement with the author.

Published in 2000 in the U.S. by arrangement with Chivers Press, Ltd.

U.K. Hardcover ISBN 0–7540–4156–5 (Chivers Large Print)
U.K. Softcover ISBN 0–7540–4157–3 (Camden Large Print)
U.S. Softcover ISBN 0–7862–2567–X (General Series Edition)

Previously published 1973 in Great Britain and the USA as *The Red Daniel* under the pseudonym *Duncan MacNeil*.

The text of this Large Print edition is unabridged.
Other aspects of the book may vary from the original edition.

Set in 16 pt. New Times Roman.

Printed in Great Britain on acid-free paper.

British Library Cataloguing in Publication Data available

Library of Congress Cataloging-in-Publication Data

McCutchan, Philip, 1920–
　　　Ogilvie at war / Philip McCutchan.
　　　　　p.　　cm.
　　　ISBN 0–7862–2567–X　(lg. print : sc : alk. paper)
　　　1. Ogilvie, James (Fictitious character)—Fiction.　2. Transvaal (South Africa)—History—War of 1880–1881—Fiction.　3. Scots—South Africa—Transvaal—Fiction.　4. Large type books.　I. Title.
　　　PR6063.A167 O38　　2000
　　　823'.914—dc21　　　　　　　　　　　　　00 028685

CHAPTER ONE

Khaki everywhere: the train, beginning slowly to move with its northward-bound freight, seemed to be chuffing through a sea of uniforms interspersed with the gay dresses of the God-speeding women. It never had taken the British Tommy long to get to know the girls. Tears, brave smiles, bursts of nervous laughter—the last few seconds that might lead to eternity.

Hearty cheers: 'Teach Oom Paul a lesson, lads!'

'Give my love to Kimberley and all those lovely diamonds!'

'Remember Majuba!'

And song; song roared out in splendid manly fashion till it brought fresh tears to women's faces:

> *Goodbye Dolly I must leave you,*
> *Though it breaks my heart to go,*
> *Something tells me I am needed,*
> *At the front to fight the foe,*
> *See, the soldier boys are marching,*
> *And I can no longer stay—*
> *Hark! I hear the bugle calling,*
> *Goodbye Dolly Gray.*

Kilts, stores, horses: all the accoutrements

of war. A real mix-up of regiments: Argyll and Sutherland, Black Watch, Seaforths, Royal Strathspeys. Tall guardsmen—Coldstreams, Grenadiers, Scots. Bush-hatted troopers of the Imperial Light Horse. Plain English queen-of-battles infantry: Northamptons, KOYLI, Northumberland Fusiliers. Gunners. The Cape Town sun shone down on them all regardless, blazing from somewhere over Table Mountain, blazing down on the masts and yards of shipping in the background. From one of the windows of the crowded troop train leaned one of the kilted officers—Captain James Ogilvie of the Royal Strathspeys.

Tips of fingers touched lightly. 'Good-bye, James. Take the greatest care—but teach the Boers a lesson!'

A laugh: 'You can rely on that, Katharine.'

'Don't forget the Red Daniel.'

'You can rely on me for that, too. Good-bye, Katharine.'

'Goodbye . . .' The engine was really pulling now, it had got its grip on the overload. Movement was a trifle faster. James Ogilvie waved and grinned, looking back at the girl on the platform, fashionable in her long dress with leg-of-mutton shoulders, extravagantly hatted and parasolled. She'd landed him with quite a task, but old French's Chief of Staff, Major Douglas Haig, had been insistent that he should give his help. Besides, he had a soft spot for Katharine Gilmour: they'd shared great danger together in the past, in India. It had brought a comradeship . . . James Ogilvie, as the station platform receded, brought himself in from the window and found his thoughts going back to India, now almost three weeks and a good few thousand miles away. From India they had been expecting a posting home on relief, and had been surprised when the Colonel had announced that the regiment had been ordered to the Cape to join the Army Corps under Sir Redvers Buller. The war reports had not been good: the telegraph had brought word that the first news to greet Buller when, on the day before the Colonel's announcement in the Mess, he had disembarked at Table Bay, was that of the defeat of Sir George White at Ladysmith. That town was already under heavy siege, and Kimberley also was threatened. The Colonel's announcement had been well received throughout the regimental lines, despite an undoubted disappointment at not going back to Scotland yet after so many long years of fighting along the North-West Frontier. There was keenness to hit back at Brother Boer. *Kruger watch out—watch out all you whiskery bastards, get back to your stinking farms, we're on our way to give you merry hell!* That was the underlying message behind the wild singing, when the news reached the men, of Soldiers of the Queen.

We're part of England's glory, lads,
For we're Soldiers of the Queen . . .

But—would it work out so nicely? *Would it?*

Ogilvie was, frankly, less sanguine than the Other Ranks on that score. All, unhappily, did not appear to a thinking mind to be set quite so jolly fair! All the Empire was converging on Table Bay, so said the news, to teach that well-deserved lesson to the unruly Boer farmers of the Transvaal and the Orange Free State. The *Times of India* had reported massive enthusiasm at home in England, of wildly cheering men and women crowding the regiments as they marched to embark, of patriotic fervour in the music halls—and in the exclusive London clubs as well—of all the blue blood in the British Isles rushing to enlist under Sir Redvers Buller or Sir George White, the latter until recently Commander-in-Chief in India. In Natal volunteers were being raised from the colonists and displaced Uitlanders. The signs had been good, the force of arms immense and colourful and impressive: but to date, sadly, the results had not been equal to the effort. The troops were strung out and dispersed—White had 8000 men at Ladysmith, and forty miles away at Dundee General Penn Symons commanded another 4000, since to have concentrated all on Ladysmith would have been virtually to abandon Natal's north-west: a purely political consideration that had

4

overridden military needs. Very soon Penn Symons had been personally under fire from the first Boer shells of the war. Through an excess of bravery that verged on stupidity, Penn Symons was mortally wounded at Talana hill—and Penn Symons had only recently fought on the North-West Frontier himself. Talana was a kind of victory, but a Pyrrhic one: Penn Symons lost 546 of his men and left the Boers holding Impati and the water supply for Dundee. On the day of the battle General French, sent out to command White's cavalry, arrived at Ladysmith, bringing Major Douglas Haig as his Chief of Staff. There followed another Pyrrhic victory—at Elandslaagte: Pyrrhic because owing to a misunderstanding as to the Boer intentions and strength, White within hours of the action ordered the abandonment of captured Elandslaagte which had been taken at the cost of heavy casualties to the Devons, the Manchesters and the Gordon Highlanders. Semi-victories were not what the British had expected, neither had they expected muddle. The British Army was supreme, all-powerful, always undefeated even in major wars. How was it that they had failed to decimate a bunch of undisciplined farmers at the very first encounter? At home in England, the public was sustaining a considerable degree of shock, and it was possible their confidence even in Buller might be shaken. Sir Redvers Buller was loved, revered, by the public, and his troops would follow him anywhere; but among the army's younger officers was a whisper that poor old Buller was too often given to leading in the wrong direction; and he looked like an apple dumpling on a horse. Buller, it was said, didn't like to out-run the champagne and caviar. And he was sixty years of age—a chicken, of course, compared with the venerable Duke of Cambridge even when the latter had yet occupied the Horse Guards—but still!

Ogilvie's mind, as the troop train chuffed out of Cape Town, now went on to the Indian Ocean, reflecting on the long haul in the transport. The *Malabar* had still been a day's steaming off Table Bay when she had been signalled by a passing freighter, by means of a blackboard slung in the latter's halliards: LADYSMITH AND KIMBERLEY STILL UNDER SIEGE. BOERS CONTROL RAILWAY FROM ORANGE RIVER TO RHODESIA. PLUMER FORCED BACK FROM LIMPOPO. WHITE SURROUNDED BY STRONG FORCES.

No depression aboard the troopship: the men were simply anxious to be in the fight. It couldn't last long now. The next day's arrival off Cape Town had given point to this belief. The roadstead was filled with ships, ships that had brought Buller's Army Corps from England, ships that had brought troops from Canada, from Australia, from New Zealand. It

6

was a mighty concourse, a sight to be seen with awe. Boats came out to greet the *Malabar* and her contingent from India, men cheered, flags waved gaily, and the sun shone down from a clear blue sky as the inward-bound trooper eased to her anchorage and let go. From one of the boats came a staff officer, who climbed the accommodation-ladder the moment it was in the water, and was met at its head by Lord Dornoch and the adjutant. Ogilvie, standing nearby, heard him remark that the battalion had got there just about in time; and wondered: just in time for what?

*   *   *

'Sir Redvers Buller,' Dornoch had told the assembled officers just before dinner in the saloon, 'has turned the War Office plans upside down—with what effect I dare say we shall see in due course.' He went on to say that the Army Corps had now been split up into three: one column would relieve Ladysmith, another Kimberley, and the remainder, which was not especially strong, would hold the outward thrust of Boers from the Orange Free State until General Buller re-formed the whole Army Corps in the Cape Midlands to carry out the original plan, which was to make a direct assault on Bloemfontein and Pretoria. 'The battalion,' Lord Dornoch said, 'is to join what's being called the Kimberley Relief

7

Force. This will be commanded by Lord Methuen. His orders are, to bring his force together at Orange River Station, relieve Kimberley and then Mafeking, which is also under siege as we know, and finally, to re-open communications with Rhodesia. Our own orders are to move up country as fast as possible by train to Orange River Station. To that end, gentlemen, we disembark at ten a.m. tomorrow.' He looked around and caught James Ogilvie's eye. 'A word in your ear, James . . .'

'Colonel?'

Dornoch walked to a corner of the saloon, stood for a moment looking out through a brass-rimmed porthole at the lights of Cape Town in the distance. A softly refreshing breeze wafted in. Dornoch turned towards Ogilvie. 'James, the officer who boarded with our orders—Major Haig, Chief of Staff to General French, and recently escaped with him from Ladysmith. He brought a message for you.'

Ogilvie showed his surprise. 'For me, Colonel?'

'For you indeed.' There was a smile on the Colonel's lips but his eyes were grave, even sombre. 'From Miss Gilmour, whom I know you'll remember.'

'Katharine Gilmour!' Ogilvie felt himself flushing foolishly. Major Gilmour's daughter . . . he'd brought her out of the Khyber after the death of her parents on the march, a dreadful march beset by cruel problems of war and personalities. Soon after arrival in Peshawar—as soon as she was fit for a journeyshe had gone to Murree and then he had heard she had left for Cape Town, where her grandmother had lived. He had thought little about her since, and had not expected to find her here in South Africa still. That had never occurred to him: she had loved England and, homesick, had wanted desperately to be back there. He could not have imagined she would remain in South Africa.

He saw the way the Colonel was looking at him. 'I'm sorry, Colonel, my mind was back in the past—'

'Yes—I understand. I had a great deal of time for Gilmour, James. I had great respect for him. It seems Miss Gilmour wants to see you on some matter to do with him and her mother. I see no harm ... I have anticipated your agreeing to see her, James. You will have leave to go ashore tonight, but you're to be back in the docks by eleven p.m., when a boat will be waiting to bring you off. Major Haig himself will meet you at the jetty at eight-thirty, and take you to Miss Gilmour.' Dornoch hesitated. 'James, I dare say I needn't stress this, but you'll do well to remember that we're on active service in what is fast becoming a major war. This is no Frontier skirmish. I can allow no ... entanglements. You understand?

We leave for the Orange River at ten a.m. I would prefer there to be no backward looks.'

CHAPTER TWO

No backward looks: so like the Colonel to say that! With Dornoch, always the regiment had come first and foremost. It was his life, as, in his regimental days, it had been James Ogilvie's father's whole existence. Ogilvie of Corriecraig was a proud patronymic; but it was subservient to Ogilvie of the 114th. As a ship's boat took him inshore Ogilvie, in mess kit still, stared ahead towards the yellow lights that spotted Cape Town, spread below the wide, flat eminence of Table Mountain. There would be no backward looks, but he was honest enough with himself to understand Lord Dornoch's stricture: on Indian service, James Ogilvie's heart had been known to flutter in more than one direction. The flame, for instance, of Tom Archdale's young widow had burned for a long time, and in burning had set light to many webs of scandal in the messes and bungalows of Peshawar and Simla and Murree. But India was India, and was now in the past.

Ogilvie smiled into the darkness, stretching himself lazily on the thwarts. Katharine . . . two years on, she might have changed. She'd been very young when her parents had died on that hell-march out of the Afghan hills . . . also very brave. Ogilvie's lazy movements became restless ones as his body started suddenly to react to thoughts of Katharine Gilmour. An attractive filly . . . very! But damn it all . . . she'd be well chaperoned, no doubt! The elderly, sharp-eyed ladies who seemed inseparable from all regimental life made amours sadly difficult for young captains and subalterns. It was useful experience, all the same: intrigue, planning, the outwitting of the enemy—it was fine background for the Staff, and eventual high command!

Suddenly the jetty loomed, and the boat headed in for some steps cut into the stone. A sailor offered Ogilvie a hand to disembark, but he leapt agilely onto the lower step, which was greasy and dappled with seaweed. At the top there was a lamp, yellow, guttering flame behind smoky glass. Here Ogilvie paused and looked around. As he hesitated, he heard the distant clipclop of a horse, and the grating sound of metal-rimmed wheels on stone. The sounds came closer; a carriage, a gig, very smart, rattled into the circle of light and stopped. Whip in hand, the driver, an officer in khaki, with the red tabs of the Staff, and a Major's crown, called to Ogilvie:

'Captain Ogilvie of the Royal Strathspeys?'

'Yes, sir.'

'Haig. Douglas Haig of General French's

staff. Get up, will you, Ogilvie. I'm a busy man, as you'll appreciate, I expect.'

Ogilvie got into the gig and Haig flipped his reins. He pulled the horse round, and they set off towards the town, going fast. Ogilvie, when they came beneath more lamps, studied Major Haig's profile. It was a squarish face, rather florid, with a firm jaw. The full moustache was greying a little; Haig, he judged, was around forty years of age. Irreverently, he wondered if there was any connection with the famous whisky. Whisky or not—trade or not—this Douglas Haig had about him an air of immense authority and Ogilvie felt instinctively that here was a man marked out for high command: Chief of Staff to a general in the field at forty was good enough going, as indeed was the fact that such an appointment had gone to a man of major's rank. Haig spoke little; Ogilvie felt obliged to start some conversation going.

He asked, 'You're taking me direct to Miss Gilmour, sir?'

'That was the idea, wasn't it?'

'Er . . . yes.'

'You've been briefed by your Colonel, I take it?'

'Yes.'

'Silly question, then.' Suddenly, Haig smiled. 'Got any others while we're about it, Ogilvie?'

Ogilvie felt slightly nettled. 'Probably only

silly ones.'

'Oh, don't take umbrage, Ogilvie. If you've anything to ask, ask it.'

'What does Miss Gilmour want with me, sir?'

'She'll tell you that herself.' They were clear of the docks now: the sight of Major Haig had been enough to have them waved and saluted past the military control at the gates. Haig now used his whip, just a flick, and they rattled on faster. 'I'm also the prod.'

'The prod?'

'I want you to do what Miss Gilmour wants. It's important to her. It'll be difficult, but not impossible. I expect you know, your column's marching on Kimberley.'

'Yes, sir. What's the—'

'You'll see the connection soon enough, Ogilvie.' Haig paused. 'I knew the father well—Major Gilmour, a fine man. You were with him when he was killed—I know all about that. I believe he impressed you as he impressed me.'

'That's true.'

Haig gave a low laugh. 'You're the man for the job, all right! You'll see.'

Intriguing! And Katharine Gilmour seemed to live some distance away, which increased the scope for Ogilvie's inner speculations, the more so as Major Haig fell into a silence which he seemed disinclined to wish broken. The gig travelled the streets of Cape Town and its suburbs for a little under half an hour. The town itself was on a positive war footing: there were troops everywhere, British, Colonials, all in khaki, some with the wide-brimmed bush hats of the Australians—surging about in groups, some silent, some singing, some drunk as lords, pouring from the bars in noisy abandon, a last celebration, perhaps, before entraining for the front. There were regimental pickets in plenty, slow-moving men commanded by dour N.C.O.'s, naval patrols, military policemen. There were sailors, bluejackets from warships berthed in the naval port of Simon's Town in False Bay, brawny-looking men wearing straw hats with the ship names in gold thread on black ribbons, bearded men largely, with flapping trousers and a rolling—to Ogilvie's eye undisciplined—gait. (He recalled something his naval uncle had once said: 'Don't expect parade-ground precision from seamen, my boy, if ever you serve with a Naval Brigade. You know what's been said—Royal Marine Light Infantry will advance in columns of fours, seamen will advance in bloody great heaps.') In parts of the town, Kaffirs moved obsequiously along the gutters.

For the first time, Ogilvie was fully aware that he had left India: had left behind him one particularised form of soldiering. Here in South Africa, he would to a large extent go back to the beginning. Much was to be learned.

'Here we are,' Haig said when they had reached the suburbs. He pulled up the gig, then added, 'I shall collect you at ten-thirty. Be ready outside. That's the house.' He pointed his whip at a low, two-storey house set in a small garden, one of many in a long, quiet street. A lamp was burning behind half-opened shutters, in a room to the right of a porch. Ogilvie got down from the gig, saluting Major Haig, who turned his horse and went off the way he had come, at a fast trot. Ogilvie, his heart thumping now with expectancy and curiosity, opened a garden gate and went up a well-kept path between lawn and flower-beds which, as he could see from a high-climbing moon, were already showing the effects of the approaching South African summer: there had evidently been little rain for some while.

In the porch, he pulled at the bell. From within, he heard the gentle dying tinkle. A native servant, a woman black as coal, shining and smiling, answered the door.

'Miss Gilmour—she's expecting me. Captain Ogilvie.'

A bob of the head, almost a curtsey: the Negro woman stood aside. Ogilvie went in, was taken towards the room where he had seen the lamp. When he was announced a girl in a jade-green dress rose from a chair at a bureau, where she had been writing. Katharine Gilmour—a girl yet, but one who had

15

blossomed in the interval.

Smiling, nodding at the servant who withdrew, Katharine came towards Ogilvie, holding out her hands. He took them both in his, feeling strangely awkward.

'Dear James! It's been so long. How nice to see you—how nice of you to come!' Her eyes were full of happiness: he would have been the dullest man not to have seen that and responded. 'Or did Major Haig bully you into it?'

He met her smile. 'Of course not—he was anxious I should, but I'd have come anyway. How are you, Katharine? And how did you know my regiment was here at the Cape?'

She laughed. 'Oh, James, as to that, it was Major Haig who told me you'd been ordered here. Since he learned the facts of my father's death, he's followed your career with some interest, I may tell you. And he's going to be an officer of distinction, I'm certain—one to be reckoned with. As to how I am . . . I am very well indeed, and so delighted to see you that I feel, all of a sudden, even better!'

Flattery? Flattery, in an attempt to procure his acceptance of whatever it was she was about to ask of him? But no: she was, surely, too ingenuous for that! She shone with innocence and honesty, as did her Negro woman with kitchen-sweat. Besides, there was always this Major Douglas Haig to push him into acceptance—which thought, to his intense

16

irritation, pricked pinlike in two ways, one of them being an awakening jealousy.

'How was Peshawar, James, when you left cantonments?'

He shrugged. 'As ever. Things don't change much. Patrols, the odd expedition, a great deal of boredom in between.' He decided to come to the point. 'Katharine, we haven't long. What's this you want—why did you want to see me? I rather gathered it was important. Not just poodle-faking.'

Lightly, she put a finger to her lips. Melodramatic: crossing the room to the door, the jade-green dress rustling with movements that Ogilvie found provocative, she turned the handle gently, slowly, and looked out.

Then she closed the shutters across the window.

'Come and sit with me, James, on the sofa.'

'So much secrecy?'

'It's necessary. Come!' Sitting herself, she patted the cushion close to her.

He moved across, frowning. 'Don't tell me Haig's given you some military secret, some campaign information—'

'No, no, no, Douglas would never do such a thing as that.' *Douglas? Major Haig was a damn sight older than her.* 'It's nothing like that, I promise you—though the campaign does come into it insofar as you'll be going up to Kimberley, James.'

'Yes.' No secret about that; the Boers must

17

know the relieving force would come. 'Can you please explain, Katharine?'

'Of course!' She had a wonderfully fresh scent: like mimosa. 'James, some years ago my father and mother were out here, on leave from India. I think I told you once—while we were in the Khyber—my grandmother, my father's mother, lived out here. She still does. She's a very old lady now. This is her house. Father was her only child—they were very close. After my parents died, I came here to live with her, only for a time originally, and then I found I couldn't leave her. Do you understand?'

'Yes.'

'When Father was here, at the time I spoke of, he was on long leave . . . he became bored I think—anyway, it was at the time of the First Boer War, the Boer Insurrection some people call it, for it was little more than that. Father attached himself to the 58th Regiment, which in fact was his old regiment—'

'Unofficially, I take it?'

She nodded. 'But no less factually, James! He fought at Laing's Nek . . . on the 26th of January 1881, nearly twenty years ago, just before I was born. It was a Boer victory, of course, and General Colley lost a large number of men. But there were also Boer casualties—fourteen killed and twenty-seven wounded in the first assault—and Father brought in one of them. He saved the man's

18

life, at the risk of his own, James.'

'I can imagine him doing that.'

'You thought well of him, James, did you not?'

'I did.'

She went on, 'That man's name was Opperman. A Boer, son of a farmer . . . a man with a mass of flaming red hair, Father often told me. When the rising was over and Father had not yet returned to India, they became friends. Opperman was naturally grateful for what Father had done and he gave him a present: a diamond, from the Kimberley diamond fields.' She laughed. 'Father always suspected he'd stolen it, even if only by finding it on another man's diggings, for Opperman was no digger himself. However, he said he'd come by it honestly and had had it cut and polished.'

'Valuable?'

'Very! Father put a value of twenty thousand pounds on it. It's beautiful, James, it glows . . . with a sort of pink glow. I can't really describe it properly. That's partly why it became known as the Red Daniel, that, and the fact that Opperman's name is Daniel, and he's known as Old Red Daniel too, because of his hair.'

'Is? He's still alive, then?'

She said, 'Yes, and apparently full of vim and vigour. Presently, he's Commandant Opperman of the Boer commandos, and he commands the Boers at Carolina in the

19

eastern Transvaal. But that's only by the way, James. The thing is this: the Red Daniel, the diamond, is in Kimberley. So is my grandmother—she has the Red Daniel with her. She went up there before there was any threat to Kimberley, to stay with friends—a Mrs Hendrikson whose husband's with De Beers. She took the Red Daniel with a view to having a proper valuation put upon it.' Katharine looked down at her hands. 'We have little money left, James,' she said quietly but with a curious inner tension. 'So little! Virtually, the Red Daniel is all that's left— that, and a little money of my grandmother's invested in England. The Red Daniel's terribly important to us, really it is. It's vital, James. And if the Boers take Kimberley—'

'They won't do that.'

'But if they do, James,' she said with insistence, looking at him pleadingly. 'If they do, then the Red Daniel may be lost.'

'I see—or I think I do! You're asking me, aren't you, to get into Kimberley, find your grandmother, and bring the Red Daniel out?'

She said in a tight, passion-controlled voice, 'Yes ! Oh, I know it's asking an awful lot—'

'A lot!' He laughed; a hard laugh. 'Let us not discuss *that* for now, Katharine! First, I'll dissect your theories. To begin with: from all I hear, the Boers are magnanimous in victory, and chivalrous towards women. I doubt if they'd take the Red Daniel from an

20

old lady! Next: if I should manage to get into Kimberley, which is pretty doubtful to say the least, then the Red Daniel will be on my person afterwards. If I should be wounded, or killed . . . then the Boers may take the stone—take it from a British officer, don't you see? Thirdly: if your grandmother is friendly with De Beers, why doesn't she hand the Red Daniel to them for safe keeping until Kimberley is relieved?'

Once again the girl looked down at her hands. 'All that . . . it is easily enough answered, James. My grandmother and I do not wish to chance the Boers' chivalry—there are Boers and Boers. You must not believe all you have been told about their chivalry! Kimberley means wealth to the Boers, James, great wealth, and all their eyes will be on diamonds, diamonds, diamonds! As to De Beers . . . well, I think there will be no safe keeping there if Kimberley should fall! As to what might happen to you, I pray to God that nothing will.'

'Many wives and mothers and children will be praying that for their men, Katharine, but men will still fall, you know.'

'I know,' she said quietly. 'I'm not unfamiliar with a soldier's life, or with his death either—'

'I'm sorry.' Impulsively, his hand closed over hers in her lap. 'I didn't mean to hurt you. If you're really set on this business, if—'

'It means my whole security, James.'

'Then, for the reason I gave, isn't it a foolish risk?'

She shook her head. 'Major Haig will arrange for the Red Daniel to be collected from you outside Kimberley, and brought direct to Cape Town by a trusted courier.'

Haig again! 'H'm. And do I take it that Major Haig will also make certain other arrangements?'

She looked at him, frowning. 'I don't understand, James. Please will you explain?'

'Yes. How do I arrange to be absent from my column, from my regiment, while I'm trying to burrow like a mole into Kimberley?'

'Oh,' she said in a low voice. 'Oh, yes, I—I believe Major Haig will see to that for you, James—'

'Why ?'

'*Why*, James?'

'Yes—why? French's Chief of Staff . . . he's nothing to do with me, French is to command on the Central Front—I don't come under his orders—'

'No. But Major Haig was my father's friend. As a friend, he asked for, and was given, permission to leave General French so he could go aboard your ship and—and ask you to help me. That's all, James.'

'Is he in love with you?' He sounded stiff and pompous, and he knew it, but didn't care. 'Is that it? Am I being made use of, to—'

'No, no!' She laughed impatiently, angrily. 'There's nothing like that on the part of Douglas Haig—'

'Then on your part? Is Haig married, Katharine?'

'He's not married as it happens, but—'

'Then he's paying attention to you. And doubtless you to him. From the little I saw of him tonight, I'd have said he'd probably be attractive to women—'

'True, James, he is. But not to me—and anyway, he's an ambitious man. When Douglas Haig marries, it will not be to a dead major's daughter, an obscure officer from the North-West Frontier—much as he respected my father as a man. In any case, he has no thought of marrying, I believe. His passion is the Army, James, and he is very single-minded, like all efficient officers. He is much too engrossed in the task on hand even to notice a woman.'

'In that case I still ask—why, Katharine?'

'I think that is something you must ask Major Haig himself,' she said after a pause. 'All I can say is, he is a kind man, and—and chivalrous.' She gave him a sideways glance, a mischievous one. 'And you, I think, are jealous!'

He laughed at that; but an edgy laugh. 'Come now, Katharine, you're fishing for compliments. Jealous or not, I'd like to know a little more about Haig's motives in this—so perhaps I *will* ask him myself. I take it, from

23

what you've said already, that I do have your permission?'

'Yes, of course, James.' She hesitated, looking into his face, searchingly and with hope. 'And does it follow from that, that you'll help me?'

'I haven't said so yet. But if I should decide to . . . how shall I establish my bona fides with your grandmother? She's not going to trust someone she doesn't know, who turns up in Kimberley to relieve her of—'

'James, you were with my father when he died. When you speak of that, she'll know you're telling the truth—you knew enough of him to talk about him, to be obviously sincere in what you say.' Again Katharine hesitated. 'I've discussed this with Major Haig. A letter of introduction would be too dangerous, clearly, and there is no means, beyond the open heliograph, of telling her you are coming. The telegraph into Kimberley has been cut by the Boers. But if you give her this, she will know you come from me.'

Reaching into her bodice, she produced a small golden locket, hanging from a thin chain about her neck. She handed this to Ogilvie. He studied a faded photograph of a young woman very like Katharine herself.

He met her eye. 'Your mother?'

'Yes, as a young married woman, James. It will mean nothing to anyone . . . with whom you might fall in on your way to Kimberley. It

24

could be your own mother's. Take it—leave it
with my grandmother when you take the Red
Daniel. That is, if you will . . . I'd be so terribly
grateful.' Her voice was low now, and he felt
there was a hint of tears. 'The Red Daniel was
always to be our security . . . my father always
said so. He had little else to leave. If it should
be lost, it would seem like a betrayal.'

*   *   *

The tug at the bell-pull had sounded
impatient. 'I don't like being kept waiting,'
Major Haig said as he whipped up the horse.
    'I'm sorry.'
    'I said ten-thirty, I meant ten-thirty.'
    'And I've said I'm sorry, Major.'
    Haig grunted. 'The army's going to the
dogs. Young officers are becoming a pest.'
    'Then, sir, I doubt if a pest can
accommodate Miss Gilmour in what I consider
a stupidly dangerous mission!'
    'Ha!' Major Haig gave a sudden barking
laugh, half angry, half amused. 'Damn it,
Ogilvie, you're a cool young man! Still—no bad
thing to stand up to your elders and betters—
to a point, that is. I'll withdraw the pest. Are
you frightened off by the thought of danger?'
    'No.'
    'Good! You've agreed to do as she asks?'
    'Provisionally, yes.'
    Haig slowed the pace a little. There was a

hard note in his voice as he repeated, 'Provisionally? What does that mean?'

'It means I want to know a little more. I want to know where you stand, Major.'

Haig said, 'I stand as a friend. A friend who can smooth certain paths.'

'So Miss Gilmour hinted. For the rest, she suggested I ask you. I'm asking now, Major.'

'H'm. Well, of course, I can scarcely *order* you to recover a diamond for a young woman in distress. When I was a young officer, anyone'd have jumped at the chance!'

'You said you can't *order* me, Major. True-you can't. Lord Methuen's my Commander, not General French. But you are *requesting* very pressingly. Will you tell me what's behind this business?'

There was a long pause, during which Ogilvie was very conscious of a close sideways scrutiny from Major Douglas Haig. At last Haig seemed to reach a decision, grumpily. He said, 'Yes, I'll tell you what's behind it, Ogilvie, on your word that you'll keep your mouth shut for ever afterwards. And that part *is* an order. Well?'

'You have my word, Major Haig.'

Haig nodded. 'Thank you. You may discuss this with your Colonel—no one else. What's behind it? Lord Kitchener's behind it—that's what!'

* * *

Kitchener.

A name to conjure with—Lord Kitchener of Khartoum. Horatio Herbert Kitchener who, having vengefully avenged the murder of Chinese Gordon, had achieved total victory in the Sudan and had celebrated it by having the Mahdi drawn in chains behind his horse at the great triumphal procession through the streets of Cairo. Kitchener the Sirdar, Commander-in-Chief of the Anglo-Egyptian Army, currently ensconced in Khartoum, loved by many serving soldiers and officers, loathed and detested by many more as 'that stinking Egyptian', nevertheless the idol, after Lord Roberts, of the British public.

Surprise was an understatement: Ogilvie was astounded. Haig saw this, and laughed quietly. 'Rumour has it,' he said, 'and for now I'll put it no stronger than that—rumour has it that there are moves afoot in Whitehall. Moves to relieve General Buller as Commander-in-Chief out here ... much depends on the conduct of the war in the next few weeks, Ogilvie—'

'To relieve Buller by appointing Kitchener?'

'No. By appointing Lord Roberts, with Kitchener as his Chief of Staff. Two very popular appointments, Ogilvie—if only Salisbury can be convinced, then they'll be made, I do believe. Trouble is, Salisbury's said to consider Roberts too old at sixty-seven—

doubts his stamina, don't you know—but that's poppycock in Bobs' case. They should never have put him out to grass in Ireland. But Kitchener, now . . .'

Kitchener! The iron-hard face, the compelling eyes, the tremendous black moustache. Kitchener was a dictator. Handsome, square-faced, glittering . . . eyes ice-blue with a cast in one of them, the result of desert experiences. Kitchener the hater of the Press, Kitchener who had most strongly objected even to the presence of Lord Randolph Churchill's son Winston as a journalist disguised as a cavalry officer in the Sudan. Kitchener, always accustomed to be master in a foreign land, Kitchener single-minded and celibate, Kitchener the big, big personality—who, when commanding an Egyptian outpost, had often dressed as an Arab and gone out alone . . . *to spy*.

When Major Haig said, 'But Kitchener, now . . .' it was to this aspect of the Sirdar's character and service onto which Ogilvie's mind immediately latched.

And he was right.

'Kitchener,' Haig said as the gig went along avenues of laurel and yellow-wood, 'and I say this with immense respect, is a schemer. He has no scruples as to means—none at all. He can be barbarous where barbarity pays. He is harsh to the point—almost—of provoking mutiny. But he is without parallel in efficiency,

28

and one of his efficiencies is to know, or attempt to know, the mind and planning direction of the enemy. D'you follow, Ogilvie?'

'I think so. The Red Daniel mission is a spying mission. Right, Major?'

'Right. There's no deception about the diamond—it exists! And Miss Gilmour, who knows nothing of what I am telling you—she knows only that I shall help you to undertake its recovery, nothing else—has told you the truth as she knows it. You will recover the diamond from Kimberley—'

'But not for Miss Gilmour? You have some other use for it, Major, some spying use?'

Haig said nothing. Looking sideways, Ogilvie saw the tight expression, the set lips. 'Come now, Major, you must tell me. From what you've said so far, it's obvious there are plans for the Red Daniel, and—'

'Oh, very well,' Haig said in a disagreeable tone. 'I suppose you'll have to be told now—at least, a little of the story. You're right—the Red Daniel won't be handed to me or to my courier. It won't go to Miss Gilmour—not directly, that is. Eventually it will be returned to her, I give you my word on that, but in the meantime, Ogilvie, there are other plans for the Red Daniel. Lord Kitchener—'

'Never mind Lord Kitchener,' Ogilvie interrupted crisply. 'What I've agreed to do, has been for Miss Gilmour. The diamond—'

'Will go back to her in the end—I've said as

29

much.'

'But this is a kind of stealing, sir—'

'Stuff and nonsense! Kindly don't be impertinent! I have given you my word as a gentleman. As a gentleman you must accept that, and as an officer you must now *obey*. If anything untoward should occur to the Red Daniel, which I doubt, then Miss Gilmour will be given its money value to a most generous valuation,' Haig added in a less acid tone. 'Again, you have my word on that—and Lord Kitchener's. Give me credit for not standing by and seeing a lady deprived of what is hers! It was I who insisted that she should not suffer.'

Ogilvie said, 'Then I apologise, sir.'

'Thank you!' Haig laughed, sounding relieved. 'Now then, please listen to me, Ogilvie. Lord Kitchener, looking southwards from the Sudan, has already assessed which way the wind is likely to blow him, and he is already making his dispositions as it were. I need hardly say how useful it could prove to a young officer ... to be in favour with the Sirdar. What are your ambitions, Ogilvie?'

Ogilvie said simply, 'To command the 114th Highlanders, sir, as my father and my grandfather did before me.'

Haig gave a chuckle. 'A naïve young man, I think! But it's an honourable ambition, though you mustn't lose sight of the horizons beyond the regiment, Ogilvie. They're there, you know!'

30

'Yes, possibly. But shall we discuss the Red Daniel, Major? What's to become of it? Am I to know that?'

Haig, increasing his pace towards the docks now, said, 'In due course—not at this moment. I had not wished to say as much as I have. You'll be contacted by a friend of mine, Major Allenby—I can't say exactly when, but it'll be along the route for Kimberley as taken by Lord Methuen's column. Allenby will give you your further orders, and as of now they *will* be orders. In the meantime, you will carry on with your duties as a regimental officer of the Kimberley Relief Force. I've no doubt you'll see your share of action, field action, before you're called upon to detach and enter Kimberley—which will be in advance of the relief. Understood, Ogilvie?'

'So far as it goes, yes. Can't I be told the whole story now?'

Again Haig gave his quiet chuckle, as they came down in the yellow lamp-light to the docks. 'You cannot! Let's take this in stages. You could be captured in the fighting—some say the Boers are chivalrous towards prisoners, but I don't know! The enemy always has methods of making people talk—as you should know! I'm told you've undertaken special missions before—what?'

Ogilvie gave a slight smile. 'I see you've looked into my career quite thoroughly, Major Haig.'

31

'Part of the job! You're known to Lord Kitchener as well. It all began with Gilmour, and my friendship with him—that's the way life goes, Ogilvie. You've spied before. You know a little of the game, I think. I decided you were the man for the job, and I informed Lord Kitchener accordingly. Do well—for all our sakes.'

They came to the gateway; once again Douglas Haig's face was the password. From gates to jetty no more was said. Ogilvie watched the water, dark, flecked with the yellow reflection of the dockside lamps, and spasmodically by a moon half obscured by cloud. The boat from the *Malabar* was waiting.

Ogilvie got down from the gig. Haig reached out a hand, which Ogilvie took. 'Good luck,' Haig said. That was all. He pulled his horse round at once, and rattled off, metal wheel-rims on stone, leaving silence behind, a silence broken only by the soft lap of the South Atlantic Ocean against the weed-covered walls of the jetty. A sudden shiver ran through Ogilvie. Intrigue, spying, war and death ... being Kitchener's man was no sinecure!

He went down the steps into the boat, his fingers touching Katharine Gilmour's locket. Melodramatic again: he felt like Nelson, leaving the Sally Port at Portsmouth in a small ship's boat, to board the *Victory* to fight for England. The thought made him laugh aloud, which was no bad thing. At least, he was learning not to take himself so seriously.

CHAPTER THREE

In the early morning the mist hung like a cloth on the flat summit of Table Mountain. The bugles brought the regiment awake at six o'clock, and there was a clatter along the messdecks as the men turned out to wash and shave and take their last more or less comfortable meal before the train journey and the march began. Comfortable was a comparative term: the crowded messes, the air thick with the sweat and breath of so many massed bodies, every available nook and cranny occupied by soldiers struggling with uniforms and equipment, were scarcely as well-ordered as the barrack-rooms of the Peshawar cantonment. During the long, slow voyage from Bombay, the men had learned in retrospect to appreciate what now seemed a placid and nostalgic routine: space to move, space to stow personal belongings, a space of uncrowded leisure before the first parade—if a man turned out of his bed in good time—and after the day's last muster. And the wonderful morning cool of an Indian summer, the best of the day before the heat struck full.

A ship was a different experience: on deck—when there was space to enjoy it—it was blazing hot or pleasantly cool according to the hour; but below it was always smelly and foetid, the apparently motionless air overlaid with emanations from galley and latrine, and no room anywhere to swing a cat. Also, although this was the fair-weather season in the Indian Ocean, there was the occasional roll that brought soldiers' stomachs to their mouths most unpleasantly.

At half past eight the *Malabar* weighed anchor and proceeded alongside the jetty. The disembarkation gangways were laid in position fore and aft. Captain Black, adjutant of the Royal Strathspeys, followed by the various company commanders, the Regimental Sergeant-Major and the colour-sergeants, walked through the messdecks, saturnine, smart as paint, sniffing and looking as though he couldn't get on deck fast enough. Probes were made, orders passed down the line of inspection, grumbling Scots were set to last-minute antics of cleaning to satisfy Captain Black.

At nine-forty-five Black reported to the Colonel in his stateroom: 'Battalion ready to disembark, Colonel.'

'Thank you, Captain Black. Start disembarking by companies at ten o'clock, if you please. In the meantime, I'd like a word with Captain Ogilvie.'

'Very good, Colonel.' Black saluted and turned about. Three minutes later Ogilvie

34

knocked and entered.

'You sent for me, Colonel?'

'Ah, James.' Dornoch turned away from the port through which he had been looking along the jetty. 'I take it you've seen Miss Gilmour?'

'Yes, Colonel.'

'And you've agreed to do as she asks? You may speak freely, James. I had a long talk with Major Haig on arrival yesterday.'

Ogilvie said, 'I have agreed, Colonel. As a matter of fact . . . I wasn't given much choice. Major Haig—'

'Yes, yes, I understand. A good deal of importance is being attached to this business, though I don't profess to follow it entirely. Damn it, James, I prefer regimental soldiering to intrigue and—and subterfuge!' Dornoch was indeed looking far from happy, Ogilvie saw. 'Standards are slipping—there's no morality left. The Army's changing fast. However, it's not up to me to preach, nor to seem to criticise men in high places. I shall give you my full backing, James, come what may.'

'Thank you, Colonel.'

'I gather a Major Allenby will make contact later.'

'Yes, Colonel.'

'And he'll pass orders. That's as much as we know.'

'Yes, Colonel.'

'I thought,' Dornoch said, 'that it might be

helpful to you if I were to brief you more fully on the overall plan for the relief of Kimberley, so that you have the background to whatever it may be that you'll be called upon to do.' He reached into a ready-packed valise and brought out a rolled-up map. This he spread on the table before him. 'Come and look, James. Here we are—Cape Town. There's the railway.' Ogilvie moved to the Colonel's side and followed the moving finger. The map, he saw, included Cape Colony, the Orange Free State, and Natal; also the southern boundary of the Transvaal. 'As you know, we take the Western Railway to Orange River Station, where we join up with Lord Methuen's column. Look now—you can see the main thrusts of the Boers to date—their invasion routes into Natal only recently. You see the arrows?'

'Yes, Colonel.' It looked a formidable penetration: the spearheads of the Free Staters running from Van Reenan's and the Tintwa Passes through the Drakensburg towards the Klip River and Ladysmith, another through Botha's Pass and the Biggarsberg range to drop down on Elandslaagte and Reitfontein, this column being composed of Germans and Hollanders, a Johannesburg commando and the Vrede State Commando, all under the command of the Boer General Koch. General Joubert had led down past Laing's Nek—where in the First

Boer War Katharine Gilmour's father had saved the life of Old Red Daniel Opperman— making for Newcastle, which was also threatened by a column from Wool's Drift. Commandant Erasmus had thrust down on Dundee, where he had been joined in victory by Meyer from Jager's Drift.

'They said they were farmers,' Dornoch said with a bitter smile. 'For farmers, James, they make first-class soldiers! But now for our part to come: Lord Methuen expects to have his force assembled at Orange River Station by the day after tomorrow, the 21st, when he will at once strike out towards Kimberley. At the same time, the Ladysmith relief column is expected to march, this column being provided from the Army Corps arriving at Durban. Incidentally, no commander's yet been appointed for the Ladysmith column. Our own line of advance will most probably be here, here and here—directly along the railway line in fact. There will be difficulties: there's a cluster of pretty high kopjes that command the line at Belmont, more again near Graspan— there's the rivers at Modder River Station, and a rather nasty triangle of hills *there*—at Magersfontein—these command the railway about five miles north of the Modder. No doubt the Boers will bring us to action at all of these points—that's to be expected. That's the general picture, then. Somewhere along the way, Major Allenby will presumably show

37

himself, and you'll leave us.'

Ogilvie said, 'I hope it'll not be for long, Colonel!'

'So do I, but that's up to Allenby and Haig now. It's out of my hands, James.'

*   *   *

To the skirl of the pipes and the beat of the battalion's drummers, the 114th Highlanders, the Queen's Own Royal Strathspeys, marched from the North Wharf to the railway terminus through the cheering crowds of Cape Town. Men, women and children ran forward to clap the Scots on the shoulders, to thrust chocolate and cigarettes into willing hands; strong Highland arms went round pretty girls, swept them up for a smacking kiss whilst on the march, released them laughing and gay: certainly to date the news had not been as good as expected, but now the Army Corps was arriving with every ship that entered, a splendid build-up of splendid men who would win the war in weeks and give Oom Paul Kruger the fine whisker-burning he so richly deserved. Flowers were flung at Ogilvie as he marched ahead of B Company. In the rear, Colour-Sergeant MacTrease was having difficulty with his step: there was a young woman boisterously on either arm. Even Lord Dornoch, leading the battalion on horseback, was not immune. Only the Regimental

Sergeant-Major, Bosom Cunningham, had a degree of exemption: he looked too formidable as he marched stiff and straight behind his stomach, eyes front and pace-stick rigid as though on the parade-ground at the depot at Invermore.

And at the station: crowds again, women who had already attached themselves to the officers of the regiments who had been a few days in Cape Town, the earlier arrivals of the great Army Corps, or to the officers and men of the local forces who were about to join the corps from Britain and the Empire overseas.

The troop trains seemed to be leaving in a continuous stream, coaches and wagons filled, crammed to capacity with men and horses, stores and ammunition and rifles. Katharine Gilmour was there to see James Ogilvie off for the front.

'Goodbye, James ... don't forget the Red Daniel.'

He would hardly do that! The chuff of the engine, clouds of steam, the surge of movement. Behind Ogilvie—Captain Andrew Black, pulling at his dark moustache.

'You're still no time-waster, Ogilvie.' Not for Black the brotherly Christian name, traditional to the 114th: Black was, as ever, Black. 'Is this why the Colonel singled you out for shore leave last night, Ogilvie?'

'That's none of your business.'

'Oh—is it not? I'll thank you not to be

39

impertinent, Ogilvie!' Angrily, the adjutant swung away.

*   *   *

Later: dust and flies, dust and flies and heat, dust in the food, in the drink, flies that seemed to be crawling on every inch of exposed flesh, heat over all, ubiquitous, insidious, enervating, different somehow from the heat of the North-West Frontier. Around six hundred miles to go, to Orange River Station alone. Through mountains, across the Great Karroo, more mountains. Chuff and pull, dead slow up the inclines, rush merrily downhill: more heat and sand, more flies. *Something tells me I am needed, At the front to fight the foe.* Discomfort, sweat, no water for washing, little enough for drinking even. The train stank; it was filthy dirty anyway. At first the men had mostly been singing heartily, just a few had made an attempt to write letters for home, to be posted hopefully upon arrival at their destination. Letters might reach Scotland before the war was over, and when it was, then the Royal Strathspeys might well be ordered home at last. So the letters anticipated this, some even hinting at being home for a roaring Scots New Year—for Hogmanay. But after the first two hundred miles the singing had stopped and the scraps of writing paper had been put away. Cunningham and the N.C.O.s

40

left them alone. They were passengers on a train, they were not on parade. But Black traversed the train, hopping from coach to coach at the stops, looking, issuing orders about unfastened neck bands and shrugged-off equipment, about crowded bodies sprawled in ungainly attitudes. When he was there: grudging obedience. When he had gone: loud insubordination.

'What the bleedin' fick-fack does the long streak o' bleedin' misery think he is!'

'Bluidy loon ... gosh, but I'd like fine to see a bluidy Boer shove a bluidy bayonet up the mon's bluidy arse!'

'Mebbe it'll no' be a Boer that does that.'

The colour-sergeants heard nothing: but they grinned widely behind discreet hands.

Ogilvie button-holed Black after one foray. 'I'd be obliged if you'd leave my company alone,' he said.

'They're slack, man! Slack and slovenly!'

'So am I. Look at me.'

'Then do yourself up, Ogilvie.'

'I'll do no such thing. And as B Company Commander, I'll have my men travel at ease when they can, Captain Black.'

'I happen to be the adjutant—kindly do not forget yourself!' Black was trembling with rage, his eyes staring. 'I shall have words with the Colonel—'

'And so shall I. Meanwhile you will not interfere with my arrangements, *internal*

41

arrangements, for my company.'

Black chattered: to swing away with dignity in a crowded trooptrain was frustrating in the attempt. His kilt became hooked up on a splinter of woodwork. Grinning, Ogilvie gallantly freed it. Black's spindly thighs became decently covered again. He thrust through the press of officers, fuming and grim. Ogilvie sighed and went on staring through the window at the passing landscape: the flat, level plain of the karroo, bare mostly but for the mimosa shrubs with their yellow ball-like blossom, or the sheep-feeding karroo bush. The occasional animal bounding away from the steamy monstrosity under South Africa's clear blue skies—wildebeest and zebra for the most part, some steenbok. When night came down, the temperature dropped considerably: it was time for men to shiver now, in the sudden change characteristic of South Africa. Ogilvie had heard of a good deal of sickness amongst the front-line troops: very possibly it had to do with these sudden shifts in temperature.

Early the following morning the trooptrain pulled in to Orange River Station. First out was the Colonel, to be welcomed in person by Lord Methuen, a tall, stooping figure with a thick red moustache, a Scots Guards officer now embarking upon his first independent command. Nevertheless, Ogilvie knew that Methuen had a good deal of campaign experience behind him.

'I'm delighted to welcome you, Colonel,' Methuen said, holding out a hand which Dornoch took.

'Thank you, sir. I'm glad to join you.'

Methuen smiled. 'Brother Scots, Dornoch. We'll work well together, I'm sure of that. How are your men?'

'In good trim, sir, and eager to march.'

'They'll not be kept waiting long. I suppose you know Rhodes is in Kimberley?'

'Yes indeed!' The great Empire-builder, Cecil Rhodes, once Prime Minister of Cape Colony, had got himself into Kimberley aboard almost the last train up from Cape Town, only two days before the start of hostilities: his interest still lay in the Chartered Company that controlled Rhodesia. 'I've no doubt he's far from happy!'

'An understatement. Rhodes is said to be in a state of fearful agitation, Colonel. He believes Kimberley to be the key town, the key situation in this war. I fear that his opinion of military strategy is poor, insofar as there has been no relief attempted earlier. There has been a stream of almost hysterical messages—this may have influenced General Buller's decision in the matter, I dare say—'

'There's urgency in the air?'

'No town's big enough to hold a Rhodes in confinement, Colonel! Urgency—yes. We march tomorrow at four a.m. I'm sorry for the short notice, but there it is . . .'

The senior officers moved out of earshot; all along the track now, men were tumbling out, glad enough to be free of the packed, cramped train, to breathe fresh air. The colour-sergeants and corporals shouted them into line; Ogilvie saw B Company fallen in and mustered and when the battalion was formed up with its animals and its baggage, a corporal of military police guided them to their lines in the encampment, riding ahead of the now silent pipes and drums. On arrival at their allotted ground, the men were fallen out and set to the task of pitching their tents. That day they were left very much to themselves: Dornoch went off with Major Hay and Andrew Black to wait upon Lord Methuen at his field headquarters tent, and that was all. When they returned, no conference of officers was called. The battalion seemed to return, temporarily at any rate, to a degree of normality, like a day of rest in India. Men sat outside the tents that afternoon, yarning and smoking their pipes. The odd song was struck up, and there was the sound of the occasional mouth-organ playing some popular music-hall ditty. After a while Ogilvie heard the first strangled whine as air was puffed into bagpipes, and then saw Pipe-Major Ross coming into view, walking up and down and playing by himself. 'The Campbells Are Coming', 'The Old 93rd', 'The Rowan Tree',

44

'The Badge of Scotland', 'The Heroes of Vittoria'. Challenging, a sound of war and courage, nostalgic, remindful of Scotland and of India. The men fell silent, listening. Ogilvie studied some of the faces, trying to read the thoughts behind the sun-tanned masks: thoughts of home, thoughts of the morrow, thoughts of who would and who would not go back to Scotland when the war was over? For though the war would be short, men would fall: the casualties had been high already. There was no reason to suppose they would not continue high, and the Royal Strathspeys might well lose more men than they had become accustomed to during patrol activities along the North-West Frontier . . .

Ogilvie became aware of something approaching an earthquake immediately in front of him: R.S.M. Cunningham, slam-slam to attention as usual. 'Sir!'

'Yes, Sar'nt-Major?'

'Nothing special, sir. I just thought to myself, Captain Ogilvie's looking pensive. Sir!'

Ogilvie grinned. 'Perhaps I am, Sar'nt-Major. It's Pipe-Major Ross's little effort, I expect.'

'Aye, sir. The pipes do induce it.' Cunningham paused; Ogilvie saw his look straying across the lines of tents, across the sprawling, lazing Scots soldiers, across the dun-coloured, dried-up terrain beyond the fragile-looking railway line that led back to

Cape Town and on north the other way to Mafeking and beyond. The R.S.M. expressed something of Ogilvie's own thoughts, earlier ones and ones that had again entered his mind now. 'It's a different sort of soldiering, Captain Ogilvie, sir. A very different sort.'

'I agree—but why, in your view?'

'A different sort of enemy, sir. A white enemy, men like ourselves. Men with a good standard of living.'

'Basically honest men.'

'Yes, sir, indeed. There are some at home who do not like this war, sir. Politicians and other gentlemen.'

'Plenty didn't like all we did in India, Sar'nt-Major.'

'Aye, sir, that's true. Quite true. You'll never get agreement from everybody, not in this world, and that's a fact.'

'And you, Sar'nt-Major?'

'Me, sir?'

'Yes. Do you like the war?'

Cunningham said, 'If you're asking me, sir, I'll say this and say it honestly: I see the Boers' point of view. It's their land—'

'The same applies to India and Afghanistan, Sar'nt-Major!'

Cunningham nodded. 'Yes, sir. Yes. But out there, we saved them from murdering each other, and also we tried to teach them our ideas as to honesty and straight dealing and—and truthfulness. I'll not say we succeeded—

but you'll see what I mean. You'll see the difference in the kind of man we'll be fighting soon.' He added, 'There's a difference of terrain, too, sir, and that'll tell.'

'Yes . . .'

'But I've a feeling we'll win. We always do, sir, do we not?'

Again Ogilvie grinned. 'We rather tend to, I think, Sar'nt-Major. But I must say I'm surprised at you . . . for a Boer lover, you're—'

'Sir!' Bosom Cunningham's face was suddenly scarlet with indignation. 'Sir! I must ask you—'

'All right, Sar'nt-Major, all right—only pulling your leg!'

'Sir! I should hope so, sir! See their point of view I may, sir. I still fight for the Queen, sir! *Sir!*' Slam-slam, salute, about turn, quick march. Ogilvie shook his head at the retreating angry back, the kilt swirling out shocked annoyance. Dear old Bosom, nothing would be the same without him! He was like the Rock of Ages, firm, reliable, tolerant beyond the tolerance of most Regimental Sergeant-Majors. It was a rotten shame to tease the old buffer, really. But Ogilvie had been slightly irritated himself: the Boers were a whiskery set of bastards, say what you liked about it being their land and all that. Ill-fitting workaday clothes, or Sunday-best clothes for the posed photographs of the leaders, high white collars, black coats, wide-brimmed black hats. They

47

were like a gathering of chapel dignitaries. Really, it was a damned insult to think they had stood up to the British Army, thin red line and all. An insult that they had killed so many British soldiers, fighting for the Queen. Not for much longer, though! Ogilvie thought of Major Douglas Haig, Staff Officer to General French. French was a cavalryman, and first-class at his job. Ogilvie had heard that there were two things above all that the Boers were really scared of: British cavalry, and cold steel. Well—French had his Dragoons and Lancers and Hussars; and the Royal Strathspeys loved nothing better than a bayonet charge. Very wild at that, they were!

*　　　*　　　*

At four a.m. the regiments moved out as planned. There was secrecy in the air: Lord Methuen even left his camp-fires burning behind him, as he advanced on the march up the line of the railway. 'We shall be in Kimberley within the week,' he said to Dornoch when he rode down the column. 'And I intend to put the fear of God into those Boers!'

The relief force left Orange River Station that early morning in good heart, with 8000 men of the Guards, the Northumberland Fusiliers, regiments from Yorkshire and Lancashire, the Argylls, Black Watch, Royal

Strathspeys ... a sprinkling of cavalry including the New South Wales Lancers from Australia; they were well supplied with transport animals, many wagons, and lines of artillery; while an armoured train forged ahead of them along the railway track. How could the Boers stand against such a force? Ogilvie wondered. They advanced sweatily and without the uplift of their military music across a hot land, flat country of low scrubby growth with a wealth of thornbush to jag and tear. From time to time they came across the native populations of South Africa, the black-skinned people, almost naked figures who mostly fled from their dusty approach, people who had the aspect of strangers in their own warring land, a vague and pathetic backcloth to the Whites' struggle. By the time they had reached Belmont, still south of the Modder River, they had been joined by a Naval Brigade, khaki-clad sailors sadly out of their natural element. They had also been overtaken by a rider with news from the telegraph at Orange River Station and the word spread down the column that, by the very afternoon of their departure on the march, the Boer newspapers had carried the news that the British were on their way to the relief of Kimberley.

'So much,' Black said sardonically, 'for secrecy!'

This was not the only news: the Boer General Cronje was believed to be heading south from Mafeking with a large army, but on account of deviations and the necessity of forming supply laagers along the Orange Free State border, the blocking of Methuen's column was being left to one Commandant Prinsloo, with orders to delay Methuen until Cronje had brought down his full strength. At Belmont the column was halted and Lord Methuen called a conference of commanding officers. On his return from this conference, Dornoch assembled his own officers.

He said, 'Between here and Kimberley there are three defensive positions available to the enemy—three clusters of kopjes, steep and stony. We're hard upon the first of these now—it's over there.' He pointed towards his right. 'There are breastworks along the top, and Lord Methuen believes Prinsloo's holding it. He doesn't mean to leave his communications exposed, so he's going to clear the kopje. The Guards Brigade are to lead an attack tonight—using the darkness as cover. We shall go in in support, gentlemen. Detailed orders will be issued shortly. That is all.'

Soon after this, Black held his own conference: a little pep-talk to company commanders and senior N.C.O.s. 'Our first action in South Africa,' he said. 'We must acquit ourselves well—and not let down our reputation gained in India. We shall show the rest of the column, the Guards especially, what

50

we can do. Captain Ogilvie?'

'Captain Black?'

'I have noticed signs of slackness in your company, Captain Ogilvie. I—'

'What signs?'

'Ah ... unpressed kilts, boots not decently cleaned, slovenly marching. And a tendency towards bawdy song—'

'Bawdier than other companies, Captain Black?'

There was a laugh.

'Yes! And I will not have it!' The adjutant swished the air with his hand, angrily. 'I shall—'

'I'll speak to the men,' Ogilvie said solemnly, his tongue in his cheek. 'Clean boots, pressed kilts, no vulgarity. Are there any other action requirements you have in mind, Captain Black? If the men should swear during the attack—'

'Shut your mouth, sir! You are being insubordinate in front of N.C.O.s and I will not have it!'

Somehow, Ogilvie kept his face straight.

*   *   *

'Quiet, now! Dead quiet, d'ye hear?'

Colour-Sergeant MacTrease crept along at Ogilvie's side, leading B Company of the Royal Strathspeys, spread out in rear of the Guards. Before the light went, Ogilvie had been sent by the Colonel to reconnoitre the

51

position through binoculars: he had found the kopje a formidable objective, a steep-sided bastion with no cover whatsoever beyond scraggy, leaf-free bush growth and a few grassy tufts and scattered boulders. They moved on, slow and quiet, advancing into total dark, for there was no moon as yet, and total silence also.

Nerve-racking silence.

Absolutely no sound from the Boers. Just nothing. An advance into a vacuum, was what it felt like to Ogilvie. They had covered the distance, surely to God? So damn dark—yet the moon, if and when it came, could prove a disaster unless they had reached the kopje first.

On and on, strung out, long lines of cautious men putting one foot before another and not knowing what it might be descending into. Scrub and rough grass, thorn, small animals that slithered drily away over Army boots, faint rattles from equipment, water-bottles, rifle-slings, bayonets, ammo belts. On and on, wonderingly. Then—a runner coming back, back from the Guards' commander in the van of the advance, to make contact with Lord Dornoch.

After that, the word spreading: *'The bloody maps are wrong!'*

Heading the wrong way! No wonder the Boers were doing so well! Ogilvie swore into the darkness, vividly. The Guards altered their direction—only a little, but the error had been enough to have put them dead wrong to date. The next impediment: a fence guarding the railway line—and they had to cross the line to reach the kopje. Methuen had been less than efficient. Had the maps not been faulty, they might have crossed in a better place.

They would need, now, to cut their way through—*but there were no wire cutters*.

The order came: 'Cut down the fences, using axes.'

Fine! But it all took too long. Within two more hours there was the first hint of dawn in the east. And, as that dawn came up, the van of the advance was still a long way from the kopje. And still there was silence, silence broken by the Guards' commander: 'The Brigade will advance in line. Company commanders will spread out their men to minimise the target.'

Slow, steady, rifles aimed towards the silent kopje. It was the silence that strained men's nerves. Ogilvie could almost feel his heart-beats, could smell the sweat of fear emanating from the ranks as they stepped forward through the lightening day, advancing across the open plain. The kopje's defenders were giving no sign of their occupation: it seemed a deserted place.

'Could they have buggered off in the night, d'ye think, sir?' MacTrease asked in an uneasy whisper. 'Will it be a bloodless victory?'

53

Would it be victory at all?

Ogilvie was about to give some sort of answer to his colour-sergeant when he saw the horse of General Fetherstonhaugh, who was leading the support brigade, suddenly rear up on its hind legs—and then he became aware of the ripple of concentrated fire that ran like a necklace along the kopje's crest, a killing fire that crackled into sound, raking through the mass of the advance, turning it temporarily into a holocaust.

CHAPTER FOUR

The order was passed, as General Fetherstonhaugh, gallantly but too blatantly riding his horse up and down before the men, fell to the Boer shots: 'The Guards will advance—at the double!' What was left of them, after that appalling opening fire, did precisely that—running, stumbling, falling, played bravely on by their regimental band. Behind them, pressing ahead hard and fast, were the pipes of the Royal Strathspeys; and soon the Scots and the Guards were mixed together, running shoulder to shoulder, storming on through the screen of whining bullets for the steep side of the hill. All around Ogilvie men were going down screaming, their bodies mutilated and ripped by the weight of the shot, their khaki uniforms spreading crimson. As the British force reached the foot of the kopje, they paused for breath—and to fix bayonets.

Then, with a mighty roar from the Scots, and the challenging sound of the pipes playing 'Cock o' the North', they climbed on hands and knees up the glacis towards the breast-works above. Many more died as the Boer defenders, black-hatted, shirt-sleeved, collarless, leaned over and aimed at the helmets. Those helmets, falling, rolled back down the hillside, their wearers' limbs spreadeagled. Ogilvie, reaching the top with his revolver in his hand, shot straight into a gaping, whiskered mouth and saw brief daylight through the back of the throat before the horrible gush of blood came. At once he was set upon by a huge man with a full, sprouting beard, and found himself in mortal personal combat, with the big Boer's fingers tight around his throat. His assailant fell away when Bosom Cunningham suddenly appeared behind him, and struck with a bloody-bladed claymore.

By now the bayonets had reached the crest: behind those bayonets, grim-faced and blood-lusty, the British soldiers jumped the defenders, falling upon them hand-to-hand, cutting, thrusting, carving flesh that cringed from the shining steel. The rush, the bayonet charge of the Guards and Scots and their support brigade, carried that kopje and the others. The Boers began a general retreat, fleeing the field on their ponies, to live and fight another day.

Later, in Belmont camp, Lord Methuen issued his personal congratulations. 'Complete success,' he said. 'Complete success—in spite of the Boers' dirty weapons, about which I intend to protest most vehemently to Commandant Prinsloo, in writing.'

The 'dirty weapons' were the dum-dum bullets—expanding bullets that inflicted terrible injuries, bullets that had been, by international agreement, banned the previous July. Nasty work—but, under certain circumstances, the British had themselves reserved the right to make use of them. This time, used against the British force, the dum-dum bullets had helped to kill or wound three hundred men. Complete success: one set of little hills emptied of Boer farmers, three hundred British casualties!

During the remainder of that day the medical orderlies under Surgeon Major Corton were kept more than busy; so were the burial parties. It was whilst he was concerning himself with the sad business of the dead, with gravediggers and firing-parties and pipers who would play the Highland lament 'The Flowers of the Forest' over the forlorn, dun-coloured hummocks, that James Ogilvie was sent for by his Colonel and introduced to a man whom at first he took for a Boer prisoner: a good-looking man of around forty, with a strong chin behind a fringe beard, a man with straight eyes above a straight, dominant nose, a man clad in sweaty shirt, waistcoat and trousers.

Dornoch said, 'Major Allenby of the Dragoons.'

Allenby, smiling, reached out his hand. 'So this is Captain Ogilvie. You look surprised, Ogilvie!'

'I am, sir—'

'You took me for a Boer?'

'I'm sorry, yes—'

Allenby laughed. 'No apology required, my dear fellow. It's a compliment! Now—we'll not waste time. You know, of course, why I'm here. As a matter of fact, I'm not going to give you your further orders myself, Ogilvie—that'll be seen to later. But I am going to escort you into Kimberley.' He looked Ogilvie up and down, critically, an amused look in his eye. 'For a start, you'll have to take off the glad rags. No more of the regimentals for a while . . . you're Piet de Ruis, and I'm your Uncle Koos . . . Koos de Ruis, farmer from near Potchefstroom in the Transvaal. I have brought clothing for you.' Allenby glanced towards Lord Dornoch. 'If your Colonel will release you to my care at once, we'll prepare to ride.'

*　　　*　　　*

57

Goodbye to the regiment: words with Captain Black, and out, alone with Major Allenby, pony-mounted and dressed like any dyed-in-the-wool Boer, into the vast empty spaces along the western boundary of the Orange Free State, with Katharine Gilmour's locket safety stowed away on his person. It was some sixty miles from Belmont direct to Kimberley. They would be moving ahead of Lord Methuen's column, keeping clear, as Methuen would not, of action along the way. To this end they would deviate whenever reconnaissance proved the necessity: the sixty miles would grow accordingly, but Allenby expected to be approaching the Kimberley siege lines within three days at most. The ponies, and themselves, he said, would be pushed hard.

'What's going to carry us through the Boer lines?' Ogilvie asked soon after they had set out. 'We'll not be able to outflank them, that's one thing sure!'

'We'll pray for luck,' Allenby said. 'That, and a little essential instruction, in case we can't slip through and I'm forced to talk our way into the Boers' confidence.'

'Instruction, Major?'

Allenby nodded, swatted at flies that settled to feed on sweaty bodies. 'Instruction on how to be a farmer's boy! I take it you've no Afrikaans?'

'None.'

'Then *you'll* do no talking! You're dumb, Ogilvie—a serious speech defect, the result of a recent shock. I say recent, since obviously there's no time for you to learn the sign language of the mute. Nevertheless, you should have some understanding of the life of the Boer farmer, which is your background, young Piet de Ruis—the crops, the animals and the morality! Otherwise you could betray us by your reactions to what you hear said. I shall be your mentor.'

And this he was. As they struck out across the sun-drenched plain towards the Modder River, Allenby talked and Ogilvie listened dutifully. Allenby the dragoon was a man of agile and receptive mind, a fast learner. He had seen African service before this, as he told Ogilvie: he had taken part in the Bechuanaland expedition under General Sir Charles Warren, and had served in the Zulu War in 1888. This alone, however, did not explain his detailed knowledge of the Boer: he had clearly done immense and painstaking research into his new, if temporary, character. This alone told Ogilvie how great was the importance of his mission—and even now, Allenby refused to discuss that.

'Better not,' he said with finality. 'It's a long way to go, to Kimberley!'

Ogilvie, knowing what he meant, was forced to agree: capture by any Boer raiders en route, or at the siege perimeter, might lead to exposure and questioning, and, as Douglas Haig had suggested, some of the Boer methods of interrogation were known to be far from pretty. So, shielded by ignorance of the wider issues, he concentrated on learning the mechanics of the part he had to play. In addition to instructing him in all the aspects of the farmer's life in the Transvaal—more properly called the Z.A.R., or South African Republic—Allenby crammed in the political and social background, telling him of the effects of the discovery of gold in the Witwatersrand, going back earlier to speak of the Boer movement in the thirties, the movement under Potgeiter and others from Graaf Reinet in Cape Colony to the veld north of the Orange River; of the annexation of the Transvaal by the British government, of the passions aroused, of the Uitlanders who followed the gold. He spoke of the seasons, of the high summer pasturage of the Hooge Veld, of the keen bracing air of the uplands, the hot and sometimes malarious low-lying districts, of soil that was rich and deep, of the plentiful water supply, of the deep gorges and splendid scenery of the Kaap Mountains in the east, of the Magaliesberg range stretching west of Pretoria, of Pretoria's iron and Pretoria's diamonds, of the native African tribes who had been dispossessed by the Boer encroachments over the years and who were now reduced to sorry groups of suffering bowed heads, Blacks

60

who had become virtual nonentities in the midst of war; and of many, many other things. He instructed Ogilvie in the ramifications of the fictitious de Ruis family until he was word perfect.

The first deviation from the route came when they were nearing Graspan, on the railway line fifteen miles north from Belmont.

'There's a Boer force holding more kopjes between Graspan and Enslin sidings,' Allenby said. 'For my money, it'll have been reinforced by Prinsloo's men from Belmont by now. We have to avoid them, so we'll head west and outflank.'

'And Lord Methuen?'

'Oh, I've no doubt he'll engage.'

'Result, more casualties—'

'Quite so!'

'And so little gained.'

Allenby looked at him hard. 'The Boers are across the direct route for Kimberley, and Kimberley has to be relieved. That means mopping-up along the way, does it not, Ogilvie?'

'Yes, of course. It's . . . just that my regiment was due for posting home—that's all.'

'They're soldiers, Ogilvie. They understand.'

'They still die.'

'Don't I know it! And I'm as sorry as you. But there have been so many misconstructions, so many misunderstandings . . . you know, I was never one of those who thought this would be an easy war or a short one. It'll not be either—but you may be instrumental, if you're lucky, in making it less long and less painful than it might otherwise be. So, while we're outflanking the Boers at Graspan, Ogilvie, let's continue with your education—but let's also keep our eyes and ears alert at the same time!'

They moved west and, riding their ponies down behind low hills, moved apparently unobserved. Soon after this the day began to grow dark; they were well past the Graspan and Enslin sidings when Major Allenby called a halt. 'We'll sleep for an hour or two,' he said. 'We've made good progress and the ponies need rest even if we don't. But one of us must stay awake while the other sleeps.'

The ponies were tethered to heavy boulders on the hillside and Allenby opened up a pack of iron rations. Ogilvie did likewise; and Allenby produced a flask of whisky, from which each took a draught, and then another. Weariness, the weariness of the saddle, flowed out of Ogilvie; the temporary warmth of the whisky kept out the night air's chill. In his turn, he slept; and in his turn he kept watch, keeping on the move unless he should fall asleep, flinging his arms about his body as the cold encroached. The brooding silence of the plain, of the hills behind the sleeping Allenby, the silence that rustled with small sounds, sounds of night animals that crept and scurried and slithered, sounds, distant ones, of the larger inhabitants going about their nightly businesses. A moon coming up now, to spread cold silver like a cloth upon the ground.

In that moonlight the sudden and brief silhouette on the top of the hill behind: a man, a mounted man. Very brief—the disappearance took place almost simultaneously with the advent.

Ogilvie rubbed his eyes, keeping dead still in all other respects.

Nothing . . .

Imagination? The lonely empty spaces working their magic on him?

He thought, on the whole, not: he had seen so many similar sights in the Afghan hills, along the high, remote summits of the Khyber Pass. Cunningham had said this would be a different sort of war: true enough—but not all that different!

He bent, and woke Allenby. The Major's reaction was instantaneous and quiet: 'What is it, Ogilvie?'

'A man on the hilltop, a mounted man.'

'Where is he now?'

'Vanished. I think he's gone back, down the other side.'

'Lie low, then. Let's hope he doesn't spot the ponies if he comes back.'

'Or hasn't already.'

There was a flash of teeth in the moonlight, a grin. 'That, too!'

They waited, scarcely breathing in case they should miss a sound. Ogilvie felt a looseness in his bowels: the first test could be at hand and he felt unready for it. Dumbness sounded easy to simulate: the practice might well be harder. Sometimes a man made a spontaneous reaction, without thinking.

Then they heard a movement, a horse's hooves, coming from their right. Allenby lifted his body a little, and stared along the track. 'He's skirted the hill, I think. We're asleep, Ogilvie. Both of us.'

He lay back on the hillside, curling his body in the lee of a boulder. Ogilvie copied his example, tried to appear relaxed in sleep, but was conscious of the hard tautness of his body, poised to spring into action if necessary. The sounds, the clopping horse-sounds, grew louder—then stopped. There was the distinct snick of a rifle bolt, and then a slower resumption of the hoofbeats. The rider would have seen the tethered ponies now. Once again, the sound stopped and a man's rough voice called out in Afrikaans.

'Who's there, who is it?'

Allenby and Ogilvie lay still, silent.

'Answer, damn you, answer!'

Allenby whispered, 'We wake now—convincingly!' He sat up, called back, also in Afrikaans: 'Tell us first who you are, friend—if you are a friend.'

There was a pause. They heard the horse

64

moving forward, slowly. Then they saw the animal and its rider in the moonlight: a tall man by the look of his torso, with a wide-brimmed hat. The man said, 'I am from Commandant Prinsloo's commando. And you?'

'Koos de Ruis from the Transvaal, and his nephew Piet de Ruis.'

'Whose commando?'

'Vorlang's commando in Potchefstroom—where there is no fighting. We're on our way to help defeat the British at Kimberley—'

'Why not Mafeking?'

'I have a brother outside Kimberley. We are keen to join him, my nephew and I.'

There was no response, but the horseman rode forward. Soon his features were visible in the moonlight: a hard face, with a pointed, neatly-trimmed beard. When he spoke again he sounded unfriendly. 'They must be well supplied with men, in Potchefstroom! Prinsloo will be glad enough to have you with him—that is, if you aren't running *from* a fight rather than towards one!'

Allenby got to his feet, with Ogilvie beside him. As the horse came up to them Allenby said, 'We're not runners, friend. I'll fight with anyone who'll have me, against the British soldiers. But I have a reason for wishing to reach the siege line round Kimberley, so if it's all the same—'

'What's the reason, eh?'

'My brother is there, as I have told you

65

already, with Commandant Wessels.'

'Wessels needs no more men, to my knowledge. Prinsloo does. A strong British force is advancing from the south. If Prinsloo has to fall back on Kimberley—why, then that's when you'll see your brother! Meantime, I say you'll come with me, the pair of you.'

'You've no right to press-gang free citizens,' Allenby said coolly, staring up at the horseman's rock-hard face. 'I'll fight where I please, and no permission from you needed! My aim's for Kimberley, and that's where I'm going.' He put a hand on Ogilvie's shoulder. 'Come, Piet, we've been brought awake, we'll be on our way again—'

'Hold!' the horseman snapped. Allenby and Ogilvie, who had already turned towards the tethered ponies, found the Boer's horse being ridden into them. 'You'll do as I say. Leave the ponies where they are, and walk ahead of my horse. I don't want any trouble, but if you do, well, then I'm here to give it!'

'Is that so?' Allenby asked with a laugh. Standing beside the horse now, he said, 'One question first, then.'

'Well, what is it?'

'This.' He reached up, the palm of his right hand open. 'Do you see that hand, friend?'

'Yes.'

'It's held a gun and fought in the past, friend. Back in eighty-one. It has killed men. Has yours?'

'Mine has fought, yes.'

'But killed?'

'Can't be sure of that,' the man answered.

'But I can. Touch your hand against mine. Go on—touch. It's a soldier's hand. You called me a coward, a runner.' Ogilvie was watching Major Allenby closely, waiting for some sign as to the next move. He was aware of some curious magnetic power in the Major of Dragoons, something oddly compelling in the man's eyes as they reflected the cold moonlight. Allenby said again, 'Come now, touch hands.'

Looking uncertain, the horseman brought his right hand away from his rein and touched the fingers lightly against Allenby's. At once Allenby's grip closed on the hand like a vice, and he jerked hard. Taken utterly by surprise, the Boer came off his horse in a heap, legs flailing wildly. One of his feet, heavily shod, caught Allenby on the side of the head before the Major could dodge it. Allenby went down, and as he did so the Boer recovered himself with remarkable agility, swinging a rifle-butt at Ogilvie as he leapt to his feet, catching the Scot a heavy blow on the shoulder. Swiftly he aimed the rifle at Allenby; but, when a shot came, it was the Boer who went down, his rifle clattering on the ground.

Allenby got to his feet, holding his revolver. He bent and examined the Boer.

'Dead as mutton,' he said. 'Well—he asked

67

for it! I didn't like doing that to him, though.'

'The hand?'

'Yes, the hand. An old trick, but it worked, rather to my surprise.' Allenby looked around, seeming to sniff the air. There was something of a wind now, and the night was extremely cold. The racket of the shot had sounded to the two men as though it must wake the whole region; but so far at any rate there were no indications of anyone coming to see what had happened. Allenby put a hand on Ogilvie's arm. 'Away we go, then,' he said. 'While the going's good!'

They untethered the ponies from the boulders and went off fast, keeping well to the west and out of the way of Prinsloo's commandos. As they set off through the night Ogilvie glanced back. The Boer's horse was gently nuzzling the body of its late rider, and starting a fretful whinnying sound. Ogilvie recalled once again the Regimental Sergeant-Major's words about this being a different war, fought against men who were totally different from the Pathan marauders along the North-West Frontier. These Boers were, after all, men whose forebears had colonised South Africa: they were fighting for what they and their fathers had built up over the years, fighting for home and family and the right of self-government in a land they had largely made themselves. They were not raiders, they were not murderers . . .

Ogilvie shrugged, determined, after that one backward look, to keep such thoughts from his mind. It was not his business: he had his orders as a soldier to attend to with diligence, and before long he was going to need all his mental resources and all his sense of duty. It would never do, to incur the displeasure of Lord Kitchener! Kitchener of Khartoum, or just plain K, his enmity could be death to any officer's ambitions.

By his side Allenby, keeping a close watch on the horizon behind and to their right as they went along, said suddenly, 'Not too good an omen—that fracas. Oh, he believed me I think—but I've a feeling he wouldn't have done so for long!'

'Perhaps he just had a suspicious mind!'

Allenby grinned. 'Perhaps! Mind you, these Boers are very family-minded, and it certainly wouldn't be out of character for a brother and nephew ... but I doubt if the same yarn'll work when we reach the siege lines. You see, being non-existent, he'll not be there, that brother of mine!'

'Then what do we say, Major?'

Allenby said, 'My hope is, we'll get clean through under cover of darkness—they've plenty of men there by all accounts, but I'm pretty sure we'll find an unguarded spot somewhere. You can't string men out *all* along the perimeter, in the very nature of things there has to be a concentration of personnel in

69

defensible sectors. But if we don't achieve a slip-through, my dear fellow, then I'm going to say we became detached from one of Prinsloo's commandos between Belmont and Kimberley.'

'Detached—or ran away?'

Allenby grinned. 'Ran away! They do, you know—the Boers. It's not always cowardice, it's simple strategy. When the pace gets too hot, they melt—ride off on their ponies, which they always keep handy in a safe spot. You see, they're so short of manpower, Ogilvie. They *have* to live to fight another day whenever they can. There are no men to spare for heroic last stands, which may certainly *be* heroic, but are generally damn silly and wasteful and seldom achieve any military purpose. So, you see, no one outside Kimberley is going to cold-shoulder us for doing the accepted thing, whatever that man of Prinsloo's said!'

Unmolested, but cold and starting to feel extremely hungry in spite of the iron rations, they rode on through deserted, scrubby countryside, flat, uninspiring and utterly desolate as, soon after, the first green-shot streaks of the dawn came across the clear sky of the veld.

*　　　*　　　*

Dust swirled around the two British officers: dust storms were just one of the hazards of the

70

Cape Midland country bordering the high wire fence that closed in the Orange Free State. This time, the dust storm was blowing rather more to the north and east as Allenby and James Ogilvie rode deeper into Griqualand West towards the diamond mines. While the worst of the dust blew, sending particles into ears and eyes and noses, finding its way into every fold of their clothing, they halted: to get lost now would be fatal. The storm past, they moved on again, crossing the Modder River by a drift well to the westward of Magersfontein Hill. After another night, and another long day's riding, Allenby reined in his pony and reached out to lay a hand on Ogilvie's bridle.

'Kimberley,' he said, pointing ahead. 'Or at any rate—the first of the diamond workings. Do you see, Ogilvie?'

'I see something on the horizon ... something that looks like a line of kopjes and yet isn't quite. Rather too regular.'

'Correct,' Allenby said. 'It's the tops of the debris heaps from the excavations—mine tailings, they call them. Seventy feet high, some of them. They've been converted into strongpoints—and they mark the perimeter of the defences. The command post is over that way—d'you see?—on the top of the hauling gear of one of the mines—De Beers' inclined shaft. There's always an officer on watch there, and he's connected by telephone to the perimeter strongpoints. As for kopjes, there

71

aren't any, which is unlucky for the Boers! All they have for cover is a few low ridges. You'll see them in due course. We've quite a way to go yet.'

'So what do we do now, Major?'

'Carry on advancing, but with extreme caution until dark. Obviously, I don't want to be seen if I can avoid it—but at the same time I don't want to give the impression, if we are seen, that we're sneaking in—d'you follow?'

Ogilvie nodded. 'I follow, Major. We still may need to be joining up from Prinsloo's commandos!'

'Correct. Well then—on we go!'

They moved forward. Ogilvie was conscious of a looseness in his stomach again: the time for parley, a very tricky parley, was possibly close at hand now. He looked ahead at the great dumps of mine tailings, so slowly growing in his vision, great heaps of blue-grey as the sun went down; through field-glasses he looked with fascination at the curious crow's-nest on its square support at the top of the De Beers' mine shaft—the crow's-nest that formed the headquarters of Colonel Kekewich of the 1st Loyal North Lancashires, commanding the Kimberley defence. At dusk they began to raise the low ridges that Allenby had mentioned earlier, and the Major once again called a halt.

'Now we wait for full dark,' he said.

'And then?'

'We go ahead dismounted, but leading the

ponies in. We'll reconnoitre, try to find a gap in the siege line.'

'And go straight through it?'

Allenby nodded. 'That's the idea. We'll head for one of the perimeter strongpoints- and hope to reach it before we're shot down.' He studied Ogilvie's face. 'It's going to be touch and go, I'll not deny. But this isn't your first experience of breaking through enemy lines—is it, my dear fellow?'

'No. Don't worry about me, Major.'

'I won't. A good effort, then.' A smile spread across Allenby's face. 'I dare say the lady's worth it to you, even if K isn't!'

* * *

Allenby was imprecise as to the distance they would find between the siege line and the defence perimeter of the diamond town: it would depend, he said, on just where they found that gap, if ever they did. 'It should be something between say two and four miles,' he said as they lay flat on the veld. 'We'll probably, from here, come down on them in the region of Carter's Ridge, more or less. That's about four miles from the perimeter. We'll avoid the actual ridge, of course—it's a Boer stronghold. I'll aim probably to the north of it—avoiding the railway line, you see. I believe the main Boer strength is to the south of the town, from Carter's Ridge through

Wimbledon and the railway line to Aban's Dam.' Already he had shown Ogilvie his map of the area, and Ogilvie had a fair picture in his mind. 'I rather think—' Allenby broke off as a shaft of light beamed out from ahead, sweeping the countryside. 'See—the first of the searchlights from the defences. Good for Kimberley, less good for us, but that can't be helped. Well—it's time to go. Are you ready?'

'All ready,' Ogilvie said. They got to their feet and, leading the ponies, headed for the Boer lines. Ogilvie was thinking a good deal of Katharine Gilmour: he wanted to do his best for her, his best as a man for a woman's wish, but he felt that with the involvement of Lord Kitchener the Red Daniel had now become more an instrument of war and strategy than a young woman's security in a changing world; and he would not stand by and see Katharine's hopes perish in a trap of deceit, to become another casualty of war and of a kind of treachery to a girl's trustfulness.

CHAPTER FIVE

Cautiously, they moved ahead over scrubby grass and patches of bare earth, skirting round to the north. The searchlights did not, as yet, bother them: the probing beams were directed only onto the area between Kimberley's defences and the inner circle of the siege line confronting the perimeter. Moving on, Allenby and Ogilvie soon made out the camp-fires of the enemy in the distance, saw the movement of men outlined against the glow.

'More to the north yet, I fancy,' Allenby said, after a look through his field-glasses. 'You see where the camp-fires end? There's a gap there, I believe. When we're abreast of it, we'll reconnoitre inwards and see what we find.' He put a hand on Ogilvie's shoulder. 'I've a feeling we're going to be lucky!'

On slowly, walking the ponies in. They heard the snick of rifle bolts from time to time; sometimes snatches of song came to them, song roared out by rough voices. After a while they began to come into line with the ending of the camp-fires, and Allenby turned to the east shortly after they had passed the last of them.

'Just for a preliminary look,' he said. He brought up his field-glasses again, but made no comment. Some three hundred yards closer in, he halted for another examination of the siege line. He nodded, as if pleased with continuing luck. For his part Ogilvie felt that luck was too good to hold; he advanced beside Allenby with a tingling spine, advanced into darkness and silence. The singing, away to their right once they had turned, had stopped.

The searchlights, the only apparent sign of life now, were going on with their sweeps.

Ogilvie cursed those probing beams of brilliance: they were going to endanger their lives the moment they broke out across No Man's Land on the ponies. They would become targets for the practice of Boer and British alike. Allenby had told him they were expected by the Kimberley defence, that all strongpoints and sentries would have been warned; but Ogilvie, knowing well the propensity of even seasoned troops to fire at shadows, had little confidence that the irregulars who formed a large part of the defence of the town would hold their fire when they saw what could be the spearhead of a night attack. When he had mentioned this, Allenby had replied, tritely enough but with asperity, that risks must be taken in war . . .

'We've chosen the place well enough,' Allenby said suddenly a moment later. 'If I'm not mistaken, there's a gap of around half a mile—take a look for yourself.' He handed his glasses over. 'Bare ground, and empty. Well?'

'You're right, Major. What I don't understand is—'

'Why they leave a gap? I told you— manpower shortage! They're forced to choose . . . but it'll be well covered by artillery, you may be sure!'

'And we run the gauntlet?'

'Correct, we do. But, given luck, Ogilvie, we'll be too fast for 'em. Now listen carefully.' He took back the field-glasses and stowed them in their leather case, slung around his neck. Ogilvie shivered in a chilly wind that suddenly came to ruffle the long grass. 'There may well be isolated men posted on watch in that space, and nicely hidden. I don't suppose for a moment we're going to have an easy run. Keep a very sharp look-out, and fire to kill the moment you see any movement. Keep well down on your pony's neck if you can—reduce the target. When I give the word, we ride. We ride like the wind, straight through that gap and into No Man's Land. Don't keep to a dead straight line after we're through—keep zig-zagging. Follow my movements. There's a heap of those mine tailings—over there, where the searchlight's just starting to sweep from now. D'you see where I mean?'

'Yes . . . a little to the north of us—'

'That's right. That's the direction I shall head in. It's about the closest point we shall find—between two and three miles.' Allenby looked closely at Ogilvie's face, peering through the thick darkness. There was, fortunately, no moon. 'A long ride I'll grant you, but we're going to make it. We have surprise in our favour, and I repeat, we're expected by Kekewich's sentries. Are you ready?'

Ogilvie took a deep breath, and nodded. 'I'm ready, Major.'

Allenby reached out a hand. 'The best of luck,' he said quietly. 'Now—mount.'

They mounted the ponies.

'Ride!'

Ogilvie pressed his heels to the pony's side, riding fast into the wind close behind Allenby, heading down into the siege ring's gap, expecting to be mangled in a hail of bullets if not a concentration of Boer artillery. The very fact of being mounted on a pony instead of a horse was in itself a frustration: their jogging progress was surely lethally slow and foolish! But they appeared to bounce on unseen and unheard, miraculously. Surprise was working, not for the first time in the history of war. They swept down between two gentle inclines, one of them topped by a deserted, shell-shattered building—a farm probably. Ogilvie saw, briefly, the torn walls and the gaping holes where windows had been. He saw this in the swathe of one of the busy searchlights as it moved for a moment beyond its customary range, and then, by another miracle, moved away in the other direction leaving the mounted officers to the safe shroud of the night.

They came, still unseen, to the edge of No Man's Land. Away to their right they saw the glow of the camp-fires: more of them to the left, on the far side of rising ground. Along the siege line, more shattered buildings showed up in the searchlight beams. They could see no men, no sentries, though they knew that not all the Boers would be sleeping. Allenby rode on furiously for the defence perimeter, with Ogilvie following. They had covered some five or six hundred yards by Ogilvie's estimate when he heard the shout from the Boer lines behind, and then a moment later the firing started. The British searchlights had been far from kind: the two riders had been silhouetted, briefly but for long enough.

Ahead of Ogilvie, as bullets smacked into the ground behind his pony, Allenby swung hard to his right. Now the searchlights were co-operative: they sent their beams farther, playing down on to the Boer line, blinding the riflemen, leaving the two Britons to ride on into thick darkness. Soon after, as Allenby continued zig-zagging towards the Kimberley perimeter, a long ripple of fire, sudden pinpoints of light, crackled from ahead. Looking dangerously over his shoulder for the likely target, Ogilvie saw a party of Boers, who had ridden out in pursuit, highlighted in the garrison searchlights: as the British bullets struck, men and ponies fell. Allenby and Ogilvie rode on, heels digging hard into the ponies' flanks. They had not much farther to go before they saw the British troops riding out to bring them in, and heard the shouted order for them to halt.

They brought up the ponies in a lather of sweat. A voice called: 'Who goes there?'

'Friend.'

'Advance and be recognised.'

Allenby walked his pony ahead. The officer commanding the mounted troopers, men of the Kimberley Light Horse, came on to meet him.

'Major Allenby, and Captain Ogilvie of the 114th Highlanders, at your service.' Allenby paused, looked round as Ogilvie came forward to join him. 'We wish to see Colonel Kekewich as soon as possible.'

*   *   *

The immense shadow of Lord Kitchener of Khartoum, casting itself down from Egypt in the north, quite clearly lay over that night's events in Kimberley: Colonel Kekewich was present in person at his crow's-nest H.Q. on the De Beers' inclined shaft, and this was where the two officers were taken while the British and Boers exchanged more shots 160 feet below in No Man's Land. Kekewich, who had himself proclaimed Kimberley in a state of siege almost six weeks earlier on 14th October, stared at Ogilvie with a touch of superciliousness: he was a man of supercilious aspect, a man with a round, somewhat pink face beneath a high-domed forehead and a balding head, and a thin moustache that drooped like a Chinaman's around the corners of his mouth.

He said, 'One of K's young men, one gathers—h'm?'

'So I'm told, sir.'

'H'm. Well, you were damned lucky to get through, both of you! Anyway, now you've reached us, Captain Ogilvie, we'll waste no time, no time at all.' Kekewich transferred his cool stare to Allenby. 'Major, I think your part in this affair is done now—what?'

'It seems so, sir.'

'I understand you left General French advancing upon Naauwpoort. One presumes he is still doing so—no damn reports seem to have reached me! In any case you'll have to remain here in Kimberley, Major Allenby.'

'Sir, I—'

'You'll have to do as I say, my dear fellow. I'm sorry, but there it is. You'd not break through the siege line on your own, and I can't spare any men as an escort—they'd be cut to pieces and so would you. I need every man I can lay my hands on, and that includes you— you'll be invaluable. Kindly make yourself comfortable in the headquarters mess—I'll send an officer with you. My adjutant will make the necessary provision for you.'

'Very good, sir.' Allenby saluted Colonel Kekewich and turned to Ogilvie, holding out his hand, which Ogilvie took warmly. 'Goodbye for now, Ogilvie. You may be thinking all the instruction in Boer history and so on was wasted after all. Let me assure you it won't be—in the future. I'll say no more,' he added as a staff officer came forward to take

81

him, at Kekewich's bidding, to the mess. 'Those further orders you were so anxious to hear . . . I've no doubt Colonel Kekewich will satisfy your curiosity shortly.'

When Allenby had left with the staff captain, Kekewich moved across to an observation window and stood for a few moments looking down broodingly on the perimeter, on the strongpoints linked with barbed-wirc fences, on the strategically sited abattis, on the searchlights still keeping up their nightlong vigilance against the Boer siege ring. Then he swung round on Ogilvie.

'Strange times,' he said. 'Strange times, when a bunch of farmers can block in our British infantry and cavalry!'

'Yes, sir.'

'And strange men too, my dear fellow.' Kekewich gave a sudden laugh, a sound of no humour. 'You're about to meet a pretty strange one yourself!'

'Sir?'

'Perhaps strange is not quite the word. Tiresome—troublesome—bloody nuisance half the time, though he's done some good. I'm speaking of Mr Rhodes, Mr Cecil Rhodes.'

'Rhodes! He's concerned in this, sir?'

Kekewich raised an eyebrow. 'This? You mean Kitchener's proposals?'

'Yes, sir—though I don't yet know precisely what those proposals are—'

'Then Rhodes will tell you, Ogilvie, Rhodes

82

himself will tell you, for it's partly his scheme. I shall take you to him presently. In the meantime, I shall tell you something about him, and I shall not disguise the fact that we don't see eye to eye. Mr Rhodes is not a soldier, though he is a brave man—I'll not deny that. He has been pestering me constantly, insisting I demand a relief force. He is constantly sending his *own* messages direct to Lord Milner in Cape Town, urging the sending of a relief force. He has even telegraphed to the De Beers office in Cape Town telling them to cable Lord Rothschild in London—urging Rothschild, who is also no soldier, to bully the Cabinet into arranging immediate relief—as though a military campaign were to be run by damn businessmen with minutes and an agenda and a show of hands! Why, Rhodes has even had his own heliograph made here in Kimberley so that he has his own means of communication with the outside world—and damn it, Ogilvie, his system bears more damn traffic than mine! Half of it's share dealing, I'll be bound!' Kekewich simmered gently for a moment, then said, 'Now the good—I'm a fair man, I hope! Rhodes has put all the resources of De Beers at our disposal ... he's even provided rifles, 450 of them. He's got his engineer, an American named Labram, to start building a big gun. They're going to call it Long Cecil. You see the searchlights?'

'Yes, sir?'

Kekewich swept his arm down towards No Man's Land. 'Rhodes's Eyes. He provided 'em! He's given us Company's water, when the pipes to the reservoir were cut. He's allowed the women and children to take shelter in the mine tunnels during bombardments. Oh, he's a patriot, I'll grant! But with an amazing ability to infuriate! A man who has been very great, Ogilvie, and believes himself still to be so, when in fact his prestige is much declined today. All this you must remember in your dealings with him—I think it's important to understand the man, and also to have some appreciation of the position ... *my* position vis-à-vis Mr Cecil Rhodes.'

'Yes, sir.'

Kekewich said gloomily, 'It's possible he may *restore* his greatness, I suppose—his prestige, at any rate—as a result of the current Kitchener proposals. I don't know. I know only this: he and K will make the strangest bedfellows!' He shook his head. 'Too alike in many ways. One is bound to kick the other out of any bed they find themselves sharing!' He banged a bell on a trestle table and another staff officer entered. 'Ah, Phillips. Kindly telephone to Mr Rhodes. Tell him I propose calling upon him in fifteen minutes' time, with Captain Ogilvie.'

*　　　*　　　*

84

Kimberley, silent in the night but obviously alive in its watchtowers and strongholds, Kimberley under siege and waiting hour by hour for a Boer attack, Kimberley and its wealth of diamonds and its Cecil Rhodes, its heartbeats provided by the men of Empire: Royal Garrison Artillery, a detachment of the Loyal North Lancs—just 500 regular soldiers out of 4000 men under arms; volunteers of the Diamond Fields Horse, the Kimberley Regiment, the Kimberley Light Horse and the Town Guard to defend a total of 13,000 Europeans, 7000 coloured and between 20,000 and 30,000 Bantu mine labourers. Riding through the streets with Colonel Kekewich, Ogilvie found the town surprisingly peaceful, a place largely of trees and gardens—put there, Kekewich told him, by Mr Rhodes.

'A man of vision—so they say! He's made himself a very great deal of money at all events. In a sense, this town of Kimberley will be his monument.'

The meeting place with Mr Rhodes was to be in the Sanatorium Hotel. Riding on through those quiet streets, past residences and business premises, bungalows of wooden construction, more imposing buildings of stone, past occasional squads of marching soldiers, Ogilvie was encountering for the first time in his career, that curious existence, that state of being under siege, of being cut right off from the world, on one's own territory yet held in isolation at the mercy of the enemy. But those few marching men, troops proceeding from their barracks and quarters to the relief of their comrades at the perimeter defences, were the only signs of war apart from the continually sweeping searchlights, those Rhodes's Eyes ever vigilant. Ogilvie was conscious also of a sense of history, of a certain awe in the fact that he was about to meet the great Mr Rhodes, a man already a legend throughout the Empire. For almost a quarter of a century Cecil Rhodes had been the dominant personality on the imperial scene so far as South African politics were concerned. A former member of the Cape Assembly, acquisitor of Bechuanaland and Matabeleland, he was the man who had, three years earlier, ended the Matabele rebellion by going alone and unarmed into the very midst of the rebels to effect a so-far lasting peace; the man who, until the scandal of the Jameson Raid, had been Premier of Cape Colony.

What was his connection with Lord Kitchener of Khartoum, the equally fabulous K? What was his connection with the Red Daniel, and Katharine Gilmour?

What intrigue had he, James Ogilvie, got himself involved in by remote order of the distant Sirdar in Egypt?

*   *   *

Tall, commanding, impressive in correct black coat and grey trousers, Rhodes, standing before a vast open fireplace, greeted Colonel Kekewich and Ogilvie in the Sanatorium Hotel. The black servant who had shown the British officers in, withdrew, closing the door noiselessly behind him: the white rulers were alone.

'So you're Captain Ogilvie. I'm delighted to meet you.'

'Thank you, sir.' Ogilvie felt awkward, and slightly overawed; awkward because he was unaccustomed to meeting highly-placed civilians and was thus to some extent unsure of himself. Some of his old diffidence had come back to plague him: with colonels, with generals, an officer knew precisely to the last point of detail how to conduct himself, how to respond, how to react. It was not so with civilians, especially civilians who had both the ear of Lord Kitchener and the evident dislike of the Kimberley defence commander . . .

'I've no doubt you're anxious to hear what's being asked of you?'

'Yes, sir.'

Rhodes made an impatient gesture, then smiled. 'My dear young man, do please relax! You've no need to stand to attention for me, you know—sit down, and have a drink if you'd care to, and then we'll talk. What—'

'I imagine Captain Ogilvie is hungry, Mr Rhodes,' Kekewich said. 'He's—'

'Of course, of course—'

'He's come a long way, from Belmont, on iron rations—'

'Yes, yes, indeed.' As the other two sat in comfortable armchairs, Rhodes stalked over to a bell-pull, which he jerked. Almost at once, the native servant appeared. Rhodes simply and in so many words ordered dinner for one, not bothering to ask what Ogilvie would like to eat nor indeed to specify what was available: there was a pre-occupied look in his eye, and there was also a certain gleam, a gleam of passion. A dedicated man, Ogilvie thought, to whom much of normal life would come as a mere interruption to his dreams and ambitions. The question of food dealt with, Rhodes brought a decanter and glasses of crystal from a corner cupboard, and poured whisky.

'Your very good health, gentlemen. And that of—Lord Kitchener.'

They drank to this; Kekewich seemed moody, with a scowl on his face. Rhodes, smiling, asked, 'Is there any further word from London, Colonel?'

'About Kitchener? I fancy your personal heliograph is better informed than mine, Mr Rhodes, so perhaps you can answer your own question.'

'There is a rumour,' Rhodes said, still smiling at Kekewich's irritation, 'that Roberts is about to offer his services . . . he's said to be tired of his Irish backwater and is not happy as regards General Buller's competence. Poor Buller! His despatches have always had a pessimistic ring, have they not?'

Kekewich sniffed. 'Your friends in Whitehall . . . do they tell you that?'

Rhodes shrugged, but didn't answer directly. He went on, 'As I said—poor Buller. He's never before had an independent command, as we all know—for that matter, no more has any other general in South Africa. Yet—and here I quote Roberts, gentlemen— there are now more men in the field out here than ever Marlborough or Wellington commanded. In fact—double! Anyway, it's all in Lord Salisbury's perfectly capable hands, and I feel confident we shall have Bobs in command before much longer. And that, of course, brings me back, naturally, to Kitchener. I dare say you know Lord Salisbury will find it easier to appoint Roberts if Kitchener is appointed Chief of Staff at the same time.'

'So I believe,' Kekewich said.

'And Ogilvie . . . are you with me, my good young man?'

Ogilvie hesitated. Back in Cape Town, Major Haig had told him of this Whitehall background to a possible fresh appointment to the high command; but Haig had also said he was never to speak of what he had been told. He said, 'I follow what you say, sir, yes.'

Rhodes gave a curious snort down his nose. 'The loyalty of the military is very touching!'

'I beg your pardon?'

'Oh, never mind, never mind—I apologise, Ogilvie. But you may speak freely. I know already that Major Haig found it necessary to tell you rather more than he was originally supposed to. I'd be obliged if you'd tell me, now, exactly how much you *do* know.'

'About what in particular, sir?'

Rhodes looked angry. 'Why, about the Kitchener plan, of course—and the Red Daniel!'

'I know only that I am to take it out of Kimberley, on behalf of its owner, Miss Gilmour.'

'You're to take it out of Kimberley, certainly—but not to Cape Town! Miss Gilmour, I believe, will have told you the history of the Red Daniel, and of Commandant Opperman?'

'Yes—that her father saved Opperman's life, and—'

'Yes, yes, I see you have the facts. Now, I—' Rhodes broke off as a knock at the door heralded Ogilvie's meal: dinner, wheeled in on a trolley by the black servant. Ogilvie stared at it in some concern and much disappointment. It looked highly unpalatable: a hunk of greyish bread, a very small portion of meat, potatoes, and a tureen of soup.

Rhodes, studying his expression, gave a loud

laugh. He said, 'My dear Ogilvie, I realised you were surprised I'd not asked what you'd like, or shown you a menu. Do you not understand that Kimberley is under siege?'

'I—'

'The military mind never ceases to amaze me—what, Kekewich?'

Kekewich scowled bleakly.

'I say it again: *under siege!* Why, our soldiers, our townspeople, our women and children even, are close to starving, do you not know that? Soon the meat ration must go down to no more than four ounces, and there will be horseflesh included in that! I am even now considering organising soup kitchens! Do you not also know that we are suffering very badly from disease—scurvy, dysentery, enteric fever? The infant mortality rate is approaching 800 per 1,000 white and native children, and yet you look askance at your share of the food!'

'I'm sorry,' Ogilvie said, flushing. He felt nettled at Rhodes's tone, but knew he had been stupidly insensitive. 'I'm grateful enough—'

'Oh, never mind the gratitude, just get on with it and fill your stomach as enjoyably as you can!' Rhodes turned away abruptly and strode back towards the fireplace, where he stood looking down at the two officers with a sardonic look on his face. 'While you're eating, we'll leave the Red Daniel and you can tell me

91

how Lord Methuen is getting on and what he's doing about us.'

'Lord Methuen,' Ogilvie said, 'is advancing to your relief with all possible despatch.'

'And pray what, exactly, does that mean?'

'It means he's coming as fast as possible, sir,' Ogilvie said, reddening. He had formed a dislike already for the great Cecil Rhodes, and felt immensely sorry for Colonel Kekewich, commanding in such circumstances. 'We have already beaten off the Boers at Belmont, and were about to advance again when I detached with Major Allenby. All that can be done is being done. I might add that my own regiment suffered heavy casualties. They are all men from my own part of Scotland.'

'So?'

'I dislike seeing them die, sir.'

'They're merely doing their duty—'

'And making little money out of it, sir. Not that such is in their minds at present, but I think they would find it galling to be criticised in their efforts by anyone to whom Kimberley means principally diamonds and great wealth!'

Ogilvie stopped, aware of three things: that he had said too much, that Colonel Kekewich approved mightily, and that Mr Rhodes was glaring at him with many conflicting emotions parading across his face. Stiffly he said, 'I apologise if I've gone too far, sir.'

'A stupid young man—'

'I'm sorry—'

'And a rude young man who begs for his come-uppance! Kimberley has never meant just riches to me, Ogilvie. However, I dare say I provoked you, and I like a young man who can stand up for his beliefs. I think you should do well, not least in the mission that now faces you. No more apologies.' Rhodes's features relaxed a little. 'We'll get straight to the Red Daniel after all. You're to take it to its namesake, its original donor—Old Red Daniel Opperman himself!'

*   *   *

That night, physically comfortable as it was in the Sanatorium Hotel, brought no sleep to James Ogilvie. The betrayal of Katharine Gilmour seemed now complete, with the proposed handing over of the diamond to a Boer leader. Ogilvie thought much about Douglas Haig's words, Douglas Haig's promise that no ultimate loss would be incurred. He felt that Haig was to be trusted, and he knew, of course, that it was the value of the diamond, rather than the stone itself, that meant so much to Katharine. This knowledge eased his conscience but left a bitter taste all the same. As to his task itself, Ogilvie felt supremely unfitted for that. Spying: he had known all along that such was to be his mission; but he felt an extreme distaste for a job that involved insinuating himself into the confidence of a man, a white man who was probably a decent enough old farmer—not some idolatrous, scheming Afghan princeling—and then turning viciously upon the trusting hand. War was war: James Ogilvie shrank from no open fight—but honour was still honour. These were changing times, when the high command, or the high command to be, could in however remote and vicarious a sense connive at such a scheme. The facts of his mission, the skeleton of what he had to do, were simple enough: on the morrow he would meet Katharine Gilmour's grandmother, and ostensibly on Katharine's behalf would take over the Red Daniel, saying that he would take it back to the grand-daughter in Cape Town. This would be the first lie: the old lady was not to be told anything further—Rhodes remarked, casually enough, that Mrs Gilmour would never approve the idea of the viper in Old Red Daniel Opperman's bosom in any case, and that he himself would see to it that no security was breached once Kimberley was relieved. Mrs Gilmour meanwhile would trust the name of Ogilvie, the man who had been with her son when he was killed in the distant Khyber Pass. Having obtained the diamond, Ogilvie would leave Kimberley under cover of darkness and move towards the Boer siege line. When challenged, he was to wave a white handkerchief, and allow himself to be taken by the Boers. He was, he would say, a deserter, a man who had stood so much and could stand no more—not an officer, but a private soldier, a volunteer of the Kimberley Regiment, an Englishman caught up in adverse circumstances whilst visiting Kimberley, visiting a friend of his parents: old Mrs Gilmour, by whom he had been given the Red Daniel after hearing its story from the old lady herself. He would ask to be taken to Commandant Opperman, saying that he had a vital message from Mrs Gilmour, at any rate one that the old lady herself considered vital, to be delivered only to Old Red Daniel in person, and that the possession of the diamond that had once been Opperman's would be his letter of credence to the Commandant's favour.

When Rhodes had told him that, he had asked, 'What if the Boers simply steal the diamond from me?'

'They'll not do that. They aren't after wealth and they're honourable men—they wish to win South Africa, not to steal diamonds for themselves. Opperman is a trusted and respected leader—they'll not do anything to impede you, I'm certain. It's because Opperman is an important man that he can be useful, do you not see, to Kitchener. Your task, Ogilvie, will be to find out all you can about the Boers' advance plans—so that Kitchener will come well prepared as Chief of Staff—and then, when you think the time is right and you have all the information you can reasonably get, you will escape and join up with the nearest British force to Opperman's commandos in the eastern Transvaal—'

'And he'll open his mind to me, sir, to a British deserter from Kimberley?'

Rhodes shrugged. 'That's where skill must come in—your skill in persuasion. You must get his complete confidence—I repeat, *his complete confidence*. How—that's up to you. The ability of the outsider, the newcomer, to see the Boers' point of view—in all conscience, there's plenty in England who do! Have you heard of the Honourable, I should say the *Reverend* the Honourable, Edward Lyttelton— headmaster of Haileybury?'

'No . . .'

'A pro-Boer, Ogilvie, in the highest degree! He believes the British to be bully boys out here—and so can you have come to believe that, Ogilvie! You'll have heard of the stop-the-war committees, of Lloyd George, that arch pro-Boer, addressing meetings—you'll have heard of Stead's pamphlet, 'Shall I slay my Brother Boer?' Oh, you'll be in first-class company, my dear young man—have no fear of that!'

Ogilvie looked as dubious, as unhappy, as he felt. He asked, 'What about this vital message, sir? I have to have one, clearly?'

'Yes.' Rhodes took a few turns up and down the room. 'The old lady, Mrs Gilmour—she's as sharp as a needle in fact, has parried all other attempts to get the Red Daniel from her—hence you, of course—but you'll say she's senile, driven crazy by the strain of the siege. She believes that Opperman, the friend of her dead son, can raise the siege with honour for the defenders. For your part, in order to get out with a kind of safe conduct—the diamond, you see—you've agreed to go to Opperman. As a man of integrity, you're honouring your word to the old woman—that's all.'

'Do I take it, sir, there's more in this than you've so far told me?' Ogilvie asked.

Rhodes gave a curious chuckle. 'My word, and I said you were a stupid young man! But tell me—why, exactly, do you ask that, Ogilvie?'

'Because it seems to me, sir, that so far all the advantages accrue to Lord Kitchener, and none to you—'

'Ah, except by way of shortening the war. Apart from that . . . yes, on the face of it you're right, my lad! But there *is* something else, and it's this: I want to see the siege of Kimberley lifted as fast as may be. The military will not move as I have urged them to move—they are slothful, dilatory, a bunch of old women with no go in them, and no initiative, and no sense!' Rhodes's eyes were blazing with that curious fervour that Ogilvie had noticed earlier. 'I have invented for your use this story of old Mrs Gilmour's supposed senility leading her to believe Opperman can lift the siege. A fiction? Yes indeed—yet in reality it is not such a ridiculous concept in its ultimate and ulterior effect, as I hope—'

'It isn't?' This was from Kekewich, and was accompanied by a supercilious arching of eyebrows. 'Opperman may be, as you say, Mr Rhodes, a figure of importance and even of influence ... but it'll take more than Opperman to change the tactics of Paul Kruger and—'

'My dear Colonel, I'm not concerned at this moment with the tactics of Paul Kruger, only with my own.' Rhodes, suddenly in a high good humour, clapped his hands together and laughed loudly. 'You see, my tactics, or rather perhaps my strategy, is going to influence the tactics of the British Army insofar as my town of Kimberley is concerned—'

'Do me the courtesy of listening, if you please. Captain Ogilvie is going to tell the Boers that he is by no means the only would-be deserter from the Kimberley garrison. He is going to tell Opperman that the troops and townspeople are in a state of near mutiny—'

'But that's not the truth—'

Rhodes held up a hand, peremptorily. 'He will tell the Boers all the things that—as he will say—the military have kept out of the heliographed reports to the outside world, because they do not want their incompetence to come to light. He will say that a surrender is fully to be expected at any moment—that indeed he himself decided to get out before the military was set upon by the angry mobs. You know as well as I do,' Rhodes said, smashing a fist into the palm of his hand to emphasise each hotly spoken word, 'that army intelligence, however slothful it may be, will very quickly pick up such reports once Captain Ogilvie has dropped his words into the ear of Commandant Opperman—for the Boers will undoubtedly see to it that heart is put into all their commandos by giving them word of the disastrous state of affairs here in Kimberley. And then, Colonel, *then* the British Army will be forced by public opinion to move very much faster to our relief, for they will never prevent such sorry news reaching the ears of the civil populations at home and in Cape Town!'

*   *   *

Next morning, Kekewich was seething still. 'I consider Rhodes to be a lunatic, no less,' he stormed at Ogilvie. 'Apart from the fact that I detest a man who's prepared to tell barefaced lies—and the fact that I detest being lied about—I consider his wretched scheme to be wholly untenable—the product of a sick mind! Lunacy—lunacy!'

Ogilvie shook his head. 'I don't agree entirely, sir.'

'What's that?' Kekewich stared, his eyes

99

wide.

'It could work in the way Mr Rhodes expects. I think there's no doubt it'll spread to Cape Town, and public opinion certainly *will* demand action—speedy action, sir. It may well mean strong reinforcements for Lord Methuen and—'

'Damn it, Ogilvie, Rhodes is mad. Damned upstart in my opinion—though I'm not to be quoted on that. The very idea of spreading false rumours to hearten the enemy—it disgusts me!'

'Mr Rhodes's idea isn't to hearten the enemy, sir—'

'But that's the *effect* it'll have!'

'Only until it has acted as a prod to our own high command, sir. But there's another point as well: the delivery of such a message ... it gets me where Lord Kitchener wants me to be. For that purpose, sir, it's excellent.'

Kekewich shrugged, and stared unhappily out of the window, gazing across towards the distant Boer lines. 'We'll say no more about it. It'll be Rhodes's responsibility, not mine, thank God!' He brought out his watch from his pocket and studied it gloomily. 'You'd better get along to see Mrs Gilmour now.'

'Are you coming with me, sir?'

Kekewich shook his head. 'No, no, I shall keep well out of that aspect from now on, Ogilvie. It is not something that should concern me.' He added, as Ogilvie turned

100

away, 'I shall see you later—I'll send for you when I've made my arrangements for your leaving the town, which will be as far as my participation will go.'

Ogilvie hesitated by the door. 'When shall I leave, sir?'

'Tonight at full dark, unless there is too much moon. Even so, it'll be far from easy.' Kekewich frowned, and went on with an almost hysterical look in his eye. 'You're expected to exaggerate our difficulties—I realize that—but by God, that man Rhodes laid it on damn thick! As to the food supplies, I mean. We're not starving yet in Kimberley— that disgraceful meal was nothing but—but damn play-acting!'

He snorted in derision. Ogilvie hid a grin. Poor Kekewich was still furious about Rhodes's pinpricks.

CHAPTER SIX

Far from easy—nothing more true, Ogilvie thought as he made his way to the home of the Hendriksons of the De Beers Company, where Mrs Gilmour was staying. Very far from easy; getting in had been one thing, and there had been a good deal of luck around, to say nothing of the competence of Major Allenby. But he would go out on his own, right into the enemy lines—and who could say that a trigger-happy Boer would not take a pot shot at him? He knew the Boers were excellent shots, having been mostly brought up from an early age to bring down buffalo on the run at a range that would have appeared more than extreme to the majority of British marksmen.

Kimberley by day, as opposed to Kimberley by night, was a thronged town. Walking along, dressed now as an Englishman in clothes provided by Colonel Kekewich, Ogilvie rubbed shoulders with men in khaki, or civilians, both men and women, and passed by coloured people and Bantus in the gutters, ignoble natives with eyes downcast as the white rulers strode or rode by. There was little joy in any of the faces, and many of the people looked ill, with greyish, drawn features. There was fear in many of the eyes, a kind of looking-over-the-shoulder aspect as though in apprehension of a bombardment by Boer artillery, the crashing explosions of the 75-mm Creusot field guns which might soon be joined by the heavier ones of the Long Toms. Once again Ogilvie felt the claustrophobic constriction of being under siege: the knowledge of shortening food supplies and medical comforts, and the lengthening sick list, must indeed be hard to bear and yet keep smiling. It came to Ogilvie that the mendacity Rhodes had ordered him to indulge in might yet turn into the very truth. If the townspeople should decide to surrender,

Kekewich would be hard put to it to prevent the act with his comparatively small force, so overwhelmingly composed of local volunteers who in the event might throw in their lot with their families.

Reaching the Hendrikson home, Ogilvie was admitted by a coloured servant to the drawing-room, where he introduced himself to Mrs Hendrikson. 'Captain James Ogilvie, Ma'am, of the 114th Highlanders. I wonder if I may have a word with Mrs Gilmour? I ... come from her grand-daughter in Cape Town.'

'From Katharine, Captain Ogilvie? A charming child, to be sure. But—how on earth did you get into Kimberley—or shouldn't I ask that?'

Ogilvie smiled. 'It's something I can't answer, I'm afraid, Mrs Hendrikson. I'd be obliged if you'd treat the whole of my visit as confidential—it must not reach Boer ears at all events, and—'

'Of course, I understand. But Mrs Gilmour's confined to bed, Captain Ogilvie. She's very old, as you must know.' Mrs Hendrikson paused. 'She'll want news of Katharine, however. She may be prepared to let you go to her room ... I shall ask her myself.'

She left the drawing-room and was back within two minutes, saying Mrs Gilmour would see Captain Ogilvie with pleasure. She took him up the stairs, made the introduction, and left them alone. Ogilvie felt extreme embarrassment and sorrow at the deception as the frail old woman in the great four-poster bed reached out a thin white hand. She smiled at him.

'How very kind of you to come, Captain Ogilvie. My granddaughter has spoken of you in the past. You were with my son, of course.'

'Yes, Mrs Gilmour.'

'Please sit down. Draw a chair up to the bed, and talk to me.'

Ogilvie did so, smiling back at the old lady. Gentle and quiet, the impression she gave was of muffins and afternoon tea, tea in an English country garden, elegance and old lace and great kindliness. Ogilvie produced the locket, pressing it into Mrs Gilmour's hands. 'Katharine said you were to have this,' he said.

'How very kind of her—it's of her dear mother, you know—'

'Yes, I know. She—'

'Tell me about my son, Captain Ogilvie. Tell me about that terrible journey through the Khyber Pass.'

Ogilvie did so, speaking of her son's manly death in the blinding Khyber snows, under fire from the Pathan hordes. The old lady listened intently, looking into his eyes all the while. When he had finished, she nodded. She said, 'I'm so very glad to meet you, Captain Ogilvie. My grand-daughter has often told me how brave ... how brave and kind and *gallant* you

104

were. And you were the last man to know my son.' For a moment Ogilvie saw the sparkle of tears in her eyes, then she seemed to stiffen herself and went on, 'Now tell me about Katharine. She is well—she is in no trouble?'

'No trouble,' Ogilvie said. 'There is something she wishes me to ask of you, however.' He stopped.

'Then ask, Captain Ogilvie.'

'It concerns the Red Daniel.'

'Yes? Go on.'

'Your grand-daughter wishes it ... brought to a safer place than Kimberley—Kimberley under siege, Mrs Gilmour. Perhaps you'll understand. I hope you will.' He felt himself sweating: he detested the lie.

'But Kimberley's not going to fall, Captain Ogilvie!'

'No, of course not. That is, the British Army will make every endeavour to see that it doesn't. But—'

'But Katharine fears that Paul Kruger will succeed. I understand that fear very well. I confess—in spite of what I have just said—that I have it myself from time to time. It is not that I don't have confidence in the army, Captain Ogilvie, but I know the fighting spirit, and the determination and the single-mindedness, of the Boers. I know their aspirations, their nationalistic feeling.' She closed her eyes, and seemed to be thinking deeply. 'I also know what my son's plans were for the Red Daniel.

105

It was his security, and Katharine's.'

'She told me that, Mrs Gilmour.'

'And it is hers by right. It is her property. Well, if she wants it in Cape Town, she must have it.' She gave him a direct look as the opened her eyes again. 'Am I to understand you will take it to her?'

Again the detestable lie. 'Yes, Mrs Gilmour. That is, if you will trust me with it—'

'Trust you? Of course I shall trust you! Tell me: did not Katharine send the locket as a token that I could trust you?'

'Yes, that's—'

'Then she had no need to. You have a trustworthy face, Captain Ogilvie, the face of an honest and truthful young man, and your description of my son's death in the Khyber Pass agrees with Katharine's, except insofar as you were too modest in regard to your own part. You may take the Red Daniel, and may God protect both you and it. You are a brave man, Captain Ogilvie, to enter and leave this poor town whilst under siege. Bring me my jewel-box, if you please. It's in the top drawer of the dressing-table.'

Ogilvie did as he was told. He laid the jewel-box on the bed and Mrs Gilmour brought a tiny key from beneath her bed-jacket, a key on a slim chain similar to the chain of Katharine's locket, and opened the jewel-box. She shook the Red Daniel out from a small wash-leather bag. As the diamond lay in the palm of her

106

hand, a shaft of sunlight, streaming through the window, caught it: it glowed with a faintly pink light—that light which Katharine, back in Cape Town, had been unable properly to describe. Ogilvie, as he looked at it, was conscious of his own sharply-indrawn breath. The Red Daniel was beautiful, exquisite, and obviously extremely valuable. From all over, its facets reflected the sunlight so that it seemed to glow and sparkle like a living thing, some splendid glow-worm encased in crystal. And old Mrs Gilmour's shining trust in the word of a British officer and gentleman, as she handed over the family's security in that little wash-leather bag and a molehill of soft tissue paper, was like a knife thrust into Ogilvie's heart and soul. He found himself cursing the names of Haig and Kitchener as soon after, with the precious diamond in his pocket, he left the old lady's bedroom.

*   *   *

Kekewich was there in person, wearing mess dress after dining with Rhodes and some of the big men from De Beers. The Colonel still obviously disliked the business, but was there as a soldier to bid a kindly God-speed to a fellow officer. The night was moonless; in fact heavy cloud had rolled up at dusk. The conditions, Kekewich said, were the best they were likely to get. He looked critically at

Ogilvie as they stood together beside one of the perimeter strongpoints, by a prepared gap in the barbed-wire fence. Ogilvie was dressed in the khaki of the Kimberley Regiment, a tattered and dirty uniform with a tear in one sleeve where the wire would have caught him as he scrambled through, also a couple of neat round holes in one sleeve, evidence, when he reached the Boer lines, of British marksmanship.

Kekewich said, 'You'll do, I fancy. There's one more thing, though.'

'Yes, sir?'

The defence commander indicated the tear. 'Authenticity is all. Your flesh, my dear fellow, is unsullied!'

'Oh—I see.' Ogilvie, clenching his teeth hard, moved towards the wire. As Kekewich watched, he thrust his arm into the wire, set the flesh against a jag, pressed, and pulled. There was an agonising pain and a good deal of blood that soaked convincingly into the khaki sleeve around the tear.

'Hurt—does it?'

'Yes!'

Kekewich gave a grim laugh. 'It's less painful than a Boer executioner's bullet, and less final too. Are you all set, Ogilvie?'

Ogilvie nodded, turning to stare across No Man's Land and the distant flicker of the camp-fires. Kekewich squared his shoulders and tweaked at his moustache. 'Remember the drill. I'll not stop the searchlights, but they'll be careful not to find you before you're well enough on your way. Keep at the double for as long as you can, of course. The firing will start as soon as we judge you at a safe distance—safe from recapture by us, that is! That's when the Boers should take over, and we have to hope they content themselves with bringing you in alive rather than shooting to kill. From then on, it's up to you. Any questions?'

'Just one, sir. One that's just occurred to me.'

'Well, go ahead, what is it, Ogilvie?' Kekewich sounded impatient now, eager to be done with dirty work.

'Sir, supposing Major Allenby and I hadn't been able to slip through last night—supposing we'd had to establish ourselves as Boers, and *then* break away across No Man's Land? How would I then have been got out of Kimberley tonight?'

Kekewich shrugged and said, 'Oh, we'd have thought something up, don't worry!'

'I'm not worried now, sir—just curious.'

'As a soldier, you should know the British ability to improvise, Ogilvie. As a matter of fact, Mr Rhodes was banking on last night's success.'

Ogilvie nodded and said no more. He wanted badly to ask: *And you, Colonel Kekewich? Were you also banking on success?* The question remained unasked, for he saw that Kekewich was a worried man, Mr Rhodes being not the least of the indigestibles. The strains and pressures on Kekewich were immense, and his position was an isolated and a lonely one. But Ogilvie, as he took his final leave of Kimberley and its commander, felt a sense of extreme bitterness that so much, all around, was being left to an 'ability to improvise'. This outlook, he believed, could be largely responsible for the lack of fast British success against the Boers. True, the Boers were fighting from an entire basis of improvisation, but theirs was at least an inevitable, and to some extent a prepared, improvisation and indulged in solely because they had no properly constituted army in any case: the British, he felt now, were in danger of throwing away their immense military superiority by being too amateurish about the whole conduct of the campaign. Perhaps, as the nineteenth century ran out, it was time for England to wonder if the sport of gentlemen was not undergoing a change. Possibly there were, after all, grains of truth and wisdom in Mr Rhodes's pernickety prodding!

Ogilvie, concentrating upon his own survival a moment later, went through the gap in the barbed-wire into No Man's Land. At once, that gap was closed behind him.

He was on his own.

Above his head, the searchlights played

their nightly game. Rhodes's Eyes, peering through the darkness, looking for the enemy who might come at any time. There were men, invisible to Ogilvie, in the watchtowers, manning the strongpoints: there was infantry behind the wire along the perimeter, and beside the ready guns the men of the Garrison Artillery kept their own watches. But there was silence out there in No Man's Land, a silence that could almost be felt, a silence that settled with a grim tenacity on Ogilvie's shoulders as, at the double now, he made towards the Boer lines and the flickering camp-fires.

He was heading out for a sector of the siege line to the east of the town. Although he had studied the maps in Kekewich's command post, and had a precise theoretical idea of where he was going and what his surroundings were like, he was in fact very quickly lost in that thick darkness and was forced to go on by nothing better than intelligent guesswork. He had been advancing at a loping run for around twenty minutes when one of the searchlights swept on to him: at once he broke into a faster stride, dodging from right to left. This was the moment of action: the searchlight, by design, failed to find him again, but soon after this firing came from his rear. Running fast for the Boer lines, he became aware of some movement ahead and then, in the glow from the camp-fires, saw the Boer riflemen standing to. He saw the rifles come up, saw the flashes as they were fired and felt the wind of the bullets singing past his head. He shouted out, a hoarse yell in the night:

'Friend—hold your fire!'

The answer was more bullets. Ogilvie was within a hundred yards of the siege line when a sledgehammer blow took the side of his head, he saw a brilliant ball of fire that seemed to burst from deep inside his skull, and he went down flat.

*   *   *

His head ached abominably and he felt deathly sick, and the side of his head and his tattered khaki uniform were thick with blood. Painful shivers of light crackled before his eyes, but beyond the light he realised that it was still dark. He lay still, hoping that lack of movement would ease the blinding, racking pain. For a while he had no idea where he was, except that he was lying out in the open, with scrubby grass beneath him and a cold wind picking at his body. Slowly, things came back to him. *The Red Daniel . . .* making a tremendous effort he felt in his pocket. The wash-leather bag was still there, intact with a silk cord drawn tight about its neck. Rhodes, Kekewich, Mrs Gilmour . . . Katharine! He had to do his best for Katharine . . . but there was Rhodes as well, and who else?

Kitchener!

Fresh pain shot through his head as he made a sudden movement, a reaction to the very image of Kitchener. He had that very special mission to accomplish, and he had been brought down in the first phase—Act One, Scene One.

God damn all Boers! It came to him that he was being left to die, out there in No Man's Land, to bleed to death from his wound, to freeze in that bitter wind. He tried to sit up, to call out, even to crawl forward to the siege line, but the effort exhausted him and brought more agonizing pain. Then everything once again went blank. He had no idea how long that second period of unconsciousness lasted; but when he came round again it was to hear low voices, and feel rough hands lifting his body, and still the pain and the sticky drool of blood. He heard his own voice saying that he was a friend, not an enemy, but no one seemed to be heeding him. A jogging motion told him he was being carried along; and soon he saw the camp-fires again, growing larger. There were grunts and heavy breathing from his bearers as they lifted him on to what he saw dimly was a parapet, and then, from a trench, other hands reached out and took him, and his body was slid down bare earth and laid on duckboards in the bottom of the trench. A lantern was held suspended over his face, and behind it he made out a heavily bearded man wearing a wide-brimmed hat, and bending

113

closely over him. In English this man asked, 'Who are you—what is your name, and what is your purpose?'

'My name . . . is Harry Bland.'

'Harry Bland, eh. Your purpose? You were mounting a one man attack on us?'

'No.' Ogilvie licked at his lips, feeling another wave of sickness. The trench stank, which made matters worse. 'No attack . . . I tried to tell your people, I come as a friend.'

'A friend? How's that, then, a friend?'

'You see I have no rifle. There was no attack.'

'I think you'd better explain fully. Come now!' A hand reached out, and cruelly jerked his shoulder. He gave a shout of sudden pain, and heard the bearded man laugh. 'You're not badly hurt—you'll live, Harry Bland! A glancing shot across your skull, no more than that. Now.'

'Very well. I . . . I've deserted—from the Kimberley Regiment. I broke through the fence. They didn't see me for a while—long enough. Then they started shooting.' He paused, shutting his eyes as the lantern came closer. 'Thank God it was you who found me . . . and not them.'

'Why have you deserted?'

'It never was my fight,' Ogilvie said. 'I just got caught up in it, that's all, while visiting from England.' Bile rose in his throat. He said unsteadily, 'You'd better stand away . . .'

114

'Why should I stand away?'

'Because I'm going to be sick.' He was: gushingly, horribly. The bearded man went back with a bound, swearing to himself in Afrikaans. He watched from a safe distance, holding the lantern high. After a moment he turned to another man, standing with others in the shadow of the trench.

'You, Grootjens,' he said.

'Yes?'

'The doctor. This yellow-belly may have the plague from Kimberley—the enteric or the dysentery. Quickly, now!'

The man Grootjens hurried away along the trench. From the others there was an instinctive movement away from possible disease, but in the lantern's glow Ogilvie could see the watchful eyes and the ring of rifles pointed down at him.

CHAPTER SEVEN

'I am Commandant Wessels. I command the siege army.' The tone was guttural, the command of English fair but the words heavily accented. Ogilvie was sitting before the Commandant in the latter's tent behind the siege line, brought there through a bright sunny day by a field-cornet, the bearded man who had questioned him the night before. 'The doctor tells me you have no disease,

115

merely the head wound.'

'Yes.' Ogilvie lifted a hand and fingered the bandage around his head. He was feeling a good deal better physically, but had been dismayed that, when searched during the night after the doctor's visit, the wash-leather bag with the Red Daniel in it had been taken away—only for safe keeping, according to the fieldcornet, but safe keeping was a term open to fairly wide interpretation, he fancied.

Wessels went on, 'You are Private Harry Bland, deserter from the Kimberley Regiment.' He shook his head, apparently in wonderment. 'Kimberley is a strange town! Men break out, and other men break in. Last night, two men broke in. Tell me, Private Bland, who were those men?'

'I don't know,' Ogilvie said.

'There was firing. You must have heard it.'

'Yes, but there's often firing, Commandant Wessels, it's nothing remarkable.'

'There were no rumours?'

Ogilvie hesitated. 'Well, there was a vague rumour that someone had come in with despatches for Rhodes—someone to do with De Beers, probably. That's all I know.'

Wessels nodded, seeming satisfied. Ogilvie was aware of a curious naïvety about the Boer: he appeared unused to stratagems and deceptions, which was perhaps just as well for Ogilvie's task. They were simple farmers, after all, these people—not diplomats or

116

politicians—accustomed to looking after their lands in a God-fearing community. Wessels went back to his earlier point. 'You are a deserter. I am told this already.'

'And you don't like deserters?'

'I have not said this. Oh, you British! You are a *military* race. We Afrikaners are Boers, farmers,' he added as if in reflection of Ogilvie's own thoughts. 'We have turned into soldiers only from necessity. No, I do not dislike deserters as you British would! And now I am more interested in *why* you have deserted, than in the bare fact that you have done so. You will tell me, please.'

Ogilvie did so, giving him the prepared story.

'Things are bad, then, in the town?'

'Terrible. It doesn't bear thinking about. Starvation, sickness . . .'

'The sickness I have heard about. The starvation—this surprises me. I have understood the De Beers Company had large food stocks.'

Ogilvie shrugged. 'This may be so, I don't know. All I know is, it's not being distributed—except to the officers and the high-up town officials and so on, perhaps. As for the natives, the Bantus, they're getting next to nothing!'

'And as a result, are discontented?'

'More than that! As I said, Commandant— mutinous. Of course, none of this has been

117

allowed to leak out—the British authorities outside Kimberley know nothing of the real truth!'

'It has not been reported by the man Kekewich? His telegraph station is destroyed, but I know he is able to communicate by means of his heliograph, with the next telegraph station—'

'He doesn't want it known that he's not in full control. He has his career to think about, and he is relying on a fast relief by General Buller. But it's my belief the town will fall long before the relieving columns can arrive.'

'Fall?' Bright eyes stared into Ogilvie's face. 'Do you mean—surrender?'

'Yes, I do, Commandant. The whole town's ripe for it.'

'And your Cecil Rhodes?'

Ogilvie laughed. 'Not him! He's said to be all for sitting it out until Buller gets there. Kekewich more or less does what Rhodes tells him, so he'll not surrender either—but I think his hand's going to be forced before much longer!'

'I see.' Wessels drummed his fingers on the packing-case he was using as a desk. 'In that case, why did you not wait for all this to happen, rather than risk crossing No Man's Land, with the British guns behind you, and ours in front?'

'I didn't mean to wait to get caught up in the panic—or the reprisals afterwards! As I said, Commandant, it's not my war. I hold no brief for what the British want out here. As far as I'm concerned, it's your country. The war's bloody stupid and bloody wrong too!'

'Yes. Then why did you join the British Army when you reached Kimberley?'

'Well—I *had* to. I don't mean I was conscripted . . . but a man has to do *something* in a siege situation! After all, it's a defensive situation, isn't it, purely for survival and—and all that. But in the end, you see, I just couldn't go on taking it any more . . . so I got out. That's all.'

'Not quite all,' Wessels said with a sly look on his face now. 'No?'

Ogilvie said, 'No, you're right. There is something else. A mission I've been asked to undertake.'

'To do with—this?' Wessels reached into a pocket and brought out the wash-leather bag. Opening the neck, he shook the diamond with its tissue-paper out onto his palm. He removed the tissue-paper. The Red Daniel glowed in the daylight coming through the tent flap, glowed as it had in Mrs Gilmour's bedroom the previous day. 'I think you had better tell me, Private Bland.'

'That diamond . . . it's known as the Red Daniel.'

'I know this. It is a famous stone.'

'Then you know its history?'

Wessels nodded. 'Oh yes, yes! But you are

119

telling me, not I you. Go on, please.'

'Commandant Daniel Opperman, after whom it's named, gave it to a Major Gilmour, years ago, after the battle of Laing's Nek. Major Gilmour had saved Commandant Opperman's life.'

'Yes. You know what you are speaking of. Go on.'

'It now belongs to Major Gilmour's mother—or at any rate, it was in her possession. She's in Kimberley. She has a message, which she believes to be important, for Commandant Opperman. She has asked me to go to him with this message, and she gave me the Red Daniel as proof that I come from her.'

'*This* is why you deserted?'

'No! I keep telling you, Commandant—it isn't my war! I'm not interested really. The old lady—Mrs Gilmour—she . . . well, she befriended me from the start. I used to talk to her, she was like a mother. I got to know her very well. I told her what I meant to do. At first she didn't believe me. But in the end she realised I was determined—and she asked me to do this for her, you see. Well, naturally, I agreed.'

'Why naturally?' Those keen bright eyes stared into Ogilvie again, penetratingly.

Ogilvie said, 'The diamond meant a sort of safe conduct to me. I knew it would . . . help me into your lines. And it has—hasn't it, Commandant?'

Wessels laughed. 'Quite a sharp young man! Yes, it has, in a sense. Well—now what do you want? To be allowed to go free, to rejoin the British somewhere else—with a king's ransom in your pocket, after perhaps buying me off with a promise of a share in the sale of the Red Daniel? Is this your plan?'

'No, it isn't.' Ogilvie looked up, full into the Boer's eyes. 'I may be a deserter, but I mean to honour my word to Mrs Gilmour. I want you to give me a safe conduct to Commandant Opperman, wherever he may be. Naturally, I'll expect to be escorted by an armed party—that would be only reasonable of you to insist upon. Will you do that?'

Wessels asked sardonically, 'This message—what is it?'

'It is only for Commandant Opperman. I am sorry.'

'You refuse to tell me?'

'It's not so much that I refuse, Commandant. I have given my word that I will tell only Commandant Opperman.'

'You split meanings, young man. Now split some more.' Wessels leaned heavily forward across the packing-case. 'You have sworn not to reveal this message, so you will not reveal it. Yet when you joined your regiment in Kimberley, you would have sworn loyalty and allegiance to your Queen Victoria, sitting on her golden throne in Buckingham Palace, and wearing her golden crown, and wagging her golden sceptre over all her subject peoples . . . yet you have deserted, and thus broken your word to her! What is the difference—eh?'

Ogilvie said, 'I've never met Queen Victoria. I knew Mrs Gilmour well.'

Again Wessels laughed—uproariously, slapping a heavy hand against a thigh. 'Well split indeed! Oh, you British, I have a strong feeling that you should all have been comedians! It is a shame to kill you, for the world needs laughter!' He sobered down. 'Is this a message that will please Old Red Daniel Opperman?'

'Yes, and bring him much credit if he is able to make use of the information. And no doubt, Commandant, *he'll* pass on credit where it's due.'

That, it seemed, was the wrong thing to say. Wessels growled, 'Young man, do not make me slap your tender face for having the impertinence to suggest I can be swayed by bribes. If I send you to Commandant Opperman, it will be simply because I have a high regard for him as a man. If this message is as important as you say, he must hear it for himself. If there is any trickery, he will know well enough how to deal with it—and with you, Private Harry Bland.'

'Then you'll send me?'

Wessels nodded. 'Yes, I'll send you—I can't really spare the men, but I'll send you. Do you know where Commandant Opperman's to be found, eh?'

'No.'

'Well, he's in Carolina, over in the eastern Transvaal. It's no short distance. I'll send three men, but there will be no delays permitted—you will ride fast. The British are not far off Kimberley now, as perhaps you know.'

Ogilvie said, 'We've heard rumours, that's all. The high command doesn't keep the troops too well informed, which—'

'What rumours?'

'That General Buller has ordered our relief.' Ogilvie grinned, and waved a hand in the direction of the distant town. 'Or rather—their relief, seeing it doesn't affect *me* any longer!'

'That's all, is it?'

'Broadly, yes. Lord Methuen's said to be not far off, coming up from the Cape.'

'True—he is. That's why I want to be at full strength, though I've not the smallest doubt Methuen will be stopped before he reaches us!'

'Have you any news of Lord Methuen, Commandant Wessels?'

'He had his cavalry badly cut up near Enslin sidings—cut up uselessly too, for they achieved nothing!' Wessels gave a deep laugh. 'I believe Lord Methuen was so angry that he dismissed his cavalry commander, Colonel Gough of the 9th Lancers!'

'He's got as far as Enslin, has he?'

123

'Yes, but he'll get little farther, my friend! General Koos de la Rey is waiting for Methuen and his troops at the Modder River, and if Methuen should cross the Modder itself he will be halted at Magersfontein hills . . . and let me prophesy, it will be those blue hills of Magersfontein that will bring Methuen to his Waterloo!'

*　　　*　　　*

Wessels wasted no time: with the Red Daniel restored to him, Ogilvie was sent on his way astride a pony during that morning, with a heavily armed escort of three mounted Boers. They rode out into a splendid morning, heading directly east from the siege line, and Kimberley was soon well behind them as they crossed the border into the Orange Free State. It was pleasant riding, in invigorating air, a day for shooting—not men, but game. Hares, buzzards, coveys of small birds started up at the ponies' approach; and all was peaceful. Ogilvie's thoughts were split between the job ahead of him and his regiment in rear, marching with Lord Methuen for a hot reception, if Wessels was to be believed, at the Modder River. Wessels probably was quite correct: the Modder, and the Magersfontein hills, were the last obstacles before Kimberley itself, and in these locations the Boers would mass their artillery and their best riflemen.

This was to be expected. But knowledge of the due and proper expectations of war brought no peace of mind to Ogilvie. His highlanders would fight well and bravely, of that there was no doubt at all, and willingly too; but he would have wished with all his heart to be with them, rather than to be sneaking off in the guise of a deserter into comparative safety, to act as a spy.

Carolina was some four hundred miles as the crow flies, through high ground and across the Vaal River below Johannesburg. The journey could take as much as twenty days, and the four ponies carried meagre rations to last this time, together with water-bottles that would be used sparingly. To a large extent Ogilvie and his escort would be able to live off the country, shooting game as they went and cooking it over a camp-fire. This they did successfully for the first three days, keeping the iron rations in reserve, eating reasonably well, and sleeping for a few hours each night beneath the stars, in sleeping-bags. They yarned all the time during the riding days, and Ogilvie stored away all the information he learned about the Boer ways and outlook, continuing the lessons begun by Major Allenby—whom he had not met again before leaving Kimberley. They encountered no British patrols, no penetrative probes—and very few Blacks. On one of the rare occasions when they spotted the crinkly-haired heads, and the few tattered garments, and the spears, Ogilvie asked where all the natives had gone.

'Oh, they're hereabouts and thereabouts,' the Boer said dismissingly and without interest. 'They keep out of our way—they don't like us, nor we them. This is *our* land now.'

'Whose side d'you suppose they're on?'

'If any side at all, Mr Bland—the British side, for what that's worth.'

'Do they ever attack?'

'Attack us? Oh, they've come at us with their spears from time to time, yes. Paying off what they think of as old scores. But they're only rabble, and make no impression. You can forget them, Mr Bland, just as we do.'

They rode on, interminably as it seemed. Then, on the fourth day, they had a stroke of luck that saved them a wasted journey: they fell in with a party of Boers who told them that Old Red Daniel Opperman had left Carolina and was moving south into Natal to place himself and his commandos under the orders of General Louis Botha outside Ladysmith which was still, like Kimberley, under siege.

'Oho! Where's Old Red Daniel making for precisely, then?'

'Towards the Tugela River.'

'That's a long river. Whereabouts on the Tugela, eh?'

'I can't say. Maybe Colenso. There's a rumour that Botha's building up a force around there, between Colenso and Spion

Kop. But that's just a rumour.'

'Where do we pick him up, can you tell me that?'

'He's making for Reitz in the first place. He'll be there a few days, so they say ... recruiting.'

Reference to the map indicated that they could be in the town of Reitz in the Orange Free State within seven to eight days with luck, hard riding and the minimum of sleep. They made it, in fact, in seven: seven days of slogging, punishing days for ponies and men, seven days of intermittent plaguing from the wind-whirled dust devils that came twisting up from the dryness of the veld, seven days that brought them wearily into Reitz. The first townsmen they met told them where they would find Commandant Opperman. He had arrived only the day before, this man said, and was busy forming a new commando of Free Staters to oppose General Buller, who had recently placed himself in personal command of the force that was expected to march on Ladysmith.

Following the directions given, noting the stares of curiosity and of hostility at his tattered, filthy British uniform, Ogilvie rode with his escort to a church hall on the eastern outskirts of the town. There they found Opperman with his officers. From descriptions given there was no mistaking that fiery red hair ... Ogilvie felt that the years could scarcely have touched it, that, although Opperman was no longer young, that hair was probably no less fiery than when, twenty years before, Opperman had given the Red Daniel to Major Gilmour.

CHAPTER EIGHT

'Who is this, a prisoner? This is a recruiting centre, not a prison camp!'

'Commandant Wessels outside Kimberley has sent him to speak to Commandant Opperman,' the leader of the escort said. 'He's all right, I'll vouch for him. Will you tell the Commandant?'

'I can *tell* him, yes.'

While the man went over towards Opperman, Ogilvie looked around the hall. For a church building, it was remarkably warlike. The chairs and benches had all been stacked away, except for those occupied now by Opperman's recruiting team, who sat behind packing-cases similar to that used by Wessels outside Kimberley. Rifles were piled in one corner, belts of ammunition in another. Outside the porch, Ogilvie had seen machine-guns and a couple of the Creusots. There was an air of bustle from the recruiting team, who were under the eye of Old Red Daniel Opperman personally, but in truth there did not appear to be many recruits forthcoming. Perhaps they had all joined up already, and Opperman, coming from his own district of Carolina to a strange place, was getting only the dregs, the bottom of a very well-scraped barrel . . . certainly the few who were being enrolled in his commando were weedy-looking enough—gangling youths with largely vacant expressions and little hair upon their faces, which in many cases were pale and spotty and clerkly. Major Allenby had spoken of manpower problems facing the Boers: now, Ogilvie could well believe that there was indeed a problem.

After a word with Commandant Opperman, the messenger came back and told the escort to bring Ogilvie forward. Halting him in front of Opperman, the leader handed over a sealed envelope from Wessels. Opperman broke the seal, brought out a letter, and read it quickly, glancing from time to time at Ogilvie.

'You are Private Bland of the Kimberley Regiment, a disillusioned soldier—yes?'

'Yes, Commandant.'

Opperman tapped the letter. 'I gather you haven't come to join me as a soldier.'

'No, Commandant. I am no soldier.'

'No stomach for the fight, eh?'

'No,' Ogilvie answered boldly.

'You're like many of our burghers, then!' Opperman's nostrils flared and he glanced with disdain towards the pitifully thin columns

129

of recruits. 'Well—at least you're honest, Private Bland! All day I've listened to excuses—farms that can't be left, old parents who are sick—and half of them, even when they do join and are sent to the front, they lurk behind in their laagers and leave the fighting to their comrades of better spirit!'

Opperman had spoken loudly; his words rang around the walls of the hall, and men glanced uncomfortably towards the angry red-haired figure, standing like a rock amidst shifting sands. More quietly Opperman said, 'This is a time of great courage, but it is also a time of dismal cowardice. I don't know in which category I should place you, Private Bland. Can you enlighten me?'

Ogilvie shrugged: he affected carelessness but felt a sharpening of all his senses as he realised that now was the vital moment when he would determine the fate of his mission, the moment when Opperman would get that first important impression. He said, 'It's not of any concern to me. I think you must decide, Commandant Opperman. I got out of Kimberley because I detested the way we—the British—were trying to impose our will and our ways on your people, whose land this is. Not only because I disliked starving! And I came also with a message . . . no doubt Commandant Wessels mentions this in his letter.'

'Yes, he does. I see you know Mrs Gilmour.'

'Yes. You see, I came partly for her sake.'

130

'And risked the guns of both the British and the Afrikaners?'

'It was the only way.' Ogilvie laughed. 'Who can ever say, Commandant, where to draw a precise line between courage and cowardice?'

Old Red Daniel gave an approving nod. 'Well said, young man. And the message?'

'I'd prefer to deliver it in private, Commandant.'

'It is not a written message?'

'No.'

'I see. Very well—in that case, it shall be done as you wish. I'm wasting my time here anyway. Have I your word that you'll behave yourself—and not try to kill me, or run away?'

Ogilvie said, 'I had no need to come at all, if I wished to run away when I'd got here.'

'True! But you could have come to kill me, couldn't you?'

Ogilvie looked him in the eyes. 'I haven't come to kill you, Commandant.'

'You swear that, a Bible oath?'

'I swear it, upon my honour.'

'The honour of a deserter, Private Bland?'

Ogilvie flushed angrily. 'I may be a deserter, but I still have my standards, my personal honour, as a gentleman—'

'A gentleman, Private Bland?'

'You should know, surely, that there are many of my station serving in the ranks at this moment, as volunteers.'

'Yes,' Opperman said. 'Yes, I do know that.'

131

Suddenly he reached out and clapped Ogilvie on the shoulder. 'I think I shall trust you. For one thing, you have no arms to kill me with!' He gave a deep, throaty laugh, and looked at the escort. 'Your Commandant writes that he wants you back quickly—I'll not detain you. You may leave your charge with me now. Refresh yourselves and your ponies, and then ride back to Kimberley. Give my regards to Commandant Wessels—and tell him I know he'll hold the siege line at Kimberley as General Botha will hold it at Ladysmith! Mr Bland, you'll come with me to my hotel.'

*   *   *

They walked through the streets of the town together and alone. Ogilvie's pony had been left with the escort to go back to Kimberley where, Opperman said, Wessels would have need of all his transport. Making their way through the throngs of towns people, all of them wearing Republican colours and once again looking with hostility at the British uniform, Ogilvie and Opperman talked little. Ogilvie was aware of the sharp sidelong glances, summing-up glances, that Old Red Daniel kept giving him as they went along. He felt somehow that Opperman was well disposed towards him, and for that he guessed he had to thank Wessels' invocation of the name of Mrs Gilmour. This guess was

132

confirmed once they were in Opperman's room and seated at a table before very welcome glasses of Dutch lager. Opperman started by saying, 'You come from Mrs Gilmour. I am pleased to know she is still living, though she must be very old. How is she?'

'As you said—very old.'

'But well?'

'Physically, yes. Her mind's no longer strong.'

'I'm sorry to hear that.' Old Red Daniel shook his head with apparently genuine sadness, then went on, 'Wessels wrote of the diamond. You have it?'

'Yes.'

'May I see it, please?'

'Of course.' Ogilvie brought out the small wash-leather packet, extracted the diamond and unwrapped the tissue-paper. He handed the stone to its namesake, and Old Red Daniel took it with a curious tenderness, placed it in the palm of his hand, and stared at it in silence for a long time, moving it a little so that it caught the light and its facets shone and glittered with richness.

'So many, many years ago ... I was a younger man then, and eager, and full of vigour! If it hadn't been for Mrs Gilmour's son—you know, of course, about that?'

'Yes. You know that the son is dead, do you?'

Opperman nodded. 'I do, and am deeply sorry. I'm told he died in India, fighting the Afghans—in the Khyber Pass to be exact. His wife too.' He examined the diamond again, and there was a far-off look in his eyes. 'So the Red Daniel went to his mother, though I know he had a daughter. You knew this?'

'Mrs Gilmour spoke of her. I gathered ... she wants the diamond to go to her grand-daughter eventually. I brought it only at her own insistence, as a password to yourself, Commandant Opperman.' He hesitated. 'I feel responsible for its safe keeping. May I have it back?'

'Of course.' Opperman handed the stone back. 'Guard it well, Mr Bland. Guard it with your life! It belonged to a brave man whom I much respected. If anyone should steal it, he will have me to reckon with. And now the message: what is it?'

'Mrs Gilmour wished me to tell you about the conditions in Kimberley.'

'They're bad?'

'Very bad.' Ogilvie, doing his duty for Mr Rhodes, painted an appalling picture of starvation and disease and disaffection, conditions which, he said, were bringing the garrison close to the point of abject surrender. Opperman listened with full attention, nodding his head at intervals.

'How does Mr Rhodes find his dealings with the military?' he asked when Ogilvie had finished.

'With Colonel Kekewich, you mean? Oh, I've heard talk of disagreements, but that aspect is rather above my head really. I believe Mr Rhodes will oppose any suggestion of surrender, though.'

'And Kekewich?'

'I think he'll have his hand forced. I think it could become a case of mob rule.'

'Which will also overrule Mr Rhodes?'

'Yes.'

Opperman sat in silence for a while, deep in his own thoughts. 'And Mrs Gilmour?' he asked eventually. 'What are her views, her personal views?'

Ogilvie said, 'She's very old, Commandant. She's still patriotic, of course—you'd not expect anything else of her—but her age is making her see things differently. I believe she has had enough of death and trouble and fighting. I think—indeed I know—that she would much welcome the ending of all hostilities so long as the end was honourable for both sides. But that's going ahead too far: her current wish is to see the lifting of the siege—'

'A wish in which she'll not be alone!'

'No, indeed. But she goes farther than others—inasmuch as she's sent me to you for help.'

'How can I help, Mr Bland?' Opperman ran a hand through his fiery red hair. 'How can I help, except perhaps by seeing to it—for I have enough influence—that Mrs Gilmour is brought out in safety when the town falls to Wessels and his commandos?'

'No, she's not asking for that. It's ... Commandant, this is hard to put to you satisfactorily. I've already said, Mrs Gilmour is old and her mind is failing. She is, frankly, bordering on senility, I believe. She is obsessed by an idea ... a deep belief that you, and you alone, Commandant, can arrange for the siege to end—that is, in victory for your people, an entry into the town—but, and this is I believe the point, with complete honour for Kimberley's defenders.' Ogilvie spread his hands wide. 'That's the best I can do, the closest I can get to what she wanted me to tell you.'

'And you left Kimberley for this?'

'No. Only partly. I told you, I'd already made up my mind I was getting out.'

Opperman seemed bewildered, not entirely to Ogilvie's surprise. 'Has the old lady any suggestions as to how I can possibly effect all this?'

'None. She—'

'A siege can end only two ways: in its lifting by its relief, or in a final assault by the besiegers!'

'Three ways—the third being surrender.'

'Yes, three ways then.' Opperman pushed his chair back, shaking his head in what looked like real regret. 'I can't help, Mr Bland. The information you've given me as to the state of life in Kimberley is useful, and will be passed to the right quarter. You may have done a service to the people in the town in perhaps bringing their ordeal more quickly to an end. But as for poor Mrs Gilmour's fancies . . .' He threw his arms up. 'What can I possibly do, Mr Bland?'

'I've no idea. I've passed the message, I can't say more. But I wish you could help, though of course I know you can't. I tried to say as much to Mrs Gilmour, not wishing to raise her hopes, but there was a point I couldn't pass without being cruel. Maybe I was a coward—but I couldn't leave her entirely without hope.'

Opperman nodded. 'You did right, perhaps. Yes, I think you did right. But I repeat, I cannot help. I too am a patriot, Mr Bland, and I can't weaken our effort. Kimberley must be brought down by any means available, so must Ladysmith and Mafeking. No other consideration can be allowed—this would be an indulgence and we can't afford indulgences! Do you understand my position, Mr Bland?'

'Of course I do. We'll say no more about it. My job's done in any case.' Ogilvie finished his lager.

'And you, Mr Bland? What are your plans for yourself ?'

'Isn't that rather up to you, Commandant?'

Opperman didn't answer directly; he stared

137

sombrely at Ogilvie for a while, frowning and running his powerful fingers through his hair. Then he said, 'You have guts, Mr Bland! You have delivered yourself along with Mrs Gilmour's message, you have walked into enemy hands, well knowing what the result might be.'

'Not enemy hands, Commandant. I don't regard your people as enemies. I have no quarrel with you, none at all. And there's one thing certain now: I can't fall in with British troops, nor can I go home to England.'

'You realised this before you left Kimberley?'

'Of course.'

'Then what do you want, Mr Bland?'

'Why, to stay in South Africa! It's all that's open to me now.' He laughed. 'I'd not be welcome anywhere in the Empire, would I? Australia, Canada, New Zealand . . . no, I must stay here, and hope for an Afrikaner victory.'

'And the Red Daniel? Do you sell that, Mr Bland, and live on the proceeds?'

'Certainly not!' Ogilvie flushed with anger that was not entirely simulated. 'I shall see it's returned to Mrs Gilmour, or perhaps to her grand-daughter.'

'Have you any other money?'

'In England. Not here. I may be able to get some sent out, but it'll be a tricky business, Commandant.'

'For a deserter, yes! And if it proves to be . . .

too tricky, Mr Bland, what then?'

Ogilvie shrugged. 'Really, I've no idea. I'll just have to find work, won't I? I dare say I can turn my hand to a number of things if I try. Farming, perhaps. I'd sooner that, than work in the cities.' He hesitated, scanning Old Red Daniel's face for hopeful signs but failing to find them. 'If you have any ideas or suggestions, Commandant Opperman, I'd be glad to hear them. As a matter of fact ...'

'Yes, Mr Bland?'

'Mrs Gilmour did suggest you might be willing to help me get settled.'

Opperman gave another deep laugh. 'Settled—in time of war? We are all of us *un*settled to a very high degree, Mr Bland!'

'Yes, but surely—'

'I am sorry.' Opperman lifted a hand. 'I know of no way in which I can help. You are from England. Even though you say you have sympathy for our people, I think our people would find it hard to help you in conditions as they are today. Nevertheless, I will say this, Mr Bland: since we share a friendship with Mrs Gilmour, I shall see what there is I can do— but I make no promises of success. In the meantime, of course, there is the question of your personal safety.'

'I'm in danger, Commandant?'

Opperman smiled. 'You are in enemy territory, Mr Bland, whatever *you* care to regard it as! Certainly you are in danger, and I can't very well put a placard on you, can I, saying "Approved by Commandant Opperman" !'

'Then you do approve me?'

'I like the look of you, yes. You have tried to do a service. I am, of course, bearing in mind other possibilities—for instance, that you could have stolen the Red Daniel from Mrs Gilmour and are making use of it to get my help so that you can live. But I confess I do not see this in your face when I look at you, and I am accustomed to summing men up.'

Ogilvie inclined his head with a touch of irony in the gesture. 'Thank you, Commandant.'

'I shall trust you therefore. In any case, any untruths will emerge when Kimberley is relieved, for I shall get in touch with Mrs Gilmour then. Now—let us consider your safety. There is only one thing I can do, and that is, to hold you as a prisoner of war, at any rate for the time being—'

'No, not that!' With an almost involuntary movement, Ogilvie got to his feet. As he did so, he saw Opperman's hand slide towards the revolver-butt in its holster, but Ogilvie remained standing, staring down at the Boer leader. A prison camp would be the end of his mission, and up in Egypt Lord Kitchener, if accounts of him were to be believed, would froth at the mouth.

'I didn't get out of Kimberley just to go back into something similar, let me tell you—'

'Similar but different. No fighting, and an assured supply of food. I would probably send you to Pretoria, where we have many British—including your Mr Churchill of the *Morning Post*, son of one of your politicians. A brave young man, who worked for an hour under fire to free a locomotive that one of our commandos had ambushed with boulders. You would be in good company there, Mr Bland.'

'Perhaps! I'd sooner stay here—'

'We have no compound here and there aren't the men to spare for guards—'

'You'd need to escort me to Pretoria and that takes men.'

'Three only, Mr Bland, three only, and on temporary duty at that. I'm sorry, but there it is. You have my assurance that it'll not be known to your fellow prisoners that you're a deserter.' Old Red Daniel got to his feet, ponderously, and stood facing Ogilvie. 'Come now—take this in good part! I shall have you in mind, and when the time is right, I shall do what I can to help you. When the war is over, and we have won South Africa, I shall be your good friend, Mr Bland.' He laid a hand once again on his revolver. 'Now I'm taking you to the police station, to await an escort. Come.'

Ogilvie could do nothing but obey. His orders were clear: to win Old Red Daniel Opperman's confidence, which would not be done by strong-arm tactics. Thinking fast, he decided on a move that should be a step in the right direction: much as he disliked parting with it, he brought out the diamond and thrust it towards Opperman. 'Take the Red Daniel,' he said. 'It'll be safer with you than in a prison compound—if that is where you're determined to send me.'

Opperman nodded, and took the diamond in its wash-leather bag. 'Thank you. You have my complete assurance of its safety. I promise you that.' Smiling suddenly, he took his hand away from his revolver-butt. 'I shall not need the gun,' he said. 'Let us walk out as friends, eh?'

'All right, Commandant.'

They left the room together, side by side, and went down the stairs into the small entrance hall where a native woman was on hands and knees brushing the carpet. Out into the street, beneath a hot sun, into a mixture of smells, of mimosa, of horses, of corn from a nearby store. There were not many people about: a few women, shopping with their children, some natives going about their masters' business, a handful of farmers in from the country, and a couple of wagons creaking slowly past along the dusty street. Ogilvie saw the man from the corner of his eye, the man standing back against the wall at the angle of the hotel, a man with madly staring eyes who came away from the wall and began shouting obscenities at Opperman, a man holding a rifle pointed at Old Red Daniel's heart. In the next second as the shooting started, Ogilvie changed the pattern of his future very nicely.

*   *   *

The bullet was removed from his arm in a doctor's surgery, a painful process made more bearable by a bottle of good brandy. Opperman was present throughout. Afterwards he said, 'The bravest act I've seen, Mr Bland, to take the bullet yourself. I haven't the words to say thank you properly.'

'It was just instinctive.'

'An instinct that saved my life! I tell you something, Mr Bland: instinct, in many men, would have worked the other way—a quick dash for safety! You are going to be a hero now, Mr Bland.'

'Rubbish, there was nothing heroic in it.'

Opperman smiled and waved towards the window. 'Can't you hear? Don't you know what's waiting for you?' There was in fact some considerable noise from the street, a loud and growing murmur as men and women gathered. And it was far from a hostile sound. Ogilvie reckoned he had undoubtedly scored a point, but was in two minds as to whether or not he had helped the British Army much by saving the life of one of the better of the Boer leaders, though it would presumably bring joy to the hearts of both Rhodes and Kitchener.

He asked, 'What about the man? Do you

know who he was?' 'Yes, I recognised him. Piet Kries, a man whose son was killed whilst fighting in my commandos.'

'Poor beggar! Can't you feel for him?'

'Oh yes, I can. I'm sorry enough for any man who loses a son, but that doesn't excuse what he tried to do.'

'What'll happen to him?'

'Oh, he'll be tried by a military court, and shot.'

Ogilvie felt sickened. 'Can't I plead for him?'

'Why should you? He's nothing to you.' Opperman dismissed the would-be assassin from his mind. Justice would, as ever, take its course. 'Do you feel fit to walk now?'

'Where to?'

'The hotel. I'll make the arrangements.'

'Not Pretoria, and the prison compound?'

Opperman grinned. 'By no means! The townspeople wouldn't hear of that. Didn't I tell you—you're a hero now! Take my arm, Mr Bland.'

Opperman held out his arm. Ogilvie leaned his weight on it; he felt groggy but quite capable of motion, and also quite capable of finding some grim humour in the situation as he and Old Red Daniel emerged from the surgery into the midst of a frantically yelling crowd who clearly wanted to slap him on the back, wring his hand, and heap figurative garlands upon him—and probably would have

144

done but for the restraining and protective hand of Commandant Opperman. A noted Boer leader, whose death would much have helped British morale in South Africa, arm-in-arm with a captain of the Queen's Own Royal Strathspeys ! Kekewich—Ogilvie reflected as the plaudits of the crowd beat on his eardrums—Kekewich, who had spoken of Rhodes and Kitchener as being strange bedfellows, really should have been here now!

One thing was sure enough: the Boers loved their Old Red Daniel, and a good deal of that love was rubbing off on James Ogilvie, alias Mr Bland, deserter.

*   *   *

More mutual trust was solemnly formalised in Ogilvie's hotel bedroom: the Red Daniel was once again transferred with a flourish. 'Now we are friends,' Opperman said.

'I still don't know how I'm going to live.'

'As to that, I have some ideas, now.'

'Oh?'

'You have said you sympathise with us Afrikaners—like your own Lloyd George and many, many others of all classes in England, though I think they're mostly careful enough how far they let their opinions be known. But since you see our point of view, and appreciate our right to run our land in the way we want, then perhaps you would care to work with us,

145

Mr Bland?'

Cautiously Ogilvie said, 'Work, yes. Fight, no! I've done with fighting.'

'Yet you are a brave man.'

'Oh, I happened to take that shot—'

'You threw yourself in its path. That was very brave. No, you are not avoiding fighting because of cowardice. Why?'

'I don't want to kill people. That's all, really.'

Opperman nodded. 'Very well, that is your outlook, I shall accept it. No fighting—no killing. But would you object to . . . shall I call it, staff work?'

Ogilvie pursed his lips and studied Opperman's face. 'What sort of staff work? Staff work in the field?'

'No, no. Not that, no.'

Opperman was being mysterious. Ogilvie felt a strong and insane desire to burst out into loud laughter, for he had a feeling he was going to be asked to spy. A spy in the pay of both sides at once? It would be comic opera! But Opperman's next words killed that conjecture. He said, 'Recruiting.'

That, too, took Ogilvie's breath away for a moment. 'Recruiting? Me—a deserter from Kimberley, trying to sell the fighting spirit? I doubt if I'd be much good, you know!'

'But you would. You would be invaluable! A Briton, Mr Bland, a Briton who has taken sides with us because he knows we are right. A

146

Briton who can address public meetings moreover—and tell of the horrors in besieged Kimberley—heartening our less valorous men with eye-witness accounts of the low state the British have come to! If there is any man in South Africa who can convince our people that victory is near, and that one extra push will bring it about, that man is you, Mr Bland!' Opperman, who had been looming like a war-cloud over Ogilvie, dropped back into a wickerwork chair, his eyes shining with his beliefs. 'Now—will you do it? *Will you?* Did you not say you wished to help?'

'Yes, I did say that, Commandant.' Ogilvie lifted a hand to his forehead: he was, he found, streaming with sweat. 'All right. I'll do it.'

Opperman jumped to his feet again and took Ogilvie's good hand, seized it, pumped it. 'Thank you! You will not regret this, when the war is over, I promise you! Thank you, from the bottom of my heart. Now, hurry up and get fully fit, Mr Bland, for time is precious—in war, it is always that, but even more so at present, for we have to consolidate our position by making sure of the fall of those three towns—Mafeking, Ladysmith, Kimberley!'

Opperman talked on for a while, excitedly, then at last left Ogilvie alone—to rest, he insisted. But no mental rest came to Ogilvie after Opperman had clattered down the stairs to set up the machinery for public addresses and recruiting campaigns *par excellence*. Worry nagged at his mind: in acceding to Opperman's plan, he, James Ogilvie, would be in a very positive sense bringing comfort to the enemy, which was an act of treason. He could only hope that Lord Kitchener would approve his emissary's interpretation of his orders! That evening, when a servant brought him his supper, he had fresh worries. The servant brought newspapers, with word of Lord Methuen's column as it had fought through towards Kimberley. Ogilvie sent down for someone to translate the Afrikaans, and when a young man came up to do so the reports made bitter hearing. Methuen, it seemed, had been halted at the Modder River as Wessels had predicted. It was there at the Modder that the Boers had made their first real defence line: there would be no more strategic withdrawal, as had to some extent been the pattern at Belmont and Enslin. At the Modder the Boers had stuck, digging themselves in along the south bank of that river and of its tributary the Riet, where a preponderance of trees and bushes gave them fine cover. Reinforced by more Free Staters and by Cronje with some commandos from his main army, the Boers numbered 3500 men; Lord Methuen had advanced upon the Modder with some 8000, but poor reconnaissance had failed to inform Lord Methuen that the Boers were massed behind that pleasant-looking green foliage along the river bank. And the next morning—with the Guards Brigade leading the British advance and the Royal Strathspeys in the centre of the line behind them—the Boers opened with artillery and well-directed rifle fire, the new automatic one-pounder guns sending out necklaces of shells that had a startling effect on the surprised attackers. Methuen's force was enfiladed and quickly brought to a full stop, finding what cover they could—which, the newspapers said, was little enough. Many of the British, driven half mad with thirst after lying for hours in strong sunlight—sunlight so strong that rifles had to be lain upon to keep them cool enough for use if they had the chance against the concealed Boers—died as they ran back without orders to the water-carts. For no advance at all since the start of the battle, the British had ended that day with 500 dead and wounded; and during the night, having achieved the desired delay, the Boers had pulled back in safety to the Magersfontein hills to join the swiftly congregating reinforcements for a magnificent stand before Kimberley.

His mind numbed, Ogilvie dismissed the translator.

*   *   *

'Why so gloomy, Mr Bland?'

Ogilvie, deep in thought about Dornoch and

149

the rest of the battalion, looked startled. He said, 'I've been reading the newspapers, Commandant. Or rather, listening to a translation.' This he could scarcely conceal: the pages littered his bed; and in any case instinct warned him to act naturally. 'I may have deserted, but I'm still British. You know I'm not seeking a British victory in the war . . . but all those casualties are pretty sickening!'

Opperman, advancing into the room, shrugged and sat again in the wickerwork chair, which creaked under his weight. 'Just so. I understand, of course. Nobody likes war and killing, but it has to be in such days as these. Had you friends amongst this British force, Methuen's force, at the Modder River?'

'No friends,' Ogilvie said, sick at heart at the lie. 'I came straight to Kimberley from England, and there I stayed when the war broke out.'

Opperman grunted. 'That is as well, Mr Bland, for Lord Methuen will be mauled again at the Magersfontein hills. He will not be allowed to relieve Kimberley—certainly not at this stage when victory is within our grasp.' He reached out and put a hand on Ogilvie's shoulder. 'Your report of the terrible state of things in the town has been passed on, Mr Bland—'

'Will this affect your strategy, Commandant, your plans?'

'Not our strategy or plans. Kimberley was

150

always to be occupied. But the word, which will be widely spread, will greatly hearten our commandos as they make their stand against Methuen ... and fortunately for us, his attributes as a general make his own task the harder!'

'How's that, then?'

'Why, he's a typical British general of his generation, Mr Bland. He is predictable—so predictable! For one thing, he's no flanker or rearer ... always, always he can be relied upon to mount *frontal* attacks—'

'What do you regard as a typical general, Commandant? Is there really such a person?'

Opperman laughed heartily. 'Well, they may *look* different—like Buller and Methuen. But thin, fat, short, long—they are all the same inside! Very little imagination, plenty of courage but small of brain, hardly any ability to think and plan, to use initiative or to improvise. In a word, they are hidebound.' He chuckled, unaware that he had virtually paraphrased Rhodes's opinion of the military, and started to fill a pipe that, when lit, filled Ogilvie's room with reek and thick blue smoke. 'I have a theory. Our generals, who are farmers mostly, have so far outwitted all your British generals—if we'd had the numbers, you would all have been driven into the sea long ago! And our farmer-generals, Mr Bland, are plainly-dressed men in shirt sleeves and waistcoats and broken boots—so

151

I say this: the more the plumes and the helmets and the scarlet coats and the swords, the less the resilience of the brain! You see, the brain grows tired and weary with its main military pre-occupation, which is formal dress, and ceremonial, and parades, and marching in step, and saluting, all the trappings which do not ever concern us! Am I not right, Mr Bland? Give me an honest answer!'

Ogilvie couldn't help a smile. 'You may be right, Commandant. You may indeed.' The smile broadened as his mind went back to India, and Lieutenant-General Francis Fettleworth—Commander, by the grace of God and Queen Victoria, of the First Division in Nowshera and Peshawar. How Bloody Francis had loved parades! He would never remotely have understood the mind of men like Old Red Daniel Opperman—and the fact that the army contained so many Fettleworths perhaps held at least part of the reason for the British failures. Casting General Fettleworth from his mind with a certain gladness, Ogilvie asked, 'Have you heard of Lord Roberts, Roberts of Kandahar?'

'Who has not!'

'There's nothing unresilient about him, Commandant.'

'No, that's true. If ever that man comes out here, things could go differently, I'll grant, but we shall still win in the end—'

'And Kitchener?'

'Kitchener!' Opperman growled something in Afrikaans; his face had grown darkly ominous and surly. 'I pray nightly to God in heaven that He should keep that terrible man busily occupied in Egypt—and at the same time have mercy on the suffering Egyptians!' He went on scowling blackly for some moments, then asked, 'How are you feeling, Mr Bland?'

'A lot better—'

'Good! There is work to do, Mr Bland, and no time for delay. I've arranged that tomorrow morning at eleven o'clock you will address a meeting of our burghers, and fire the first shot in my recruiting campaign to defend Ladysmith and Mafeking against relief.' Opperman stood up. 'You're ready to do this?'

Ogilvie nodded. He said, 'I'm at your disposal, Commandant,' and felt his heart give a sick lurch at his own words. Tomorrow truly was to be a time for treachery.

CHAPTER NINE

Following a cold night it was stiflingly hot in Reitz. After a late breakfast Opperman came to fetch Ogilvie, who was now dressed in civilian clothes of Boer origin provided by Opperman himself. During the night Ogilvie had tried to sort out in his mind what he was going to say to the assembled burghers, how far he would go in satisfying Opperman's wishes. He fancied he had a fair scope: Rhodes's own plan, after all, would be followed insofar as he would be expected to repeat Rhodes's exaggerations about the food supply and the various sicknesses in Kimberley. That part would be all right; James Ogilvie's reservations were more concerned with the rest of it: the exhortations he would be expected to give about joining Opperman's army to reinforce Louis Botha. If his words caused just one man to enlist under the banner of the Republic, he would be the indirect cause of God knew how many British deaths.

Even so, it had to be.

He must accept it, had already accepted it by implication in his initial acceptance of Lord Kitchener's demands, so nicely put as His Lordship's requests.

'You're nervous, Mr Bland?' Opperman swatted at the buzzing, crawling flies that came up like clouds from the horse dung lying in the street.

'A little. To be honest—very. I've not done any public speaking, you know, and my position's a little tricky.'

'You mean as a deserter?'

'Yes.'

Opperman said reassuringly, 'Don't worry about that aspect. No one else will!'

154

'I'm glad to know it!' They walked on; there was quite a stream of people making the same way. Most of them had a word for Old Red Daniel, a cheery greeting, a respectful salute. Most were men, but there were some women, bold-looking ones mainly, potential Amazons perhaps—there had been stories in the newspapers he had read back in Peshawar of the Afrikaner women fighting alongside their menfolk, in the field even, though mostly in defence of their homes. Those women handled rifles, it was reported, with astonishing expertness and an incredible lack of fear. It was unseemly, of course, for women to kill, but the Amazons of South Africa didn't baulk at it. Ogilvie asked Opperman about them.

'Yes, we have women in our commandos, Mr Bland. There's been some exaggeration of their numbers—but they exist.' Opperman gave Ogilvie a sidelong glance of appraisal. 'Who knows—you're a good-looking and upstanding young man—you may bring many more women into the fighting today!'

'God forbid!' Ogilvie said involuntarily.

'God will not forbid, if He thinks it right. So far, He has not forbidden.'

Ogilvie felt in some way reproved. God, he knew, loomed very large in the lives of the Boers—Allenby had made much of this point. Their ways were puritanical, sober, and Sunday-ridden. Here, indeed, was one of those 'differences' that the Regimental Sergeant-

Major had spoken of: here in South Africa, the Royal Strathspeys were fighting a very Christian enemy! Ogilvie, who was not a deeply religious man in any obtrusive sense—though he had an innate belief in, and respect for, the Holy Trinity—nevertheless felt that this did alter his concept of fighting. Until the action at Belmont not so long ago, he had fought and killed only the heathen. In India he had never thought about the matter, since he had never been called upon to put a Christian to death. Now, however, as he walked along with Opperman towards the hall where the meeting was assembling, he reflected with a sense of some unease that in the sight of God all men were equal, even the heathen . . .

Ogilvie and Opperman went into the crowded hall together and marched straight to a dais at one end, where there was a plain deal table, with three white-bearded men seated behind it. The proceedings started with a hymn, dirgely sung but with sincerity, and this was followed by a lengthy prayer in Afrikaans. This over, the meeting got under way. The chairman eulogised Opperman, and Mr Bland from Kimberley, who had bravely broken out and away from starvation and disease and dictatorship to come along and tell the burghers about the iniquities of the British. Opperman said a few words by way of further introduction, though by this time he scarcely needed to, for Mr Bland's heroism the day

156

before was widely known, and then Ogilvie himself was called upon to the evident pleasure of the impatient meeting.

The moment he stood up, pandemonium took charge. There were loud cheers, shouts of 'Bravo, bravo!' and both men and women came forward to shake him warmly by the hand. He was taken aback by this demonstration, tried to smile but felt almost hysterical at his own treachery and duplicity. The welcome, the pleasure, was so genuine, so sincere, so spontaneous, yet he was here to do these people immense and perhaps fatal damage. Helplessly after a while he turned to Opperman. Old Red Daniel rose at once, laid a hand on his arm, and turned a smiling face to the excited audience. He held up a hand, commanding, peremptory, when the noise didn't stop.

'Friends, friends!' he roared. 'You are embarrassing Mr Bland. Please go back to your seats, all of you—and listen to what he has to tell you.'

The immediate response was a loud rendering, in very throaty English, of 'For He's A Jolly Good Fellow'. After this, sobriety and propriety returned and the meeting settled down to listen. Throughout, as he stumbled and stuttered his way through his speech, Ogilvie was aware of an extremely pretty young Amazon who didn't take her gaze from his face once. There was a vague familiarity about the girl that he found tremendously disturbing and the result was a poor delivery of an uninspiring speech—or so it seemed to himself.

He was evidently wrong.

At the end of it there was another demonstration, this time of hand-clapping, and foot-thumping that made the boards hum. Both the chairman and Opperman pumped his hand in turn, smiling and happy. Opperman said, 'You sounded so honest and true, Mr Bland. You have helped us enormously. There will be many more such occasions. You have put much heart into the burghers by your description of the miseries of Kimberley and the feeling of the people there. Wonderful!'

Ogilvie said nothing. There was a vote of thanks, and then he watched the meeting disperse while the committee members congratulated each other on the big success. In his mind's eye he saw those good, solid Boer farmers speeding along to the recruiting centre to take up arms against the British. He could only hope Kitchener would find it all worth while. As they left the church hall, Old Red Daniel suggested that Ogilvie should ride out with him to visit one of the commandos exercising to the south of the town.

'Yes, I'd like to.'

'Then *opzaal*—saddle up, Mr Bland! To the ponies!'

Outside by the door, the young woman

158

Ogilvie had been aware of earlier was waiting. She was wearing a black dress, with a white shirt-like garment beneath it, the high collar of which gave her a very clean-cut look; but the wide-brimmed hat shielded her face a little, so that it was in shadow. As Ogilvie passed she touched him lightly on the arm with a riding-crop.

'May I be allowed to congratulate you?' she asked, in an upper class, purely English accent. 'That was a splendid lecture, and very, very stirring!'

'Thank you, Miss—er—'

'Do I understand your name is—Mr Bland?'

There had been something faintly mocking and sardonic in her tone. Aware suddenly of some possible danger, Ogilvie nodded. Then Opperman, to his immense relief, took his arm and drew him away. He felt the girl's gaze on his back, mocking still. Opperman said, 'Many people will want to talk to you now—you will need to be strict with them and with yourself, even to the point of rudeness if necessary.' Then he chuckled. 'A well-built young woman, that! Tall and sturdy.'

'Yes.'

'And a pretty face.'

'Yes, indeed.'

'And you are a man, and young. Oh, well, a man has always had a way with a maid ... but be careful, Mr Bland.'

'Is she one of your fighting women,

Commandant?'

Opperman shrugged. 'I don't know. I don't know her, I've never seen her before. I've not been long in Reitz in any case.' He added warningly, 'I said—be careful! Keep your heart inside your body, Mr Bland, for there are sterner things to do now than attend women's tea parties and suchlike. Women are distractors of men, they prattle and make silly noises, and expect to have attendance danced on them. But this I dare say you know without my telling you.' Old Red Daniel seemed a human enough man, but yet there was a sort of moral stricture in his tone—the emergence once again of the native puritanism of the Boer, with his hatred of ungodliness and anything remotely pertaining to womanising. There was, as Allenby had remarked one day, a very curious juxtapositioning of the Bible and the gun in the Boer way of life.

Ogilvie and Opperman rode out together on ponies, making their way over sun-baked country for some two miles out of town. There had been a light rain during the night, and the scent of the mimosa was strong. Ogilvie asked about the training of the commandos and what their state of readiness was. When Opperman answered that he would shortly see for himself, he remarked, 'The Orange Free State itself is pretty peaceful, isn't it? I mean, you have no British troops in your territory?'

'No. There have been raids, and the British

have stolen our cattle and our sheep, sometimes our grain has been destroyed and farm buildings set on fire. It is possible that this devastation may grow worse, Mr Bland, as the British begin to sense defeat! But in the meantime we must always be ready for them to invade us. You see, they can come in from Griqualand or the Cape routes—or, with more difficulty perhaps, they could cross the Drakensberg from Natal. There are strong forces in Natal—and Buller's there in person, as perhaps you've heard. Buller intends to relieve Ladysmith himself—but I shall be there to stop him with my commandos!'

Ogilvie grinned. 'And General Botha?'

'Oh, I shall find Louis Botha's help invaluable!' Old Red Daniel gave a broad wink. As they jogged along, not hurrying unduly, Opperman grew a little mysterious, looking intently ahead, seeming excited and in a high good humour, judging from his anticipatory smile, but said little, answering Ogilvie's questions in a preoccupied manner. In due course they began to come up to some low hills, lying stark and purplish beneath a high sun. Before the hills there was low, scrubby bush and a few ragged trees dotted about at random. Nothing stirred anywhere: there was no wind to shake the trees and bushes, there were no animals even to bring movement to an utterly lethargic scene. But all at once, as they came up towards the scraggy

161

bushes, and rode in among them, the veld exploded into action. From those unlikely pieces of sorry cover, men materialised as though raised by some magician's wand—a horde of them, shirt-sleeved, waistcoated, aiming rifles at the two riders, who were completely surrounded. Had those rifles been aimed with intent, a much larger body of men would have been cut up long before they had had a chance to open fire themselves.

The Boers moved in, grinning, as Opperman and Ogilvie pulled up their ponies. Opperman was shouting with laughter. 'My good Mr Bland, you didn't see a thing till they came out, did you, eh?'

'Not a thing! It's unbelievable.' Ogilvie was indeed mightily impressed by the Boer field craft. 'How do they do it?'

'We know our country, Mr Bland, we know it better than the British ever will. We are a pioneering people, and we have lived hard, and lived close to the land.' Opperman lifted an arm in greeting to a field-cornet who approached his pony, a rifle held in the crook of a sun-browned arm. 'Hullo there, Jan Kloops.'

'Good morning, Commandant. I think we scared your friend. Who is he, eh?'

'Mr Bland, from Kimberley.'

'The one who saved your life yesterday?'

'The same.'

Jan Kloops reached up and shook Ogilvie's

162

hand, grinning at him from a black-bearded face. It was a hard face, tough and square above a thick chest crossed with heavy belts of cartridges. He and Opperman spoke together in Afrikaans for a while, then the field-cornet went back to his men, who began streaming away towards the hill behind. 'Going for the ponies, who carry the commissariat,' Opperman said. 'Jan Kloops is going to get a meal ready for us—we'll eat out here, in God's good fresh air. All right, Mr Bland?'

'Fine.'

'Jan Kloops gave me some news,' Opperman said.

'Yes?'

'The Modder River battle was some days ago now, as you know. Kloops has fallen in with a man from that battle, one of our Free Staters who was slightly wounded and had decided to return home—this is one of our greatest difficulties, our burghers being men of independent mind—they insist on taking leave when they feel like it, chiefly when their own affairs need their attention, you understand. However—this man brings news, Mr Bland: General Cronje and Commandant de la Rey are going to hold Lord Methuen finally at the Magersfontein hills. They're digging twelve miles of trenches—four feet deep, narrow as a protection against shrapnel, and well forward from the hills so that the British are expected to waste their artillery bombardment on the

163

sangars behind—and well camouflaged. I warrant Methuen will not cross those trenches, Mr Bland, but will lose most of his men in an attempt to do so—frontally! He won't have the wit to try to outflank. I tell you—' Opperman broke off. 'What's the matter?'

'I've told you before. I'm still British.'

'It does no good, to hide your head in the sand.'

'Perhaps, but there are still things I'd rather not see, Commandant, or hear about either. All I want to hear is that this senseless war has come to an end!'

Opperman gave him a shrewd sideways look. 'It'll do that, my friend, if God smiles on our plans.'

'What plans?'

'Plans for a quick victory.'

'I can't see it being quick. You're very heavily outnumbered, aren't you?'

'Surely!' Old Red Daniel gave a hard laugh. 'Much outnumbered, Mr Bland, but we have that inestimable advantage of knowing our country as you have just seen—and therefore of being able to surprise the British troops in an ambush. We fight by hiding—the British fight always in regimental formations! I'll tell you another thing: our intelligence is good.'

'Better than the British?'

Opperman laughed again. 'For the British, it scarcely exists. They've never paid enough attention to that side of the war, you see! For the British, soldiering is a game, the sport of English gentlemen. They sneer at subterfuge—you see this physically illustrated by your Lord Methuen and his obstinate love of frontal attacks—don't you? To attack from the front, where you can be seen, that's sporting and gentlemanly. Only sneaks go round the side or the back! Or tradesmen—to the tradesmen's entrance! Well, Mr Bland, we Boers are not gentlemen, we are tradesmen, and that's why we shall win, and quickly!'

'For my part,' Ogilvie said, 'I wish you luck in regard to the speed if not the killings. But what's the overall plan of campaign to be?'

Opperman said promptly, 'We haven't one. Not in the field, that is. Mr Bland, we were speaking of intelligence. Do you know what intelligence consists of ?'

'Well, obviously, knowledge, on the part of a commander, of the enemy's intentions.'

'Broadly, yes, but what does this break down to, do you suppose?'

Ogilvie checked a too-ready answer. Instead he said, 'I was only a private soldier, Commandant. You tell me.'

'Very well, then.' Opperman shielded his eyes against the sun, looking into the long distances of the veld. 'Any commander, to be wholly successful rather than merely lucky, must know this: the disposition of the enemy's front-line troops, the enemy commander's strength, his supply position, the morale of his men, the kind of terrain over which the battle is likely to be fought, the number, position and availability of reserves, the character and outlook of the enemy commander himself—which latter enables your commander to assess the probable conduct of the battle on the part of the enemy—their reactions, their tactics in various situations and so on. You understand?'

'Oh, yes, I think I do. But are you telling me you know all this about the British?'

Opperman said, 'In the present areas of battle, yes. We've talked of poor Methuen. Who else is there? Buller, White, Gatacre. Let us take Gatacre, who is very much the opposite of Methuen. Now, Gatacre believes among other things that attack is the best method of defence—he can always be relied upon to attack even when to do so is unsuitable—and more often than not his attack is not frontal but flank. He is a bungler, a man for whom things go wrong accidentally. He fails to keep his officers fully informed—this is a common failing among the British, of course, and we ourselves are sometimes guilty of it. More important perhaps, Gatacre puts too great a physical strain on his men and exhausts them long before battle is joined—he doesn't spare himself either—takes twenty-mile rides before breakfast! His men call him General Backacher.' Opperman gave a deep chuckle. 'My good Mr Bland, from studying the generals a lot may be learned, believe me!'

166

'I take your point,' Ogilvie said. Looking ahead towards the low hills, he saw the Boer commando starting to re-appear over the crest of the nearer one, bringing up the ponies with the commissariat. Hunger stirred within him. He asked, 'Suppose the British know your leaders just as well, Commandant? What then?'

'They don't,' Opperman answered with assurance, 'and they never will. We have so many smaller leaders, local leaders if you like, and they tend to change quite often—more often than your British generals who have been generals for so long they have forgotten what it is like *not* to be generals!' He paused. 'Did you ever hear *my* name for instance, mentioned in Kimberley?'

'Only by Mrs Gilmour.'

'There you are, you see! Besides, we are only Boers, farmers whose unmilitary minds are not worth the effort of studying! If the British did study us, and if they could master our field craft, then they might beat us with their superior numbers.'

'But whatever you said a little while ago, Commandant, you *must* have some kind of plan, surely—and this could become known?'

Opperman said, 'For now our plan is only this—to take the three main towns at present under siege. We look no further ahead than this—and if we *have* no field plan, Mr Bland, how is anybody ever to find out our secrets?'

He winked broadly, in high good humour. 'Our broad strategy will be found not so much upon the field as upon . . . let us just say, upon other scenes, Mr Bland.'

*   *   *

More than this, Opperman would not say; and Ogilvie decided not to press. It was early days; he had yet to insinuate himself much deeper into the Boer leader's confidence; but, as the appetising smells of cooking meat came to him from the camp-fire that had now been lit, he pondered a good deal on the possibilities inherent in Opperman's remark about 'other scenes'. Naturally enough, the first thing that came to mind was the political scene, but Ogilvie could find little help there. Of course, it was common knowledge that there was a fairly strong pro-Boer movement at home in England, and the home-grown pro-Boers could well be gaining some more support as a result of the British casualty lists and the failure of the generals in South Africa to secure the hoped-for speedy victory. But Mr David Lloyd George, perhaps the leading pro-Boer, was, despite his heretical opinions about the morality of the war, still basically a patriot. Ogilvie could not remotely envisage him being involved in any underhand bargaining with the enemy, though no doubt he could prove a powerful mouthpiece for Oom Paul Kruger, a mouthpiece set right upon the doorstep of Whitehall . . .

'You don't seem hungry, Mr Bland. Don't you like our food?'

Ogilvie brought his thoughts back from their speculative wanderings. 'It's very good,' he said, 'and I'm hungry enough, Commandant. I was just thinking, that's all.'

'What about, eh?'

'Home.'

'Homesickness, Mr Bland?'

'Perhaps, yes. It's hard—not to go back.'

Opperman finished munching a thick cut of steak. Watching this joyous mastication, Ogilvie found himself thinking of the tins of bully beef that would be the main luxury of Methuen's rank-and-file just now. The mouthful finished, Opperman said, 'Don't weaken, Mr Bland. I understand your feelings for home, but don't weaken.'

'I can't anyway. I'm committed. What I did . . . it's irrevocable, final.'

'Yes. Where's your home?'

'In Scotland.' It was useless to prevaricate; his knowledge was of Scotland. Except for Sandhurst, and a few periods in London, he had little experience of England. 'My family comes from—near Carrbridge in Inverness-shire.'

'Your father, what is he?' Opperman gave one of his deep laughs. 'Apart from being, as you said, a gentleman?'

'He's a factor. He manages estates, as an

agent.' This description would scarcely fit Sir Iain Ogilvie, still commanding the Northern Army of India in Murree; but it should pass Old Red Daniel.

'There are soldiers from Scotland fighting with Methuen,' Opperman observed. 'Among them, the Scotch Guards.'

'Scots Guards. Yes, so I've heard.'

'Those terrible bagpipes, and they call the British civilised!'

Ogilvie said with a snap, 'It's a matter of opinion.'

'You like the sound of the bagpipes, Mr Bland?'

'Yes, very much.' At that moment, Captain James Ogilvie would have given almost anything just to hear those wild, strange notes in the distance, closing, coming nearer and nearer across the sun-drenched veld, to see the kilts a-swing around brawny highland knees as the Scots came over the hill and poured down, yelling, with bayonets shining, to cut up this over-confident commando! The sounds of home and victory, even victory on so small a scale, would have been very, very pleasant. Much more pleasant, he thought wryly, than the sound of the Boer songs that the men of the commando sang when the meal was finished and they were lying back, puffing lazily at their pipes, watching the smoke from them and the now dying camp-fire spiral up into a clear, windless sky. After this open-air impromptu smoking concert, Ogilvie and Opperman rode back into Reitz with the commando. Opperman was at its head, and Ogilvie rode by his side. He had the feeling that already the Boer was looking upon him as a kind of lieutenant, an aide-de-camp whom ultimately he might even persuade to fight, though this was something Ogilvie would refuse resolutely to do, Kitchener or no. They rode into the little township, past the hotel, past shops—a general store with ironmongery, a haberdasher's, a pharmacy—for the church hall where recruiting had been in progress. That day, no less than seventy-two new men had been enlisted under Opperman's command, and he was mightily pleased about that. As the commando dispersed, the men going to their own homes, he took Ogilvie almost affectionately by the arm.

'Well done,' he said. 'You've done fine work for us, and we're all grateful. There'll be more occasions before I ride south for the Tugela River.' He hesitated. 'I'm hopeful you'll come with me, Mr Bland, when I join General Botha.'

Ogilvie shook his head. 'No fighting for me. I'm sorry.'

'I am sorry too.'

'Couldn't I be more use here, to carry on recruiting for you?'

'Perhaps. Perhaps!' Opperman frowned, and clapped him on the shoulder. 'We shall see. By the time I leave, we may have exhausted the Reitz reservoir—such as it is. But we shall see, Mr Bland.'

*   *   *

To have seemed too eager would have been a mistake, but in furtherance of Lord Kitchener's wishes he knew that in fact he must ride on towards the Tugela with Old Red Daniel Opperman. A meeting with Louis Botha, one of the biggest names among the Boers, would be a chance he must not miss. Ogilvie decided he would let matters drift until Opperman's departure was imminent, and then raise no further objection to leaving Reitz with him. After that, he would simply have to use his wits to avoid having to use a rifle against his own side. If necessary as a last resort, if and when a rifle was thrust into his hands, he would have to abandon Kitchener and Mr Rhodes and try to fight his own way out to join the British lines.

When he returned alone to his hotel he found he had a visitor: sitting in the little entrance hall was a young woman—the one he had seen that morning during his recruiting drive. As he came in she rose from a chair behind a large potted plant, and came towards him, smiling.

'Good afternoon, Mr Bland. I hope you don't mind my presumption in calling upon

172

you?'

He was aware, once again, of danger. 'Not at all,' he said.

The smile was faintly mischievous now. 'But you'd like to know why? And I shall tell you, Mr Bland. You appeal to me. I hope you're flattered?'

Frankly, he was embarrassed. But he asked lightly, 'Where does my appeal lie, Miss—er—?'

'Smith, Mr Bland. Maisie Smith—from Hounslow. Your appeal? Oh, I admire your courage, I think—what you did for Commandant Opperman, what you did in leaving Kimberley and showing so honestly and bravely where your true sympathy lies, that is, with the Afrikaners.'

He cleared his throat. He had an idea the hotel staff were listening and were laughing at him. He said, 'Er—yes.'

'That is where your true sympathy lies, isn't it?'

'Why yes, of course—'

'Mine too, in spite of Hounslow. I've no doubt Hounslow is being immensely patriotic on the British side.'

'Yes, indeed, Miss Smith.'

She looked at him reflectively for a few moments, shaking her head a little, and biting at her lower lip. She really was immensely pretty, and not a bit Amazonian in spite of her lithe and healthy build. Suddenly she reached out to him as she had done that morning, and

173

put a hand on his arm. 'Let us talk, Mr Bland. In private. We can go to your room.'

'I think that would be hardly proper.'

She laughed. 'Nonsense, it would be perfectly proper. That bandage needs attention, and I'm a nurse. As a matter of fact, I'm Dr Heinik's dispenser as well—yesterday 'I had gone to the hospital at Bethlehem. Had I been here in Reitz when you were shot, Dr Heinik would have sent me to you. Come, Mr Bland, don't be shy of me!'

CHAPTER TEN

'Well, here we are,' she said, looking around Ogilvie's bedroom. 'Proper or not!' Suddenly, staring at her own reflection in a looking-glass, she gave a giggle, a sound that Ogilvie would have thought out of character, for it was an unladylike giggle with a hint of coarseness behind it. She said, 'You're a one, aren't you— Mr Bland!'

'I don't quite understand?'

'Don't you?'

'Are you a nurse or are you—'

'Don't say it!' Maisie Smith lifted a hand, then giggled again. 'This is the Orange Free State, remember. All God and hellfire. They don't like immorality!'

Ogilvie said, 'I wasn't going to use the word

I think you had in mind, Miss Smith.'

'But you do know the facts of life—don't you?'

'Of course. On the other hand, I tend to believe ladies when they say they're nurses—until they give me other ideas.'

She giggled again. 'Go on with you! What ideas have I given you, may I ask?' There was a coquetry about her now; the upper class accent, the patrician air, had gone: she was a good actress, Ogilvie thought. The sense of danger was strong: he had no wish to be compromised in his dealings with Opperman, and he had a feeling the red-haired Boer would react badly to any scandal surrounding his curiously-appointed recruiting officer.

'You want to throw me out, don't you, Mr Bland?' Her voice hardened. 'You better not! I can make a hell of a noise when I'm crossed. They could tell you a lot about *that* in Hounslow.'

'Perhaps,' he said coldly, 'you'd better explain. Why not sit down?'

'Ho! Polite at last, aren't you? But I'd rather not if it's all the same to you. I rant better standing up, see.'

'At least you're honest.'

She laughed. 'God, that's rich! Honest!' She stared into the looking-glass again, swaying back from the hips and adjusting the large hat, making a face at herself. Ogilvie studied her in astonishment; there was still something very

175

appealing about her, and there was a touch of something else as well, something indefinable to Ogilvie: a hint of sadness, of a kind of . . . he searched for a word . . . gallantry almost, a hitting back against a hostile and disapproving world. A little girl lost? Not quite that! She looked capable of taking care of herself and she was not physically little.

She turned away from her reflection and stood in front of Ogilvie, hands on hips now, looking him up and down and clearly liking what she saw. He felt more and more uncomfortable: he was strong and healthy himself and had been celibate too long, and he knew he desired her. He wondered, briefly, if the solution might not be to allow both himself and this woman their satisfaction, and then send her packing. He had hardly reached the conclusion that a whetted appetite might prove even more dangerous than abstinence when she spoke again, and shatteringly.

Smiling, she asked, 'Remember Mrs Bates, do you?'

At first he didn't understand. There could be many Mrs Bates scattered throughout the world. Then she amplified: 'Mrs *Colonel* Bates'—Supply and Transport—Peshawar, India. Got it now? You're Captain James Ogilvie of the 114th Highlanders, or I'm the Prince of bloody Wales.'

*   *   *

He had gone cold as death: the sun of Reitz, sending its heat through the open bedroom window, quite failed to warm him. Mrs Colonel Bates, that long-tongued, spiteful woman who had tried to make trouble for him in India years before, the woman he had deliberately snubbed on more than one occasion since then. Ogilvie had detested Mrs Bates, but it wasn't Mrs Bates who was important now. It was this Maisie Smith. To start with he tried to bluff it out, saying she must be mistaken in her man.

'Oh no I'm not!' she said, loudly—too loudly. He shushed at her, and that seemed to please her. 'Don't want anyone to hear your guilty secrets, do you, Captain Ogilvie?' But she lowered her voice when she went on, still staring into his eyes, 'Let me just prove it. I'll mention some names. Bloody Francis Fettleworth. Sir Iain Ogilvie—your father! Colonel Lord Dornoch, Captain Black the adjutant. General Lakenham. Colonel Carmichael of the Medical Stall. Shall I go on, Captain Ogilvie?'

She was triumphant, grinning now like a she-devil.

'No,' he muttered. 'You've said enough. Just tell me what it is you want—and what you were doing in Peshawar, for I don't remember ever meeting you!'

'Oh, you didn't,' she said, sneering, curling

177

her lip. 'I was a nurse—children's nurse, I mean. Nanny. Major the Honourable Alastair Duff-Kinghorne, seconded from the Scots bloody Greys. Scotch, see—like you! His lady wife didn't want the kids brought up by *amahs*. Silly bitch. Oh no—*you* didn't meet nanny, but nanny saw you often enough.' Once again the giggle. 'She liked what she saw, too, and wanted to see a lot more, but she didn't get the chance. God, you were a lot of bleeding snobs! Mind, I made use of you all. I learned, my God I learned! One thing I learned was how to talk like a lady, and believe me, that's been useful enough since those days!'

Ogilvie had got his equilibrium back a little now. He said, 'Tell me about the since, Miss Smith. How did you land up here in Reitz?'

She laughed. 'I was given my notice in India. Didn't you ever hear?'

'Hear what?'

'Well, I see you didn't, unless you're pretending. I'd have thought everyone knew everything in Peshawar, but I s'pose the bitch saw to it that it was kept dark. The Honourable Alastair wanted me more than he wanted his Honourable wife—that's what! He had me once, too, but never again.' She made a grimace. 'He was horrible, you can't imagine! All hair, and his breath—stank of cigars and brandy, and he had a gut like a rhinoceros. Well, *she* found out and that was that. She paid my fare home to Hounslow. I got pregnant on
178

the way back, and when the child was born my father kicked me out. I went on the streets after that, up Soho way. It was a living! My baby was put in a home—they call it a home. Bloody institution! She's three now and I've never set eyes on her since she was a few weeks old—but I still bloody love her, that I do!'

It could be acting again, but Ogilvie saw tears in her eyes. He asked, 'But what about Reitz? How the devil did you end up here?'

'You may well ask,' she said bitterly. 'I met a young man after a while, in London. Not professionally. He didn't know any of that. He had money—he came from South Africa, from the Orange Free State. He was in London on business. Well, he fell in love with me and persuaded me to come out here, which I did. He wanted to marry me, but wanted his parents to meet me first, and we'd get married out here, see. I'm not going into a lot of detail, but we never did get married. I reckon his mum saw through me, like the Honourable Mrs bloody Duff-Kinghorne. Not so long ago, after I'd come to Reitz—I hadn't the money to go home to England—I heard he'd been killed in the early fighting.' She shrugged with a show of indifference. 'Well, that's my story, take it or leave it.'

'Didn't you say you were a nurse? I mean, a hospital nurse?'

She nodded. 'Yes. Course, I'm not a proper nurse, but I picked up enough to get by—

179

looking after the Duff Kinghorne kids! God knows, there were bloody nine of 'em! Probably ninety-nine outside of holy wedlock. And there's a shortage of any kind of nurse out here just now. Dr Heinik was glad enough, so was the hospital at Bethlehem. At least I'm a woman!'

'I don't dispute that,' Ogilvie said with a short laugh. 'Now I think you'd better tell me what you want, Miss Smith—if that really is your name?'

'Yes,' she said, 'it really is, Maisie Smith as ever was. Maisie Smith who wants to get back to England, see? Do you get it, Captain Ogilvie, or don't you? I want you to take me out of Reitz, out of the Orange Free State, out of South Africa altogether. All right?'

He knew the answer to the question before he had even asked it: 'And if I refuse?'

She said, 'Why, then I'll go straight to Commandant Opperman and tell him who you are. I'm not bloody blind. It's obvious you're here to do a job of work for the high-ups, a sort of spy. Your sort doesn't drop down to private and then desert, it's just not in you. Well?'

'You'd do that—to your own side? You're still British, aren't you?'

'Yes,' she said steadily, 'I'm still British and I hate these people with their beards and their Bibles and their bloody stuffiness and I'll wag a flag at the old Queen with the best of 'em

180

when I get back! But while I'm here, Captain Ogilvie, I'll do *anybody* dirt—just to get back to my baby again!'

Then she burst into a torrent of tears.

*   *   *

It was, in a sense, stalemate: and very dangerously. Ogilvie refused point-blank to encumber himself with a woman who, in any case, would never be acceptable to Old Red Daniel—he was certain of that. Opperman, indeed, had already warned him explicitly not to involve himself in any kind of affair. Maisie Smith was adamant that she would ruin her own life even, if necessary—she admitted that the Boers wouldn't take kindly to a knowledge that she had tried to strike a bargain with an enemy of their country, but she said she might as well be in a prison compound, or even dead, as carry on with an existence she loathed and detested. Ogilvie asked her why she hadn't brought the baby out to South Africa with her: she flew at him for his stupidity over that. How, she asked, could she confess to a man she hoped to marry that she'd had an illegitimate child? And even if she could have done that, even if she could have taken the risk, there would have been difficulties with the law unless he had married her first, and that he hadn't been disposed to do.

'But you'd have told him afterwards—after

you were married?'

'Yes. Then I'd have gone back for my baby.'

'And your husband's feelings?'

'It was my baby that counted. Nothing else.'

'So you didn't love this man?'

'No. He was a means to an end, that's all.'

Ogilvie gave a hard laugh. 'It was you who called Mrs Duff-Kinghorne a bitch!'

'Oh, I know I'm one too. I don't deceive myself! Well, what are you going to do? Better make up your mind quick.'

'I can't do it. In a way I'm sorry . . . sorry for you . . . but I can't do it.'

'Why not? *Why the Christ not?*'

'It's—it's impossible!' Ogilvie lifted his arms in a gesture of hopelessness. 'Can't you see? How can I take a woman with me on . . . on what I have to do? I'm probably riding to the Tugela with Opperman, possibly even to the siege lines outside Ladysmith. I'm heading into the fighting zone—Buller's troops will be concentrating—it's no place for a woman! Opperman wouldn't permit it anyway.'

'He would if I let myself be recruited by the brave Mr Bland. If I joined his commando! And then, at the right time, whenever that may be, I join forces with you—and you take me away.' She reached forward brazenly, mockingly, to tap him on the chest. 'If you still refuse, Captain Ogilvie, I might as well have a rifle with me now, and shoot you dead—for you will die the moment I talk to Opperman,

182

die as a spy, and your job, your mission, will die with you—*won't it?*'

Ogilvie reacted with anger: 'You're a damn strumpet!'

'Oh!' she said lightly, demurely shocked and, seeing victory in sight, going back to her ladylike speech. 'What a delightfully old-fashioned word, Mr Bland!'

*   *   *

Opperman was in a towering rage. 'Sodom and Gomorrah are let loose, Mr Bland! Nations have been lost by the enervating effects of womanising. I took the trouble to warn you personally—and what do you do, eh, what do you do?'

'I'm sorry, Commandant, I—'

'Sorry!' Old Red Daniel raised his arms towards heaven, and shook them as if in the face of a God who had unaccountably gone mad to allow such a development. 'Sorry! Bah! You've become soft in the head, that's what you've done!'

'But surely it's a very natural thing—'

'Natural? Natural? Oh yes—it's natural! But the Bible teaches us that we must control nature! This is what marriage was ordained for, Mr Bland!' He pulled at his whiskers and stared into the wide spaces of the veld, falling ominously silent. Underneath, he was rumbling away in contained fury. Ogilvie had the diverting feeling that old Opperman wanted to say quite a lot—wanted to say that a sensible young man, naturally hot-blooded and eager, would just for a short space have turned a blind eye to the teachings of the Bible and taken the young woman by storm—and then, having kept his own counsel and achieved satisfaction, would once again have remembered those responsibilities to God and His Boers and set his face against further temptation. No doubt in his youth Old Red Daniel had done similar things ... or, on the other hand, perhaps not! Perhaps a good Boer did indeed wait for matrimony, just as the Bible taught ...

'Marriage,' Opperman said, breaking suddenly into Ogilvie's thoughts.

'Yes, Commandant?'

'I must assume that you intend to marry this woman when possible.' It was a statement; not a question.

'Er ...'

'The prospect worries you?'

'That's for the future, Commandant,' Ogilvie said ambiguously. 'For the present, if it makes it easier for you to accept her when we ride south, why should she not join your commando?'

'As a woman who'll carry a rifle, and fight?'

'Yes.'

'The moment she does that,' Old Red Daniel said flatly, 'she comes under my orders, and I shall send her in the opposite direction, away from you, Mr Bland!' As soon as it was said, Ogilvie realised, Opperman regretted his impetuosity: the woman certainly wouldn't enlist now—he should have held his tongue! It was, however, equally clear that Opperman's native obstinacy would not permit any withdrawal once a thing had been said. Glaring angrily ahead across the empty countryside, he said, 'You must marry her. If she is to come, you must marry her. Not at once . . . I have no wish to take a newly-wed husband and wife with me to the Tugela—this could lead to many complications and divided loyalties under attack. But as soon as matters are more settled than they are at present. Well, Mr Bland?'

Ogilvie shrugged. 'I would like nothing better, speaking for myself. But I haven't got that far yet! Give me time, Commandant.'

There was a chuckle, and Old Red Daniel relaxed. He was not a man to hold bad temper long. 'Never give a woman time, my good young man! That is fatal. To a woman, time means only an opportunity for a change of mind. They must be taken like a buffalo—with one single shot!'

'Perhaps—once they've actually made up their minds.'

'Mostly their minds need forcing, though I will admit this—you've not let any grass grow so far, Mr Bland.'

Ogilvie grinned. 'She can come, then?'

'Oh, yes, she can come! I would have preferred she didn't, but . . . yes, she can come, with the proviso I have already given.'

Silently in his heart, Ogilvie cursed the existence of Miss Maisie Smith.

*   *   *

Three days later, as Opperman left Reitz with Ogilvie and Miss Smith for the Tugela River, the speed of rumour in time of war had achieved its tangible result: word had reached Lord Methuen that the state of Kimberley's defenders was very much worse than had been supposed and that a fast relief was vital if there was not to be an abject surrender. This word came, boastfully but with every indication of substance, from Boers who had fallen prisoner to the British column; Methuen knew that the moment the news reached Cape Town it would be relayed to him in no uncertain terms from the high command. Thus was Lord Methuen moved to immediate action; and having first pulverised—as he thought—the Boer defences at Magersfontein with an artillery bombardment, he sent out his Highland Brigade to march through the night to be in position for a dawn attack on Magersfontein Hill. Four thousand Scots under Major-General Wauchope marched into a heavy drizzle that turned into an appalling storm, lightning-lit, with drenching rain through which the beams of the search-lights at Kimberley, Rhodes's Eyes, could be seen faintly. At four a.m. Wauchope, his men brought up short by a barrier of thick bush impassable to any large body of men, and with Magersfontein now half a mile away, passed the word for the brigade to deploy. But at once his Scots were enfiladed by a tremendous curtain of rifle-fire that came at them, caught as they were in a perfect trap, from point-blank range close by from all around. The brigade withered and died, caught utterly by surprise: hundreds lay dead in seconds, among them Wauchope himself. Of the rest a large number turned and ran—ran largely into the Boer rifles. Others, advancing, reached the hillside, only to be cut to pieces by the Boer General Cronje. Towards the rear was heard the eerie sound of the pipes starting to fill with air: in a moment they came out full blast and glorious, swelling the hearts of the Scots and sending the Argylls forward to the attack. Through smoke and flame and rifle-fire, the Argylls' pipers marched and played, their regimental tartan moving bravely towards certain death, the notes of the highland challenge sounding out as though to drive death itself away in awe at gallantry. From behind, the cavalry from Methuen's main column went forward on foot, together with the guns, advancing with the Guards and the King's Own Yorkshire Light Infantry upon the

Boer centre. But by now time was not on the side of the British. The battle dragged on all through that morning, with Methuen failing to press home a decisive attack; and by two o'clock the line began to crumble. A mob of men streamed to the rear in panic, to be gunned into the ground as they ran. And down upon the broken column rained the Boer heavy artillery, held in reserve until this moment of total defeat.

On the following noon, Lord Methuen began a full-scale retreat and by four p.m. was camped once more on the Modder, his force more than a thousand men lighter. This was now 12th December. So began the week that was to be written into the annals of British military history as Black Week. Colenso was yet to come.

*   *   *

With Opperman's commandos Ogilvie rode towards the Tugela River, on the move by day and at night sleeping by the glowing camp-fires. On two occasions they were attacked, and attacked bravely in Ogilvie's opinion, by native tribesmen, Zulus wearing scanty rags and waving spears; but the Boer rifles were too deadly, and the attacks were virtually still-born. On that trek Ogilvie and his companions had a little over a hundred miles to cover, and their route led across the Drakensberg

Mountains, after which they would drop down, Opperman said, between Ladysmith and Colenso.

'And Buller?'

Opperman gave a deep-throated laugh, and spat into the camp-fire, then waved his pipe-stem towards the south. 'Buller's going to have a shock from Louis Botha. Buller's reported as likely to move north from Frere for the Tugela at any moment—oh, the British think we're too stupid, militarily, to know their plans—have I not said this already?—but we're not so stupid, Mr Bland! Buller no doubt expects an easy crossing of the river and an equally easy advance on Ladysmith, but he'll not get either. I'm told Botha expects General Buller to stick close to the railway line—so he'll cover all routes around Colenso. Botha's got about 8000 men to cover them with. No, Buller will be held and soundly beaten, you may be sure!'

Soon after this, Opperman turned in. Ogilvie sat on by the fire with Maisie Smith, listening, after a while, to raucous snores from Old Red Daniel. He was very aware of the girl by his side, aware of her scent in the night, of the softness of her body, of her warmth. She said suddenly, 'I'm frightened. Bloody frightened!'

'What of? Ghosts, bogies?'

'Don't laugh at me,' she said.

'Well—tell me, then.'

'I'm frightened we're going to lose this war,

189

that's what—'

He put a hand on her arm, suddenly frightened himself. 'Sssh! For God's sake, keep your voice down, you fool!'

'Opperman's sound asleep.'

'Others may not be. Use your common sense!'

'Oh, all right.' She snuggled closer to him, and spoke in a whisper into his ear. 'Things aren't going very well, are they?'

'Well enough. We'll get our teeth into Brother Boer before long. It's early days, you know—'

'It was going to be a short war.'

'Yes, I know. That was a miscalculation, I admit. We'll win in the end, though!'

'What makes you think that?'

He said, and he believed it, 'We always do, Maisie.'

'That's a laugh. I mean, it's been true in the past, I s'pose, but it doesn't have to stay true, does it?'

'It will. You know the saying—we lose every battle but the last! There's something in that. Didn't you pick up any military history in Peshawar?'

She giggled. 'No. Not military history.'

'Well, don't worry about the outcome. All we have to do is get our second wind.'

'All right, if you say so.' She shivered suddenly, as some animal sound came to them from the distance. 'My God, it's lonely out here, isn't it! Lonely and dark—and bloody cold.'

'Sorry you came?'

She shook her head. 'No. Not so long as I go in the right direction in the end, and you know where that is.'

'Yes. Tell me about your baby, Maisie. I don't even know her name.'

'Alexandra, after the Princess of Wales. My God,' she added, 'what that poor lady must go through, with 'im gallivanting about with all those women! I bet his mum doesn't like it either. Can you *imagine*?'

'It does stretch the mind a little, but I dare say the stories are exaggerated. Tell me about your Alexandra.'

'Why?—'

'I'm interested, that's all. Shouldn't I be?'

She moved against him. 'No reason why not, really. Getting to like me a bit—are you?'

'I wouldn't mind wringing your neck, frankly.'

'Well, that's nice, I must say!' There was a sound of indignation. 'And here's me thinking you were getting more sort of matey like!'

He said, 'One has to keep up appearances, that's all.'

'How d'you mean?'

'I'm supposed to be in love with you, aren't I?'

'No need to sound so angry about it.' She hesitated, and moved even closer to his body.

191

It could have been for warmth: Ogilvie knew it was not. 'Couldn't we, well, get to know each other better? Couldn't we? You're lonely just like I am ... and I know what men want. I could make things easier for you, you know, if you'd let me.'

He said between his teeth, 'Maisie, stop making things worse, which in fact is what you're doing. If Opperman woke up and caught us in flagrant disregard of the Bible, he'd probably shoot us on the spot—or something!'

'Strewth,' she said witheringly, 'it makes you wonder how the bloody Boers ever spawned themselves all over South Africa, doesn't it!'

*   *   *

She did talk for a while, before they slept by the fire's embers, of her baby in the institution so far away in England. A bundle of love, she called the baby without any ironic intent. Sweet-tempered, always gurgling with happiness, and a lovely smile and a dimple. She hadn't cared a bit about the man who'd fathered little Alexandra, he was just a bird of passage, a satisfier of a need who at the same time had given her something very precious. As they rode on next day, through a damping cold rain now that made Opperman morose and taciturn, Ogilvie thought a good deal about Maisie Smith. For good or ill, she had

192

become his responsibility, and he had to see her through to the end. A confounded nuisance she might be—and was—but she couldn't be escaped. Nor could she be disregarded. Not only had he, as he had said the night before, to show her what might be called a statutory love, which meant he had to keep on raking up occasions for showing his feelings before Opperman by means of continually dancing attendance on his beloved; she was also in very fact getting, as it were, beneath his armour. James Ogilvie was no ascetic: women he had had, and loved too. Maisie Smith was undoubtedly attractive and made no attempt to be otherwise. His imagination bloomed; in his mind he saw a milk-white body, with softly rounded breasts and a flat stomach. He saw firm buttocks, sleek thighs, a titillating area of soft hair ... but always, as soon as he began pondering on them, the buttocks turned into the irritable Kekewich-prodding face of Mr Cecil Rhodes, and the soft hair into the bristling brush that grew from the face of Lord Kitchener of Khartoum. For uppermost in James Ogilvie's mind was the successful outcome of his mission. He had to find out the Boers' advanced plans: nothing must stand in the way of that, but he had a depressing feeling that this was what Maisie Smith would, even if unwittingly, do.

Meanwhile there was the Red Daniel—the

diamond as well as the man. That precious cargo seemed to burn into Ogilvie's side as they rode on across the interminable veld, coming down on to the mighty Drakensberg through bush and scrub, swamp after rain, the smell of the all-pervading mimosa, hill country and river—and finally into the mountain passes themselves. As well as with Kitchener and Rhodes, he meant still to keep faith with Katharine Gilmour, never mind Haig's promises of monetary compensation if the Red Daniel should be lost; and he was beginning to feel beset and hedged about with problems of conflicting interests . . .

Once through the Drakensberg, they heard the sound of gunfire in the north, heavy artillery. 'The Long Toms, bombarding Ladysmith,' Opperman said. Later they heard more rumbles, heavy gunfire to the south, from which Opperman deduced that Buller was engaged on the Tugela. A few more miles after this they saw dust clouds ahead, dust raised by the galloping hooves of ponies. The men of the approaching commando waved hats and rifles as they recognised the red hair of Commandant Opperman, and there were cheers from both sides as the parties met.

'What's the news from General Botha?' Opperman called out.

'The British are upon the Tugela,' was the answer.

'Buller?'

'Yes—'

'It was his guns we've been hearing, then?'

'Yes, that's right. He's bombarding our lines—and much good will it do him!' The man laughed. 'His shells are falling nowhere near us, for he can't see us and doesn't know where to aim!'

Opperman seemed to smack his lips. 'Where does Louis Botha want us to go?'

'Down to Colenso, Commandant.'

Opperman lifted his right hand. His face was alight now, filled with eagerness for battle. 'To Colenso !' he roared. As the commando surged forward, as anticipatory as Opperman himself, Old Red Daniel turned his face towards Ogilvie. 'Now you're going to see the British given one damn good beating,' he said.

*   *   *

Sir Redvers Buller had advanced towards the Tugela from his base at Frere with 18,000 men. Despite a numerical superiority his initial intention had been to undertake a flanking march around the Boer positions at Colenso, for he regarded these positions as virtually impregnable. The news from other fronts—Magersfontein in particular, and Stormberg—which came in as he was about to begin his flanking movement, caused him to change his mind. He halted his column in their tracks and for two days directed a heavy bombardment of

195

artillery against the Boer lines. On the evening of the second day of bombardment he called a conference of his subordinate commanders.

'Speed's the thing now, gentlemen,' he announced. 'Speed of relief for Ladysmith and those poor fellers of White's. They're my first consideration. The flanking march will be totally abandoned, and it's my intention to force the passage of the Tugela tomorrow morning.'

Louis Botha, who had correctly assessed the mind of the British Commander-in-Chief, had in fact expected precisely this: and was very ready to meet it, with his strong Colenso entrenchment protected on the flanks for a ten-mile stretch. There were four miles of country between the British and the Boers, the British tents being well visible while the Boers, with their genius for using every scrap of cover to full advantage, were totally concealed—so much so that Buller, trying vainly to find a sign of men or trenches, considered it not unlikely that Botha's army had taken to its heels in flight already; and next morning, 15th December, he advanced bravely into a situation that was doomed to go wrong from the very start. His tactics were simple: he would mount a three-pronged attack with the 2nd Brigade in the centre, the Irish Brigade on the left, and Lord Dundonald's cavalry brigade on the right, while his artillery moved along east of the railway. He would take the kopjes by the river, and then fight on the farside. Unfortunately he made his advance without diversionary support from Sir George White in Ladysmith. Initially the attack had been planned for two days later, and White was busily making preparations to march out a field force on the 17th. In the interest of secrecy—Ladysmith was said to be full of spies—Buller's new intention had not been notified even to Sir George White, who therefore remained biting his nails in Ladysmith when he heard, distantly, the thunder of the attacking guns along the Tugela to the south. Buller's heavy artillery had moved into position at five-thirty a.m. and three miles from the Tugela, as the marching columns advanced beneath a cloudless, windless sky towards a day of hot sun and red blood, the big guns opened on the kopjes of Colenso. Smoke rose-grey from the explosions, red from the gun-muzzles, and over all the fumes of lyddite. Then the horse-teams moved forward with the field guns. Five hundred men of the Royal Artillery and the Naval Brigade surged ahead of the infantry—thus outraging orthodoxy—under the command of Colonel Long who had led the guns at Omdurman.

But there was no sign of Botha's commandos.

Long's field batteries were within a stone's throw of the Tugela when one rifle shot came from the far side of the river—where, for all

Long could see, there were no Boers. On the heels of this single shot, however, recent history repeated itself. As at the Modder, as at Magersfontein Hill, a sustained barrage of rifle, machine-gun and heavy artillery fire blazed out. This terrible raking fire cut right through the ranks of sailors and Royal Artillery, killing and wounding. Men fell in swathes. On the left flank, the day was already going badly for Major-General Hart leading the Irish Brigade-2nd Royal Dublin Fusiliers, lst Connaught Rangers, 1st Border Regiment and 1st Royal Inniskillings—in their intended assault on Bridle Drift, from which they were to cross the river and advance from the west on Colenso. Hart—an old-time disciplinarian who had ordered parade-ground drill before marching, just as though he were back at Aldershot—had kept his men in close order, thus presenting a compact target to the enemy. In addition to this tactical unwisdom, he managed to become lost, for he had no proper maps and was forced to rely on a native guide in order to find a ford. As the Irish Brigade mistakenly approached a great loop in the Tugela, concealed rifles opened on them and, without orders from Hart, they began to deploy. Hart was furious; he ordered the Irishmen directly into the attack. By the time Sir Redvers Buller, watching through a telescope from his headquarters in the rear by the railway line, had sent word through to Hart

198

to disengage and withdraw from a hopeless action, 400 Irishmen had been cut down. Soon after this a report reached Buller that Long's guns in the centre had been deserted and all the detachments wiped out to a man. Although this was inaccurate, it was enough for General Buller.

'It's no good now,' he said, turning a strained face to his Chief of Staff. 'No good at all. We must try to withdraw the guns, and then retire.'

CHAPTER ELEVEN

'What did I tell you, Mr Bland?' Sitting his pony on some rising ground below Wynne Hill some two miles north of Colenso, Opperman looked and sounded triumphant. By his side, Ogilvie stared towards the battle. It seemed to him to be total confusion. The British cavalry appeared to be attacking a hill away to the east—Hlangwhane, Opperman told him. 'That'll be Dundonald,' the Boer said. 'He's commanding a composite regiment of horse—Natal Carbineers, Natal Police even . . . Imperial Light Horse and Mounted Infantry. By God, Mr Bland, just look at that!'

Looking, Ogilvie felt an appalling sense of hopeless frustration. His knuckles whitened from the intensity of the hand's grip on the reins. He wanted nothing so much in that moment as to take Old Red Daniel Opperman by the throat and strangle the breath from his body. He restrained himself only by an immense effort—and a thought of Lord Kitchener, whose orders he was following. The scene towards Hlangwhane was one of sheer murder, bloody and insane but touched with heroism. Thundering down on the hill, the British cavalry were brought up short by that peculiarly withering fire of the Boers, as usual in excellent cover themselves and using rifles and the new pom-poms with tremendous effect. Ogilvie watched the men and horses fall, listened to the wicked song of the guns as a field-battery gave brave support to the forlorn and halted charge. Away to the west, another brigade, this time of infantry, seemed to be pulling out, and in the centre opposite the Colenso kopjes the British guns appeared to be in a poor state, many of them lying broken and apparently abandoned.

He heard Opperman speaking to him. 'Here,' the Boer said, handing him a pair of field-glasses. 'A closer look, Mr Bland. It'll be a lesson for you in how to conduct a battle—or how not to, depending on which side you take!'

Ogilvie put the glasses to his eyes and scanned the battlefield spread before him. In the distance a stout figure on horseback was riding in the centre of a small group of other horsemen towards a donga behind the silent field-batteries of the Royal Artillery and the Naval Brigade. Ogilvie recognised Sir Redvers Buller. Some way short of the donga a Boer shell exploded close to the mounted party of staff officers. When the smoke cleared Ogilvie saw that at least one of the party had fallen, but General Buller was riding on with a hand held against his side. Opperman, who was also watching through field-glasses, said suddenly, 'You know, Mr Bland, I believe Buller intends to rescue the guns! You British, you have a reputation for never abandoning your guns— but we shall see!' He turned to the men of his commando, waving a hand and shouting exultantly. 'Charge for the guns, men—we'll stop the Britishers in their tracks and earn Louis Botha's gratitude! Follow me to the drift.' He turned to Ogilvie. 'Stay beside me, Mr Bland. If there's any treachery, I'll shoot you dead, whether or not you saved my life.'

Ogilvie saw that the Boer was almost beside himself with blood lust and the promise of action, and had no thought but to reach the British guns before Buller could withdraw them. It was unusual in a Boer to choose to fight in the open: cover tactics were better suited to the men of the commandos; but Old Red Daniel seemed to be a law to himself, to reject the tenets of his kind. As for Ogilvie, he had made up his mind that he was going to reject the tenets of Lord Kitchener and rejoin

201

the British troops at the first opportunity. The slaughter had sickened him; the terrible feeling of sitting helplessly whilst fine British regiments were cut to pieces by these surly, Bible-thumping, bearded fanatics had been too much. Buller was among the bravest of the brave, and he was in distress, and he was closer to James Ogilvie than was Lord Kitchener, safe in Cairo. When it came to the point, the hold of blood and comradeship in arms was stronger by far than that distant hold of Kitchener for all his compelling eyes and thrustful chin. Riding on with Old Red Daniel, thundering down towards the drift by which they would cross the river, Ogilvie took in the fact that they had left Maisie Smith behind. For an instant he turned his head, dangerously, and caught a glimpse of the girl sitting her pony and staring after them, looking as though she thought they had taken leave of their senses. Then they were down on the drift, and splashing the ponies through the Tugela River for the far bank—and the disorganised British troops. As they scrambled the ponies on to dry land, the British guns opened from the rear: other Boer commandos, who had been starting to follow Old Red Daniel's impulsive lead, faltered and then turned back from the river's bank, running towards a line of trenches on the ridges behind. Opperman and Ogilvie stormed on with the commando— and then, unaccountably, the British artillery fell silent.

A moment later Ogilvie saw the reason for the cease fire: British troops, two battalions apparently, were streaming down towards the abandoned field-guns. In the distance was Buller, a hand still laid upon his ribs, riding down towards the guns himself. This began to look like the end for Old Red Daniel, who could surely never stand against two battalions of infantry. Ogilvie was scanning the line, looking for his opportunity to make a dash towards his own side even if he had to wave a white handkerchief to ensure his safety from the British, when once again the Boer artillery took charge of the day. As a party of British officers came across, every Boer gun seemed to bear upon the scene and open simultaneously. The terrible racket of the Creusots screamed into Ogilvie's ears: there was something devilish in the crack and scream and explosion that always came with the firing of those big Creusot guns, with the shell a long way ahead of the sound itself. Often enough, at short ranges, the projectile would hit before men heard its warning note; while at long range—up to five miles or more across a valley—the sound went on ahead as the big shell grew tired in its flight, and then its wretched victims, cowering in the lee of rocks, wondering if the rocks were big enough to shield them from the splinters, would hear first a tremendous crash as of the heavens splitting, then a faint whistle growing quickly to a scream that filled the whole atmosphere around the target. Ogilvie that day was among the crouchers, and the shells flew over his head. Others were not so lucky: many men of Opperman's commando fell, victims of their own side's fire; the British, still making for the guns, were cut to shreds, though a party of men did in fact reach two of them, managing to haul them towards the rear. Old Red Daniel, yelling out oaths, hurled himself towards them; Ogilvie followed, getting closer to the British when he could. A moment later his pony was hit by a shell fragment, and died under him. Getting clear of the bloodied animal, he crawled along, keeping in such cover as he could. Some more distant British guns were opening now. Smoke, flame and lyddite fumes were everywhere: on all sides were the screams of horses and of dying men. His own clothing was soon torn to rags, rags reddened by a number of shrapnel wounds, small ones but painful enough. At one moment his crawling progress was halted by a figure on the ground, an officer of lieutenant's rank, badly wounded and bleeding. Scanning the face as he moved past, Ogilvie felt a sense of shock: that face was remarkably like that of Bobs Bahadur, Lord Roberts of Kandahar . . . and he had heard that Lieutenant Frederick Roberts was serving under Buller. As he emerged from the battle smoke he saw Buller himself ahead of him, Buller motionlessly sitting his horse, Buller looking pale and shaken and hopeless. He saw Buller turn aside and speak to an A.D.C. and a few moments later, as he struggled to his feet to dash towards the Commander-in-Chief, he heard the British bugles sounding retire. Before the distressful notes had ended, something took Ogilvie a searing blow on the skull and he crashed back to the blood-soaked, sun-scorched ground.

*   *   *

'Today,' the black-bearded man with the rough cloth suit and the cartridge-filled bandolier said, 'the God of our fathers has given us a great victory. This is the message I intend to telegraph to the Volksraad.' He looked down at Ogilvie, smiling slightly. 'And this is Mr Bland from Kimberley, eh? Are you feeling better, Mr Bland?'

Ogilvie nodded. 'Yes—it was just a glancing blow from a stray bullet. I'm getting used to that by now! But who are you, if I may ask?'

'Louis Botha. Commandant Opperman has told me all about you. You are welcome here, Mr Bland.'

'Thank you.' Ogilvie, lying on a camp bed under canvas, with many bandages covering the minor wounds of the shrapnel, stared up at General Botha, who had sounded cheerful and friendly. He was a good-looking man, and tall, with very bright eyes. Ogilvie, as part of his instructions from Major Allenby, knew something of the man's life. Botha was partly French and partly Dutch, but had been born in Natal as a British subject. He had left Natal when quite young, to farm in the Transvaal. A man of almost no education, he had turned into an excellent general with an instinctive flair for leadership. 'Can you tell me what happened after I was hit, General Botha? I'm told Commandant Opperman personally brought me across the Tugela—'

'Yes, that's right. He saved your life—and has thus repaid your own gallantry, Mr Bland. As to what happened after—well, Buller has pulled back. He pulled back at noon—and at five o'clock our men crossed the Tugela to bring in the guns he had left behind—'

'Buller left the guns?'

Botha nodded. 'Your Buller, I think he lost his nerve! He neither blew up the guns, nor gave time for darkness to conceal a recovery of them—and many of them still had their breech-blocks intact. He pulled his whole army back even though only half his troops had been engaged.'

'And the casualties?'

'For Buller, almost twelve hundred men. For me—less than forty, Mr Bland!' Botha shrugged. 'It is the fortune of war, of course, but if the British had proper leaders they

206

would do better, for there is nothing lacking in the men!'

'So what's next, General?' Ogilvie asked.

Botha said, 'I shall give Buller an armistice tomorrow to collect his dead and wounded who are still out there.' He swept a hand around towards the Tugela. 'Now, Mr Bland. When you're fully recovered, I shall want words with you—eh, Daniel?'

Opperman, standing in shadow to the left of Ogilvie's bed, nodded. He said, 'General Botha wishes you to extend your recruiting efforts, my good friend. If you can do for him what you did for me in Reitz, why, you will be worth your weight in gold . . . or diamonds!'

'Diamonds . . .' Ogilvie felt a rush of blood to his head. He had forgotten all about the Red Daniel; he felt in his pocket. It was, thank God, still there. He said, 'Oh, I'll do my best to help, of course.' Inside, he was cursing Opperman for unwittingly preventing his escape to the British lines, but that was past history now and had to be made the best of. The collaboration with the enemy must perforce continue. After another friendly word, Louis Botha left the tent with Opperman, and Ogilvie was alone with his temporary nurse: Maisie Smith.

'Do you want to get up?' she asked.

'I not only want to,' he said, 'I'm going to.' He put his legs out of the bed, and started scrabbling around for his boots. Maisie found them for him, and knelt to put them on.

She said, 'I think you're a fraud—Mr Bland.'

'The bullet was real enough.'

'Yes, that's true,' she said. 'So perhaps it was my nursing that made you better so quickly.' Frowning, she looked up at him: her eyes, he saw, were bright and there was an appeal in her face that touched him. She asked, 'Suppose you hadn't been hit, what would you have done? Please tell me truly.'

'Done?' he echoed. 'Why, I'd have come back on my own two feet, I imagine!'

'Would you?' Her voice was low, little more than a whisper. 'I think you would have run for the British troops—and left me to Opperman. I'm right, aren't I—Mr Bland?'

He said with a touch of anger, 'For God's sake be careful. I still have a job to do—and may I remind you, your future depends on that as much as mine does!'

'Yes,' she said. 'But across the river this morning, you were going to run out on me and the job, both. I was so frightened—that you would do that, or—or that you would be killed in the fighting. You were right when you said I was dependent on you, James—'

'*Harry*! Harry Bland—for God's sake remember—'

'Yes, all right. I'm sorry.' There was a catch in her voice, and before she bowed her head on his knee he fancied he had seen tears. Her shoulders began to shake a little, and he laid a hand on her. She was warm beneath the thin fabric of her dress, warm and vital and desirable. Gently, he lifted her face, read the mixture of loneliness and hopelessness and desire—desire for support and reassurance, for a strong arm, for love and friendship, for him. Life was becoming intolerable: a lot of her brazen façade had gone, and gone suddenly. Ogilvie believed that the day's events had shaken her badly. As she had said, she was still a Briton, and patriotic. To see the fighting from across the river, as she must have done, actually to witness the withering of the flower of the British Army, to witness Sir Redvers Buller riding off in defeat, could well have broken her. Ogilvie felt for her, very deeply; there was a strong bond developing between them now, a bond of sympathy that had superseded the bond of expedience.

'Maisie,' he said, and stopped, his blood pounding.

'Yes, James?' It was said on a whisper of breath and this time he disregarded the indiscretion.

'Get up. Don't kneel. I'm not the Monarch!' He took her waist and lifted her, catching her perfume, feeling her hair, which with a sudden movement she had shaken loose, falling like a cascade about his face. Her breath swept his ear, softly: he felt the feather-light touch of her lips, then, very gently, her teeth came together against his lobe. He felt her hand, warm and soft against his body beneath his shirt, then the pressure of firm breasts, and then, as gently as her own movements, he lifted her away from him and, getting to his feet with her in his arms, laid her down on the camp bed.

*   *   *

When it was over they lay together at peace, damp with sweat. It had been a vigorous experience: Maisie's gentleness had soon given way to a healthy abandon to which he had responded with an equal lust, but he had, to her obvious pleasure, been able to extend the act rather than bring it to a swift conclusion. During it, she had spoken words of love and passion that had aroused him strongly in their very indelicacy: he could well imagine that apelike man, Major the Honourable Alastair Duff-Kinghorne, preferring Maisie's bouncing, uninhibited love-making to that of his spouse, who was also Scots—Ogilvie's pride in his own ancestry had never blinded him to racial deficiences, and he knew that Scotswomen were often cold, cold as the snowclad mountains and high moors of their homeland; and he could imagine the Honourable Fiona lying like the Stone of Scone beneath the Major's pelt.

Maisie lifted herself on an elbow and smiled

down at him. 'Feeling better?' she asked.

'Much.'

'It was lovely, wasn't it? Really *good*. I wish *you*'d been my baby's dad, honest.' Suddenly she giggled. ''P'raps you will be, not that I want another, not out here in this bloody rotten country.' She saw his look of anxiety, and she touched his cheek. 'Oh, don't worry, it doesn't happen every time, thank God! Cheer up, do. What's the matter now—want it again, do you?'

He grinned. 'Yes. No. Not now, Maisie. We mustn't tempt fate—'

'Fate!' She was scornful. 'Not fate—bloody old Opperman!'

'All right, Opperman. Suppose he came in and found us like this? He's got to go on trusting me, you know.'

'Don't see what *trust* has to do with it,' she said, and giggled again. 'Or did you promise you wouldn't do it, swear an oath on the Bible, like? Did you?'

'Of course not,' he said impatiently. 'It's just that I have his overall trust and I don't want to shake it in any way at all. It's important to a lot of people—and I can't say more than that.'

'Oh, all right,' she said, sitting up. 'I agree you've got his trust. He'd never have taken you across the Tugela else, even though I heard him threaten you. He seems to *like* you . . .'

'You'll help me keep it that way?'

'Yes, course I will. But don't you ever get

211

any more ideas of running off and leaving me to Brother Boer, that's all!'

*   *   *

It was now England's Black Week with a vengeance: next day Sir Redvers Buller sent orders—which, fortunately, were disregarded —by heliograph to Sir George White in Ladysmith that he should burn his ciphers, destroy his guns, and fire off his ammunition— after which he should consider himself free to make the best possible terms with the Boers. And at midnight, when Louis Botha's terms of armistice ran out, Buller packed up his tents and, under a total eclipse of the moon if not of his own military position, retreated to Chieveley. At home in Whitehall, momentous events, foreshadowed for some weeks past, came to their fruition as a result of the Colenso fiasco. In London, throughout Great Britain, all was gloom; sensing the will of the people the Prime Minister, Lord Salisbury, hastened to London on the Saturday. Ignoring the War Office, ignoring even Lord Wolseley, he tendered certain advice to Her Majesty at Windsor Castle; and on Sunday evening, after an exchange of telegrams with Dublin, Field-Marshal Lord Roberts was appointed Commander-in-Chief in South Africa in Buller's place, with Lord Kitchener of Khartoum his Chief of Staff.

CHAPTER TWELVE

'They haven't got rid of Buller entirely,' Opperman said, 'and in that there is perhaps some comfort! It's said he's to remain in local command in northern Natal. But now that Roberts and Kitchener are coming out, things will never go so well again for us—I feel this in my bones!'

Louis Botha nodded, his own face grave and preoccupied as he turned to Ogilvie. 'How will your English troops see this change of command, do you suppose, Mr Bland?'

Ogilvie shrugged. 'I can't really say, General. I was a very temporary and unwilling soldier—and for a very short time at that! But I think it'll put new heart into them. Bobs has a great reputation, and he's well liked.'

'So is Buller.'

'Yes, and I think with good reason. He's a brave man, General, and considerate to his troops.'

'But not clever. Roberts is clever, and so is the terrible Kitchener.' Botha got to his feet and moved restlessly up and down. The three men, with others from Botha's staff, were resting on a hillside north of the Tugela, under a hot sun, swatting at the crawling flies that assailed them continually. 'Also, Roberts may be in a vengeful mood! I would not blame him

213

if he were!'

'How so?' Opperman asked.

'I have word that his son was among those killed in the battle the other day. He was mortally wounded, and died in hospital at Chieveley after Buller had withdrawn. It's a sad time for any man to assume the high command, and I am sorry.'

Ogilvie heard this with sorrow also: he remembered the face of the officer he had stumbled upon. He asked, 'How are you Afrikaners going to react to the new appointments, General Botha?'

'With determination! Would you expect it otherwise, Mr Bland?'

'By no means. I was only wondering if it would mean fresh plans. If I can help in any way ... perhaps by holding more meetings? You have only to ask, General.'

Botha nodded absently. 'Thank you. Mr Bland, do not be misled by our long faces! We are merely being realists, in facing up to the fact that both Roberts and Kitchener will be tougher adversaries—we must not belittle our current position, which is strong—strong, I say again! We have won a great victory at Colenso, and have seriously worried London. Possibly more important even, we have impressed the German Emperor and his—' He broke off, staring away across the Tugela. 'But you can still help, Mr Bland, by continuing to take orders from my good friend, Commandant

214

Opperman.'

*　　　*　　　*

'What exactly,' Ogilvie asked that evening, as he and Opperman were eating their supper by the camp-fire, 'did General Botha mean when he said you'd impressed the Germans?' He managed to sound casual enough; but all day he had been much intrigued by Botha's reference to Germany, a country that so far had been fairly cool towards the British over South Africa, even though, on 20th November, Kaiser Wilhelm had paid a state visit to London, apparent proof of German neutrality.

Opperman hesitated, gave him a close look, then laughed. 'I dare say it can do no harm to talk of it. We are friends—and now allies, and I can trust you. The fact is that Germany is in a mood to help us, Mr Bland.'

'How's that?'

Opperman pushed with his boot at the glowing embers of the camp-fire, and munched a mouthful of meat. 'Your Royal Navy has been stopping ships, and searching them for materials of war—chiefly outside Delagoa Bay in Portuguese East. Among the ships stopped have been German ones . . . the Kaiser is said to be angry over this and is considering breaking off diplomatic relations with the Court of St James.' Opperman laughed loudly. 'If he does—or even if he

215

doesn't go that far just yet—we stand to gain a great deal.'

'Really?'

'Yes, really, Mr Bland! Think: the Kaiser, a soldier himself, respects victory. Success, you see, brings success—for nothing in this world succeeds like success! Suppose the Kaiser should permit us the use of German South-West Africa—can't you see the strategic advantage in that? Besides which, there is the German Army itself, that excellent fighting machine that—'

'You mean the Kaiser might send help?'

Opperman nodded. 'Yes, that is what I mean. President Kruger has already been in touch, secretly, with Count Bülow, Foreign Minister of the German Empire. Bülow's own belief is that this war will end in a British defeat, complete and absolute. Other military experts in Germany also believe the same thing. Your Joseph Chamberlain has proposed an alliance with Germany—this was taken as little more than a joke by Kaiser Wilhelm, for the Germans do not ally themselves with a weak nation. I tell you this, Mr Bland: the whole world knows that one day there will be a clash of arms between the German and the British Empires, a war that may well be fought in the British Isles themselves, or on the continent of Europe. And Count Bülow and his experts do not turn a blind eye to the advantages to be gained by trying out their war

216

machine in South Africa, as a test of arms in which a great deal can be learned, and any deficiencies shown up and put right before the big war begins!'

'So this is how you are thinking, in your future plans, is it?'

'Yes. We are moving on the diplomatic front as well as the fighting one.' Opperman leaned forward and tapped Ogilvie's shoulder. 'I trust you with this knowledge. It is not to be spoken of. It is very secret. Do you understand?'

'Yes, I understand.'

The lie still did not come easily: Ogilvie hated his task more than ever, for Opperman was a genial, kindly man, and open-hearted. So was Louis Botha. No doubt even Oom Paul Kruger had his good points! Again and again, Ogilvie found his mind filled with the one thought, that the Boers, after all, were fighting only to preserve their own and not, like the British, to retain a hold over a basically alien territory. When he turned in that night beneath a cold sky brilliant with stars—turned in alone, for Opperman was bivouacked nearby—Ogilvie twisted and turned, unable to sleep, too mindful of the treachery he was wallowing in. Kitchener, who had been the distant evil genie till now, was soon to be very present in South Africa—and Kitchener would most certainly wish to know of the covert dialogue between Oom Paul Kruger and Count Bernhard von Bülow. In the morning,

217

having at last fallen into an uneasy sleep, Ogilvie awoke to a lazy, sun-filled day. It was a pleasant and peaceful scene. A light wind sent thin white cloud chasing along an otherwise blue sky. Men washed, and sang, and made breakfast. Apart from the Boers, the hills all around were empty. No British; but Ogilvie could hear the distant Boer guns keeping up their spasmodic bombardment on Ladysmith. At breakfast Opperman announced that Louis Botha had ridden off the night before to his head laager and that they, Old Red Daniel and Mr Bland, would be joining him there during the day.

'What about the rest of the commando?' Ogilvie asked.

'Oh,' Opperman said, 'they'll stay here and act as our outpost, to let us know when the British move again, if ever they do! They'll have an easy life until that day comes—though it's possible Botha will send some of them up to the siege line at Ladysmith, to help out. If so they'll have the pleasure of seeing our guns being fired on the town. Louis Botha,' he added, 'tells me that he expects visitors to come up from Pretoria to watch the bombardment.'

Ogilvie stared. 'Ordinary civilians—just to watch?'

'Yes, and why not?'

Ogilvie didn't answer; it seemed a strange way to run a war. After breakfast he walked around the bivouacs with Opperman, talking to the men, most of whom said they would take the opportunity of some leave, a right to do which at will, Opperman said, was a confounded nuisance but one that the Afrikaners, as free citizens, insisted upon—and there was little that he or Louis Botha or anyone else could do about it. Certainly this lull in the fighting while the British licked their wounds and waited for Lord Roberts's arrival at Cape Town was a good opportunity for the burghers to go home and attend to their private affairs. In the event Ogilvie and Old Red Daniel did not go that day to the head laager but went instead, at Botha's personal invitation, to an encampment on the Ladysmith heights. There they were to spend many days, still waiting for Buller to re-group; and in the meantime they took life easy. For the men of the commandos there was little in the way of military duty to be performed apart from the odd picket and now and again a fatigue party was sent back to pick up supplies of food and arms and ammunition. Ogilvie was forced to watch the Boer guns firing into the town, and was occasionally, whilst riding on visits with Opperman to the camps and outposts, under fire from the Ladysmith garrison. When this happened every Boer vanished as if by magic into cover, and the British shelling in fact caused only minimal damage, mainly to the tents. During this period of inactivity in a fighting sense, Opperman made full use of Mr Harry Bland in giving talks to the commandos on the conditions as he had so recently left them in Kimberley, talks from which they were able to deduce a similar state of affairs inside Ladysmith. He was also taken to the small outlying townships, where once again he went, time after time, into his recruiting spiel: as a result of which fresh drafts soon began to reach the Boer siege lines, building up an ever stronger force against Sir George White.

There was also plenty of time for Maisie Smith—too much time. Opperman, on one of their recruiting rides away from Ladysmith, broached the subject of marriage.

'Here is the opportunity,' he said gruffly. 'There are pastors in plenty to do what's necessary.'

'Not yet, Commandant.'

'She has not agreed?'

'No,' Ogilvie said, with his tongue in his cheek, for she certainly had not been asked. 'And I don't think I'm ready yet in any case.'

'Why not, Mr Bland, why not?'

'The war, Commandant! As you yourself said in Reitz ... split loyalties are bad for efficiency. Let me get the war done with first.'

Opperman gave a sardonic grunt. 'You are remarkably full of self-control, Mr Bland,' he observed.

Ogilvie didn't comment, but wondered how

much Old Red Daniel really knew. The Boer, in spite of his God and his biblical approach to life, was no drawing-room socialiser, no rose-spectacled maiden aunt. He knew the lusts of the body as well as any other vigorous man. Though he would be monumentally disapproving, he would quite possibly have wisdom enough never to notice. But Maisie Smith herself, as the quiet days went by, became more importunate, both in her physical desires and in her main ambition to get away from the Boer lines and back to Hounslow and baby Alexandra. Alone with James Ogilvie, she grew tearful and sentimental about home and childhood; she even brought photographs from the trunk that had followed them in a commissariat cart all the way from Reitz—photographs, old and faded, of her mother as a young girl, in service with a titled family—a young woman as pretty as Maisie, with starched white cap and streamers, an apron and a long black dress, hands demurely clasped in front with stiffly cuffed wrists. And her father, head gamekeeper ultimately at the same great house—a thickly whiskered man with a hard face, a bowler hat worn well forward, and gaitered legs. Photographs too—ones he had seen before—of her baby. He asked, looking at the small white bundle, 'How do you feel about your father, Maisie? I mean—turning you out?'

221

'He's a bastard,' she said flatly. 'I don't feel anything about him at all—except I hate him.'

'He's not unusual, Maisie.'

'Isn't he?' The tone was dismissive, but she must have known the truth of what Ogilvie had said. The majority of fathers would have reacted to an illegitimate birth in precisely the same way, assuaging their feelings of outrage, of ingratitude, re-establishing their moral image before friends and neighbours and employers. It was a highly personal matter, and reflected upon the whole family's honour. Opperman would behave in a similar manner if any daughter of his fell so far from grace. Ogilvie recalled a tenant farmer of his father's, on the Corriecraig estate, coming in tears to the castle with such a tale of his child. ' 'Tis the worst thing that can ever happen to a father, Sir Iain,' the old man had said with tears running down his cheeks, 'and I can only do the one thing, and that is, pray to God to take me.' In that case too the daughter had been turned out of the home; Sir Iain Ogilvie, though fully understanding, had with the greater tolerance and wider mind of the aristocrat much disapproved; but had been powerless to prevent it short of a threat, which he would not utter, to evict the whole family. Passions ran strong: men could do these things, but not women. Often enough James Ogilvie had pondered on the ethics of such incquality without coming to any conclusions

222

except the one of common humanity: a family in misfortune should close its ranks, and help, not hinder. Cruelty was inexcusable.

He said nothing of all this to Maisie Smith. Clearly, she had shut her father out of her mind and did not wish to discuss that aspect. It was the future that mattered now with her—and once again he shrank from the thought that it was he who had become responsible for her future.

One afternoon, when they had ridden out alone into the country, and had found a quiet hollow in the hills, a hollow shaded by trees where they could be very private, she found the Red Daniel. As Ogilvie had taken off his jacket, the little wash-leather bag had fallen from a pocket, and she had pounced upon it, holding it laughingly out of reach and then, when he remonstrated, putting it down the neck of her dress.

'It'll not be safe there,' he said, laughing back at her but with a hard edge to his tone. 'We know each other too well for that!'

She giggled. 'That's quite a point, but I could always make it look like you tried to rape me, and then old Opperman would have you buried in a dark pit full of Bibles or something, wouldn't he—'

'Be quiet, Maisie, and give it back!'

'Hoity toity!' she said with another giggle. 'What is it, then, a ring—for me, James?'

'No.'

She dived her hand between her breasts and brought out the bag. Before he could stop her, she had opened it and shaken out the stone in its cottonwool surround. She gasped when she saw the Red Daniel bared in her hand, catching the strong sunlight so that it flashed and sparkled with changing brilliant lights. 'My!' she said wonderingly. 'A bloody great diamond! Must be worth a fortune.' She gave him a sharp look. 'What's its history?'

'Nothing to do with you, Maisie.'

'Did you steal it?' She caught her breath. 'Did you *really* desert? Pinch this in Kimberley, then get out? Was that it?'

He shook his head. 'No. It's not that at all. Please give it back.'

'And if I don't?'

'I'll take it from you. If I have to hurt you, I will.'

'Then you'll have Opperman to reckon with.'

Again he shook his head. 'No, Maisie. Opperman knows all about the Red Daniel—' he broke off, flushing with anger at his own lack of control on his tongue, but it was too late.

'*Red Daniel*? It's named after Opperman himself, d'you mean?'

'Yes. I shouldn't have said that, and you must keep it to yourself—'

'Look, whose side *are* you on, James? Are you really with the Boers?' There was fear in her face now, a growing anxiety that she had committed herself to the wrong camp after all. 'Surely you wouldn't really do that, would you?'

He said between his teeth, 'What I told you—under pressure, if you remember—was the truth. I'm not with the Boers, as you put it. I'm still a British officer. I can't say any more than that. I'm sorry, but there it is. You must go on trusting me, as I trust you. We're each dependent on the other now, Maisie, and I'm going to do my part as best I can. Now give me back the diamond.'

'All right,' she said, and passed it back. There was a look in her eyes that was half hurt, half anger. 'Is this to do with a girl?' she asked.

'What if it is, Maisie? You and I . . . we're together for reasons of the war, nothing else.'

'*Nothing* else?'

'Oh, I'm sorry for that,' he said with a touch of tenderness, putting his hand over hers. 'It was clumsily put and I hope you'll forgive me. But you do know what I mean, don't you?'

'Yes, I do know. It's just not my business, is it?'

'Well, frankly it isn't, but I didn't mean quite that either.' He hesitated. 'I don't see why I shouldn't tell you just a little more, as a matter of fact. The Red Daniel . . . it's the property of a lady in Cape Town. I'm taking it back to her—that's all.'

She lifted an eyebrow, smiling a little now. '*Really* all?'

'Yes. A simple duty—to return the diamond to her.'

She nodded. 'All right,' she said, and gave a sigh, and let herself fall back into his arms. It was peaceful and utterly silent, with all the fighting very far away and no one around to bother them. In a low voice she said, 'Come on, love . . .'

*   *   *

From the Ladysmith siege lines they moved a few days later to the head laager, where General Botha was taking his physical ease but was mightily engaged in his planning for the future. Opperman was mostly in Botha's secret councils, and much was discussed in the hearing of James Ogilvie who, as the days ran into weeks, became fully accepted and whole-heartedly trusted. He was finding that in many ways the Boers were as simple as children at play: that very largely the war itself was regarded with an extraordinary lightness, however much Oom Paul in Pretoria might preach the gospel of solemnity and duty and self-denial in the most splendid of all causes, a cause in which God was firmly on the Boer side. Botha and his friends trusted Mr Harry Bland from Kimberley because they saw no reason not to. Had he not escaped at peril of his life from the British in Kimberley, had not the British shot at him in his attempt, as witness the holes in his ragged, wire-torn uniform? Had he not saved their Old Red Daniel's own life? Had he not been hit by a British bullet at Colenso? Oh yes, Mr Bland was all right and was to be trusted! He had proved himself time and again. Look at his recruiting record, for one thing!

Mostly, Ogilvie realised, Botha and his lieutenants did not think in terms of duplicity. They had their surly, close-hearted Krugers, of course—but their ponderous counsels seemed not to carry weight in the happy courts of Louis Botha.

News filtered through: the British at home had not much enjoyed Christmas, coming as it did so soon after Black Week. For Ogilvie, Christmas 1899 had passed in a whirl of hymn-singing and readings from the Bible, sonorously uttered at length by Opperman in a well-brushed, long black frock-coat, his whiskers beautifully combed for the occasion. This, and a curious juxtapositioning of laager-inspired Boer folk-singing in the encampments outside Ladysmith, drew the momentous nineteenth century towards its close. Other items of news included word that an important prisoner, Winston Churchill, son of a leading British politician, had escaped with great courage and cunning from the compound at Pretoria, being at that time in total ignorance of the fact that the Boers intended releasing him the very day following his masterly dive for freedom via the concealment offered by a lavatory. Queen Victoria had marked Christmas for her troops by sending out to every man a tin of chocolate with her own portrait on the lid, whilst the ubiquitous Mr Lyons donated a vast quantity of Christmas puddings. Boxing Day provided more stirring news for Boer hearts: the British under Colonel Baden-Powell had tried to seize Game Tree Fort, a Boer outpost at Mafeking; the attack had failed, losing Baden-Powell almost fifty men. Soon after this came small Boer victories at Dordrecht and at Upington on the Orange River. Nevertheless, to the more thoughtful Boers, other news was not so good: Lord Roberts, Fighting Bobs, Bobs Bahadur of so much Indian Frontier glory and battle experience, had by now left London's Waterloo Station amid scenes of unparalleled enthusiasm and a sea of Union Flags for Southampton, there to board the *Dunnottar Castle* for the Cape. At Gibraltar the ship would deviate to embark Lord Kitchener to join his Commander-in-Chief and plot the future conduct of the war.

*   *   *

'It's not Germany alone,' Louis Botha said, pacing up and down with Ogilvie and Old Red

Daniel, and casting glances towards Ladysmith in the distance. 'No! Russia, France—they have no love for England, and have waited for years to see the English brought down. I think the question for the English now is, not so much will they lose South Africa, but will they lose the whole Empire?'

'You mean if there were a concerted attack, war on a world scale?' Opperman asked.

Botha nodded, his eyes alight. 'Just so, my dear old friend, just so! I have the ear of Oom Paul, and that is the way he is thinking. Count Bülow is but one possible friend who may come out for us. But we shall see—we shall see!' He halted, shading his eyes and looking again towards the besieged town, gazing at the Platrand, a great 300-foot high ridge southeast of the town itself. Then he let fall another item of news, news very personal to James Ogilvie if Botha had but known. 'I have word that Buller's being reinforced,' he said. 'That must mean he intends to try again to relieve Ladysmith—perhaps before Roberts arrives.' He laughed. 'It would be such a feather in that fat little man's hat—but he'll not be allowed to wear it if I have my way!'

'Truly said!' Opperman laughed. 'What are the reinforcements, General?'

Botha said, 'Oh, a regiment from Lord Methuen's force that was to relieve Kimberley. A regiment of Scots in skirts named the Royal Strathspeys.' He added, 'I'm told they're already on their way by rail and foot across Cape Colony and up through Griqualand East—and may the good God of battles make it hot marching for them!'

CHAPTER THIRTEEN

They marched in column of route, a field-battery of the Royal Artillery and eight hundred weary Scots—the casualties had been heavy at Magersfontein and in the actions preceding that battle, and also in skirmishes after it, though in all conscience most of the warfare after the retreat to Modder River Station had been against the myriads of flies that flew and crawled over men and horses, rations and waste tips. Men's tempers were ragged now; during the rail lift along the southern Orange Free State border, the crawling train, stopped for a long and apparently pointless spell, had been attacked by a plague of locusts that no shutting of windows seemed able to keep out. The results had been unpleasant in the over-crowded, foetid carriages. After the jolting rail travel they now faced the long, long march up the whole length of Griqualand East from Maclear, where the line had ended until, if they were lucky, they might entrain again at the railhead inside Natal. Meanwhile their feet, as they struggled by forced marches to join Buller—still commanding the Second, Third, Fourth and Fifth Divisions in Natal— were sore and bleeding. They would continue to bleed, and to be bandaged by the busy medical orderlies, until the column made contact with the Third Division and found new comrades amongst the Irish and Fusilier Brigades. Then there might come some rest, and better food. Food on that march was scarce: after five days, the Royal Strathspeys were down to half rations: though now and again they fell in with friendly natives, black-skinned tribesmen, fugitives from Boer territory who had no love for the hard-fisted Dutch farmers who had taken their land and virtually enslaved many of their kind; these poor people sold the troops a little butter and some onions, individually, so that at least a few fortunate mouths were unofficially fed with luxuries. Accoutrements grew heavy, khaki jackets became drenched with sweat, kilts sagged against sun-blistered knees to add to the discomforts of an appalling march, every bit as bad as the Khyber, through sand-strewn mountain passes. They made good some fifteen to sixteen miles a day, and to achieve this the harsh, harrying voices of the colour-sergeants and corporals were a very necessary lash. Dornoch was indefatigable, riding up and down the column, always with a smile and an encouraging word for the stragglers. At sundown each evening they bivouacked with sentries manning the outposts in hastily-constructed sangars, vigilant as they faced the bitterly cold nights and heavy morning dews.

There was occasional action in the course of that Natal-ward trek north from Maclear: the enemy was making forays from the Orange Free State into Basutoland and Griqualand East. Once the Boers, sighting the dust raised by the column, appeared in some force to make a stand on the summit of a hill in their track. Lord Dornoch at once broke column, and the Royal Strathspeys advanced in fighting order against the hillside. It was an irritating delay; but in the result, after four hours' rifle fire supported by the guns of the field-battery, they dispersed the Boers, who turned and ran for their ponies. The British force suffered twelve casualties in that small action—eight wounded in varying degrees, four killed. The burial parties secured the corpses against the waiting beaks of the aasvogels; and the regiment and the guns moved on behind the pipes and drums, foot-slogging their way to the Tugela, blistered, weary almost to death, cursing belts and rifles and equipment, swatting ceaselessly at flies, blackened and shrivelled by the cruel sun as they marched, if they had but known it, towards the different discomforts of rain and mud—guarding near-empty water-bottles currently more precious by far than all the diamonds of Kimberley—

striving instinctively to straighten their sagging backs and shoulders in response to the sad but heroic wailing of the pipes which, together with the beat of the drummers, led the column out.

*   *   *

Maisie Smith said, 'Well, I see you have a problem, all right.'

'Problem!' Ogilvie lifted his clenched fists in the air and shook them. 'I'm not staying this side of the line with my own regiment on the other, Kitchener or no Kitchener! Listen, Maisie: every time I talk to the Boers from now on, every time I gain them a new recruit, I'm acting in a very definite sense, directly against my own friends—aren't I?'

'Yes,' she said, 'but so you were before, weren't you?'

'There's a difference. If you can't see it, that's your misfortune!'

'Oh, well. What's all this about Kitchener, anyway?'

He said shortly, preoccupied with his own dilemma, 'Never mind about that, forget it. The thing is, we have to find a way of getting out, and you seem to be putting difficulties in the way, Maisie—'

'Don't go on so,' she said. She gave him a pert look. 'I want to get out, just as much as you, don't I? I'm right with you, only I don't want you to blame me after, like, for perhaps making you get out before you've done whatever it is you really came to do. That's all. I don't want to seem to *push* you . . . so maybe I'm leaning over backwards—'

'Oh, all right, all right!' he snapped. While Maisie Smith sat on a canvas groundsheet, he walked up and down, trying to think things out. (Once again, in spite of a good deal of rain and mud, he had brought the girl to what they had come to regard as 'their' hollow in the hills; only this time there was to be no love-making, no dalliance.) Physically, the break-out from the Boers should be simple enough, since they trusted him. They wouldn't question his riding down to the Tugela with Maisie Smith, although it was a longish way from the Ladysmith siege lines. Trouble would come the moment he looked like crossing over, no doubt; but that was a hazard of war, and would be dealt with when it arose. No: the main problem was simply that he had not yet managed to complete his mission. So far, he had no real knowledge of the ahead planning of the Boer High Command, other than in a broad political sense; though this would most certainly be useful information for Kitchener to have, Kitchener would not consider the mission complete unless he, Ogilvie, also brought out the campaign plans, if such existed. And, whatever had been his initial reaction in his outburst to Maisie, Ogilvie knew very well that to proceed too far along the lines of 'Kitchener or no Kitchener' simply would not do at all . . .

'When are they arriving?' Maisie Smith asked. 'Your regiment, I mean.'

'I don't know. Botha's information didn't go that far.'

'What are you going to do? *Really* going to do. Because I don't think you *do* mean just to nip over the Tugela and join up with them, do you?'

'What gave you that idea?' He sounded belligerent.

She laughed and said, 'Your face! I'm used to reading men, you know. I've had to do quite a lot of that, one way and another. Well, James?'

'You're right,' he said. 'There are things I must do first, and we may not have much time—'

'We?'

'You're coming with me, aren't you?'

She nodded.

'Then you'll have to help me.'

She stared. 'Help you do what?'

'I don't know yet, Maisie. Give me time and I'll let you know!'

She said with a touch of petulance. 'I don't want to get mixed up in anything nasty. You're doing something secret and to me that means spying.'

'And if it does?'

'Well,' she said uneasily, 'like I just told you, I don't want to get involved. All I want is to get back to England and my baby—'

'I—'

'—and I'll not do that, will I, if the Boers think I'm mixed up in spying. I don't know what they do to spies, but they may shoot them, mayn't they, James?'

'I don't know,' he answered. 'But I doubt if you'll get out without me, and I'm not going till I'm ready, so you'll just have to do as I tell you. Try not to worry too much—and don't go around with too long a face, Maisie, or Old Red Daniel will start thinking, and putting two and two together perhaps, for he's certainly no fool!'

'Oh, I'll keep my end up,' she said. 'James, give me a kiss?'

Obediently, he went down on one knee and took her in his arms.

He felt the play of her hands, up and down his back, felt her hold him close, hold him like the rock upon which her whole future happiness depended. When their lips parted, she nuzzled at his ear, murmuring barely audible words of desire, but he freed himself and stood up. 'I'm sorry, Maisie,' he said. 'Not just now. We have to get back and show our faces. I told you, time may be short now.'

'Oh, but James love—'

'No, Maisie. You want your baby—don't you? From now on, we have to give our whole minds to the job—don't you see?'

She pouted, looking up at him with large reproving eyes, and sighed. Then, getting suddenly to her feet, she laughed. 'I see you're too much the bloody officer and gentleman,' she said, 'but I s'pose you're right really. I don't want to do anything to make things go wrong, not even *that*, though God knows it's a sacrifice! Come on, then: I'll race you back to the laager.'

They raced the ponies across the veld, feeling the wind in their hair, smelling the mimosa, looking across towards the distant hills and the siege ring, hearing spasmodically the thunder of the bombarding guns. Half peace, half war—and he, half soldier now and half civilian. An uneasy situation made a thousand times worse by the knowledge that the 114th Highlanders would soon be encamped across the Tugela. There was just one bright spot for which Ogilvie was immensely grateful: Old Red Daniel had never asked for his parole, nor had Louis Botha, so there would be no question of his breaking his word in any direct sense; though it lay heavily on his mind that he was so much trusted by the Boer leaders that presumably they had considered a formal parole to be unnecessary. But he had to cast all that from his mind: concentration on the objective, as he had told Maisie Smith, was all.

What was he to do?

To appear to probe Opperman's mind, or Louis Botha's—to attempt to dig too deep, might be fatal. What he had picked up so far he had picked up almost casually, without the need to seem too interested or curious. With luck, of course, that process might continue—indeed it probably would, but too slowly.

The pace had to be forced, but not too obviously. It was, Ogilvie knew, going to be devilish tricky! Perhaps some miracle would happen, perhaps God, listening with equal ear to the war-prayers of both Brother Boer and British Army chaplain, would come down on the side of Empire and the big battalions, and whisper a message into an earthbound mind, indicating what should be done now. Grinning to himself as he rode on fast with Maisie Smith, Ogilvie had the blasphemous thought that if God didn't act on the side of the British, then He would have Lord Kitchener to answer to!

Ogilvie, who was still no better a horseman than he had been in India, rode into the laager some distance behind Maisie Smith, who turned to wave and laugh as he came up. They rode together between the wagons and the tents of Louis Botha, hot and tired, and the ponies lathered with sweat. Botha himself, emerging from his headquarters tent, gave them a cheery greeting; and it was in that moment that the God of Battles spoke to Ogilvie.

*　　*　　*

After the evening meal he left the camp-fire and walked outside the laager with Maisie Smith. He said, 'What I have in mind is dangerous and I won't try to make out it isn't, but it's the only thing we can do. So hold on to your hat, Maisie!'

'I'm holding. Well, what is it?'

'We're going out with a prisoner,' he said.

'Oh, are we? Who?'

'Louis Botha.'

She stopped in her tracks, staring at him as if he had gone suddenly crazy. 'Oh, for God's sake! Don't be ridiculous.'

'It's not ridiculous—'

'Yes, it is, it's bloody ridiculous—'

'Keep your voice down!' he hissed. There was too much silence around; even the distant guns were at rest, and the laager behind them was full of ears. 'It can be done—I've been thinking it out, Maisie—'

'He's far too well guarded, and we're miles from the Tugela up here—'

'As a matter of fact,' he told her, 'he's *not* well guarded at all—just one sentry outside his tent, who's never as alert as he should be. Why should Botha be guarded? He's in his own head laager and the British are miles away, and he certainly doesn't suspect us—you and me, Maisie. Spying, if you want to use the

239

word, simply doesn't occur to him at all. As for the distance, we've got the ponies, haven't we? I'll guarantee to get Louis Botha out of here at night with a gun in his back in a brace of shakes—and then we ride for the Tugela and make the crossing before dawn, and head for Buller's camp. Once we're over the Tugela we've little to worry about, and—'

'It's a pretty big *once*, isn't it?'

'What d'you mean?'

'*Once* over the Tugela! Oh, yes, I'll agree we're all right after that! But how about the *before*? How do you get your hands on Louis Botha in the first place, I'd like to know!'

He said, 'We take him sleeping—in his tent, having first dealt with the sentry, which is where you come in.'

'Me?' She stared. 'How?'

'Enticement. Get him talking—anyway, get his attention off me—'

'Not me,' she said flatly. 'Not little me! Entice a Boer? They'd burn me as a witch, like as not!'

He said, 'It's what you're going to do, all the same. Not tonight, but as soon as I hear that my regiment's arrived and joined up with Buller. I'll get word of that from Opperman. Then we'll go into the full details—'

'Go all you like,' she flared, with her hands on her hips, 'but don't count me in! Listen, what's the point anyway? You said Opperman was no fool—well, no more am I, James, and I

240

reckon you're after the Boers' plans or some such—you want to find out what they mean to do next. Eh? Well, I don't see that you taking off Botha's going to help. You don't imagine he's going to tell your old Buller all his plans, do you?' She caught her breath. 'Or *do* you? Does the British Army torture prisoners? I used to hear in Peshawar, torture of a sort was used on the Pathans sometimes. But they wouldn't do that to white people, would they?'

'I doubt it,' Ogilvie said. He knew Maisie was right about the rebels along the Frontier: he had his own memories of that. It was not so much torture as naked brutality and the strong fist, mainly. Under pressure, the best of Britons had indulged in it, even Bosom Cunningham with Lord Dornoch's tacit permission had once threatened to castrate a Waziri tribesman with his claymore and feed his entrails to the barrack pigs. But Boers, white-skinned Afrikaner farmers? No, surely not! There would be no torture of Louis Botha, or the press would see to it that the public was properly scandalised, and Mr Lloyd George, that pro-Boer, would trumpet the facts from the very battlements of Caernarvon Castle! Her Majesty would like it no better. But there were other ways, subtler ways that would certainly be known to Lord Kitchener at all events, of breaking a man in captivity. Yet, as Ogilvie explained to Maisie Smith, this was not quite the point. He said, 'Just think of the effect on morale if one of the Boers' biggest leaders is taken in his own head laager. A lot of them aren't tremendously keen on the fight, you know—they want to be back in their own lands, their own homes. Look at the way they take leave more or less when they feel like it. Opperman's often spoken of that. No, Maisie, they'd react pretty badly to a kidnap! Quite likely they'd all desert Botha's army—and Buller would have a clear run to Ladysmith! Isn't that worth taking a risk for?'

'Well—perhaps. For you, yes. I'm not so sure about me.'

'You want to see our side win, Maisie. If I'm not mistaken, you've said as much before now.'

'Yes, that's right, I have.'

'Think of the people in Ladysmith. That bombardment ... it's been going on so long now. Pretty terrible to live under that. Even in India, we didn't have to put up with sustained heavy gunfire—or never for long.'

She laughed and said, 'Don't talk to me about India if you want to impress me. People like the Duff-Kinghornes ... if *they* were in Ladysmith I'd love to see them suffer!'

'That's not very British, is it?'

His tone had been unaccustomedly stiff; it made her give another laugh. 'You take being British really seriously, don't you, eh? If you ask me, it's a matter of class—being British!'

He was puzzled. 'What d'you mean by that, Maisie?'

'Oh, I don't know.' She shrugged. 'It's fine for the carriage folk like you, but for them like me, well, I don't know so much. We don't get so much out of it, see. Never mind, though. I'll still stick up for dear old England!'

'I'm glad to hear it,' he said.

'So long as I get my baby back. I don't want to do anything that might stop that, don't you see! My baby's all I think of, all the while—not Ladysmith, or capturing Botha, or anything else at all.' There were tears in her voice now, and Ogilvie felt the hard, almost panicky grip of her fingers on his arm. 'I don't want to take any more risks, that I don't!'

'But Maisie . . . getting out is a risk in itself, or anyway it will be once we reach the Tugela. And you do want to get out.'

'Yes. But we don't have to take Botha!'

'I have my duty.'

'Oh!' she said, stamping her foot. 'Now you're being British again!'

'I'm sorry, Maisie.'

'God, you're determined!'

He repeated, 'I'm sorry.'

'I think you're a *beast*.'

He shrugged; he could do no more. She turned away from him, walking quickly back through the night towards the laager and its flickering camp-fires. He caught her up, and took her hand, but she pulled it from him: crying bitterly now, she walked on, turning her face away. He wanted to tell her that, since his

243

mind was made up, they would have the best chance, perhaps the only chance, if she would give him her help; but to say any more now would only make matters worse, for she would never listen to reason in her present state. Reaching the laager together, but with an all too obvious constraint between them, they walked almost into the arms of Opperman.

In the light of a camp-fire, Ogilvie saw the lifted eyebrows and troubled face. Opperman said, 'Come now, young lady, never tell me Mr Bland's been upsetting you!'

Maisie gave him a glare of fury and, lifting her skirts, ran off towards her tent without a word. Opperman, after a startled look in her direction, turned to Ogilvie and took his arm. 'The way of a woman is unpredictable,' he said. 'But perhaps I was tactless to have noticed. If so, I'm sorry, Mr Bland.' He coughed. 'It's none of my business, of course, but may I ask what the trouble is?'

'Oh, just a disagreement, Commandant, nothing of any importance.'

'I see.' There was obstinacy in Opperman's tone: clearly, he was determined to do what he thought was right. 'We have spoken before of marriage, Mr Bland. You know the way a woman thinks, and feels ... marriage is security, and I'm sure the young lady favours you. God smiles upon marriage, Mr Bland. Neither He nor I would look kindly upon shilly-shallying, upon playing with a young woman's affections—'

'But Commandant ... *have* I done that?' Ogilvie was all innocence and surprise.

Opperman snorted. 'Have you done that? Look, now, when a young woman gives way to tears, there is always a reason, Mr Bland!'

'*Is* there, Commandant?'

Opperman gave him a sharp look, opened his mouth, shut it again, then smiled. 'No. No, not always. Not, that is, what a man would call a reason. To the woman, yes, there is. At least, I think so.' He let go of Ogilvie's arm, and instead placed his own arm heavily and awkwardly around Ogilvie's shoulder. 'Think well, Mr Bland. Never do wrong. She is a very personable young woman, and though usually she seems strong and collected on the surface, I think she is soft enough beneath—and can be hurt! Bear this in mind, and pray to God that He should bring you two together as soon as may be.'

Ogilvie asked lightly, 'Wouldn't it be presumptuous, to try to change His mind for Him?'

'No, no. What is prayer for? In any case, to ask Him to show a better turn of speed would be no presumption!' Opperman hesitated. 'The Red Daniel, Mr Bland. You said it had to go to Major Gilmour's daughter.'

'That's right, it has.'

'You have met her ... she is pretty?'

'No,' Ogilvie said, feeling the prickle of

danger. 'I've not met her. Why do you ask?'

Opperman shrugged. 'Oh, no real reason, just a passing thought . . .'

'A thought that I might perhaps have another commitment, other than to Miss Smith?'

'Perhaps.'

'Then you can forget it. I'm as free as air.'

'In that case I apologise humbly,' Opperman said with a broad smile of pleasure. 'Now let us forget the matter, Mr Bland. I am glad I encountered you, for General Botha wishes words with you.'

'He does? What about—do you know?'

'I understand he has a request to make. I have my doubts that you will agree, and this I have told him, but there it is. Listen patiently to him, please.'

'I'll do that, of course. What's the request to be, Commandant?'

'I think General Botha must tell you that himself. Come, Mr Bland, we'll go to his tent at once.'

They walked across the laager, past the wagons and the tents, past groups of armed Boers sitting around the camp-fires and singing, or making ready for a night's rest. A rising wind brought the night smells of the veld, and the sounds of animals, and a hint of more rain to come. Once again, Ogilvie felt the whisper of danger in his ear, and not from acts of war and espionage alone. He felt a

246

personal constriction creeping up on him, another excellent reason why he should get away fast from this Boer laager and the marriage-pressures of Old Red Daniel Opperman !

CHAPTER FOURTEEN

Louis Botha was sitting in shirt-sleeves in his tent, behind a makeshift table of packing-cases. His revolver and an ammunition-belt were on the table; four other men were with him, two also in shirt-sleeves, two in dark coats, all with bandoliers across their chests, three of them bearded, all hard-faced men whom Ogilvie had not seen before around the laager or at the siege lines outside Ladysmith.

'Ah—Mr Bland! Take a seat.' Botha indicated a camp-stool in front of the table. Ogilvie sat; Opperman pulled up another stool and sat alongside the other men. Ogilvie at once felt at a disadvantage, the interviewee confronted by the Board. The sense of danger was stronger now, though there was no really apparent reason for it. Botha seemed friendly enough, all cheery smiles and pipe smoke: it was perhaps the other men, the four strangers. Botha introduced them in rotation from right to left.

'President Steyn, President of the Orange

Free State,' he said, indicating a big-built man with a face that, though obviously strong and resolute, was perhaps less hard than those of his three companions. The sense of danger grew afresh: next to Kruger himself, Steyn was the most prominent of the Boer politicians. Steyn gave Ogilvie a polite nod, but said nothing. Botha went on around the table: 'Judge Hertzog, General Christian de Wet, Mynheer Jan Smuts.'

'I'm glad to meet you all, gentlemen,' Ogilvie said.

The beardless man—Jan Smuts, who looked a good deal younger than the others—stared at him coldly. Smuts, Ogilvie saw, had extremely penetrating eyes and seemed a man to beware of. Smuts said, 'You have come from Kimberley, Mr Bland.'

'Yes.'

'Please tell me about your experiences there, and give the reasons why you deserted.' Smuts watched Ogilvie's gaze go round towards Opperman, and he said impatiently, 'Yes, yes. You have told all this to Commandant Opperman and to General Botha. Now I wish to hear it for myself, even if you are tired of repeating it.'

'All right,' Ogilvie said. Once again, he went through his story of the hardships, the starvation, the low morale of Kimberley's garrison and townspeople, all the things Rhodes had told him to say. The Boer leaders listened politely, but the cold eyes of Jan Smuts never once left Ogilvie's face: the man had somehow the look of a lawyer, and once or twice Ogilvie saw him confer in a whisper with Judge Hertzog whilst still staring intently.

'Thank you, Mr Bland,' Smuts said when Ogilvie had finished. 'What do you think of Cecil Rhodes?'

'I beg your pardon?'

'Please answer the question, Mr Bland.'

Ogilvie hesitated. 'It wasn't up to me to think anything. I was only a private soldier—I never met Rhodes.'

'But you must have formed an opinion, even if a distant one only.'

'Well ... we regarded him as rather pompous really.'

'We?'

'The troops. We got the impression he didn't think much of the military.'

'How did the townspeople, the civilians, regard him?'

'I don't know,' Ogilvie said. 'In general, though, I think he was well enough liked. Of course, Kimberley's dependent on him to a large extent.'

'True. Now, Mr Bland. A little about you yourself. I am told you had not been long in Kimberley. Please give me your own history— and why you came out here, where you live in England, what if anything your work is. The full details.'

249

For a brief moment, Smuts' gaze flickered round the other men's faces as if assessing their reactions to his probing: watching this, Ogilvie read the danger signals: General de Wet and Judge Hertzog looked to him ready to disbelieve anything he said. Louis Botha was no longer looking so cheery: there was an anxious frown on his face as he met Jan Smuts' gaze, yet Ogilvie felt he still had a friend in Botha, and another in Opperman. And in the event he need not have worried: his story held together under Smuts' interrogation, and Opperman spoke up nobly for him, saying that he could be trusted absolutely, repeating that there had been no reason whatsoever why Mr Bland should have saved his life in Reitz, at risk of his own, had he been anything other than what he claimed to be.

The faces behind the table relaxed at last, though those of de Wet and Hertzog remained somewhat withdrawn. Steyn got to his feet, and extended a hand to Ogilvie.

'You are very welcome, Mr Bland,' he said. 'I wish personally to thank you for all you have done for our cause—which is a just one, and must and will prevail. You can do a lot more for us, if you will.'

*　　　*　　　*

Ogilvie felt almost light-headed and was possessed, as once before he had been possessed when Opperman had seemed about to suggest something similar, with a strong and insane desire to break out into peals of laughter. This time, the suggestion had been actually made: Mr Bland was being asked to rejoin the British, not in Kimberley but across the Tugela. He was to rejoin as an escaped prisoner of war, a private from another sector: a soldier of the 1st Derbyshires of Colonel Allen's brigade under Sir William Gatacre, captured in the fighting at Stormberg and taken prisoner to Bloemfontein and thence to the compound at Pretoria. From here, like Winston Churchill from the officers' prison in the State Model School, he had escaped; and had come south across country, killing a Boer on the way and taking his clothes. Before leaving, he would be fully instructed in the composition of Gatacre's force, in the names of his own officers, and the details of the fighting around Stormberg, Molteno and Kissieberg. Once established in the British lines, he was to obtain precise information as to the distribution and strength of Buller's army, its lines of communication, availability of stores, ammunition, animals and vehicles and, so far as possible, the planning intentions of its commander. Having got all this, he was either to break out and cross the Tugela again to the Boer lines, or he was to find opportunities of sending the information across by heliograph. Boer signallers would be constantly on watch throughout the hours of daylight to pick up any such messages; and if he himself had not broken out before Buller moved, he was to do so after the British had started to advance, if such was their intention.

Although delighted by the turn of events in his favour, Ogilvie felt it necessary to object.

'I've always told Commandant Opperman,' he stated, 'that I'll not use arms against my own people—'

'You are not being asked to do that, Mr Bland.'

'Not directly—no! But what you're asking me to do is the equivalent, isn't it, in the long run? I'm sorry, sir, but I can't do that. I'll help—'

'Think again, Mr Bland.' There was iron in Steyn's voice now. 'You are already pledged to help us, you are deeply committed—you must realise that for yourself. You are the only person who can do what we ask, and you must do it, or there will be sorry consequences for you.'

'What consequences?'

Steyn said, 'You have not forgotten Miss Smith?'

'Miss Smith? What has she to do with it?'

'She stays here, Mr Bland, whether you agree to go or not. If you do not agree, she will be imprisoned and kept on a low diet until you *do* agree. And if there should be deception once you are in Buller's lines, then she will be the hostage. Another hostage will be the fact

252

that you can be denounced to the British as a deserter—so you will give us your full allegiance, Mr Bland. Do you understand?'

Ogilvie, although he protested further in the interest of authenticity, had no wish to bring harm to Maisie. Maisie in fact was his only worry, and a bad one. She was going to take this hard; and for his part he knew he would be guilty of a real act of desertion in leaving her behind.

*   *   *

'I have to do my duty.'

'Oh, God, not that again!'

She was crying bitterly, held tight in his arms. Ogilvie had decided to risk outraging Boer morality that night, and she was in his tent. He had done his best to make her see that he was in the cleftest of cleft sticks, but, not unnaturally, her own plight was her first concern. He said for the hundredth time, 'I'll come back for you, I promise.'

'Bloody likely!'

'I'll get you out somehow—'

'How, somehow?' She pushed her body away, lying back from him, and in the deep gloom he felt rather than saw her eyes staring at him and into him. 'It's just words, isn't it, nothing else! Once you go, I'm done for.' She caught her breath suddenly. 'Suppose I tell Botha who you are—what do you do then, may

253

ask, Captain James bloody Ogilvie—eh?'

He said, 'Maisie, I'm relying on you not to do that.'

She gave a shrill laugh, a laugh of near hysteria. 'Rely away, then! It's what I'm going to do if you leave me here alone, and don't you think otherwise! God, you're like all the rest of your class—use us and then chuck us away! I'll go straight to Botha and that Opperman—'

'Maisie, Maisie!' He laid hold of her and shook her hard, pushed her face down into the pillows as she started to cry out. 'You've got to listen to reason now. This is war, not a bit of tom-foolery in Hounslow! You're in great danger and so am I—'

'But—'

'Hold your tongue, my girl, and listen!' He loomed over her, went on talking, quiet but firmly determined. He impressed on her that to tell Botha the truth would hardly be the best way to get herself to England in the circumstances. He, James Ogilvie, was the only man who could help her in the end. 'For God's sake, Maisie,' he said, 'keep your silly little head clear on the main issues. I—'

'You—you—'

'I've given you my word,' he said, calmly pushing her face down into the pillow again, 'that I'll get you out. I won't go back on that. I know my Colonel will back me to the hilt, so will Buller. All you have to do is stay alive and out of trouble with the Boers—that's *all*! Keep yourself in the clear—which you'll certainly not do by denouncing me—and you'll have the whole of the British Army in Natal on your side!'

She went on crying, but more quietly, as if something of reality had penetrated. She cried herself to sleep in the end, and Ogilvie, unable to sleep himself, held her in his arms with her hair falling over his face and her legs entwined with his own. As dawn slowly whitened the canvas around them, she stirred and sighed and he felt her movement as she put her head back from him and looked into his face.

'God,' she said miserably, 'I'll miss you such a lot, James. Come back as quick as you can, promise?'

'Promise,' he said, and kissed her. 'Does that mean ... ?'

'Yes,' she said. 'What you said makes sense. I'll keep my end up, don't worry, but don't let it be too long.'

'Bless you,' he said. 'And it won't be long! Nothing'll be long now Bobs and K are out here.' He kissed her again, with passion and even a little real love. She was a brave girl, and she was beautiful ... the next act seemed just to happen without volition on either of their parts, seemed to have no beginning but to emerge from the kiss and to grow from there, grow into a mingling of bodies, of long legs and flat straining stomachs and the erotic pressure of firm breasts, and a whisper of breath that became hot and urgent, and afterwards they lay exhausted but peaceful, in what promised to be the last moment of tranquillity before the Tugela once again erupted in the thunder of the guns that would accompany Buller's advance on Ladysmith.

*   *   *

He was to make the crossing of the Tugela that night, and all that day was spent in intensive cramming and rehearsing of all the details that would authenticate his position when he was picked up by a British patrol. In addition to the military details such as the names of the regiments brigaded with him—2nd Royal Irish Rifles, 2nd Northumberland Fusiliers, 1st Royal Scots, 2nd Berkshires—he was given full details of his supposed route under escort from Stormberg via Bloemfontein to Pretoria and then his lone escape trek south across the veld and the Drakensberg for the Tugela, avoiding Boer concentrations along the way, skirting the Ladysmith siege ring to drop down on the curves of the river where he believed a British force to be encamped. His instructors were Opperman and Louis Botha together with General Christian de Wet. And during the cramming session Ogilvie kept his ears open for other things beside his mentors' words of wisdom: above the teaching voice of Opperman he was able to hear at least snatches of a low conversation between Botha and de Wet: the two generals had not met recently, it seemed, and they had a good deal to discuss. And after they had departed, leaving Mr Bland to Commandant Opperman, Ogilvie guilefully managed to open Old Red Daniel's confirmatory mouth: the Boers were taking some account of the fact that they might fail to take Ladysmith after all if Buller was too strongly reinforced, and alternative dispositions were in the air. If Buller relieved Ladysmith, Louis Botha intended to make for Pietermaritzberg and Greytown, towns that were not heavily defended although they contained a large number of women and children. If this thrust should become necessary, Botha fully expected the advantage of surprise. In the meantime, as a diversion from the Ladysmith perimeter, de Wet had a plan up his sleeve to mount an attack on General French on the Central Front; whilst it was Louis Botha's intention to concentrate his own force on certain strategic points commanding the drifts by which the British might be expected to attempt the crossing of the Tugela . . .

When darkness came down over Botha's laager Ogilvie took his leave of Maisie Smith, giving her into the personal charge of Commandant Opperman. 'A trust I'll honour to the death, Mr Bland,' Old Red Daniel said with sincerity. 'When you come back to us, that will be the time for rejoicing, eh?'

Ogilvie took his hand. 'Yes, that's right, Commandant. Goodbye for now.' He turned away at once, unable to face the red-haired Boer. He had grown to like him; their trust had been mutual. Opperman had so openly discussed Botha's and de Wet's battle plans that very day—he had clearly seen no reason not to, with the man who had saved his life. He had given Ogilvie his hand in sincere friendship and now Ogilvie was going to bite that honest hand in no uncertain manner. When he came again to Botha's laager there would be no rejoicing, no marriage-feast as Opperman so obviously looked forward to: there would be blood and thunder around as the British battalions came in, and detached men to rescue Maisie Smith and start her on her long journey back to Hounslow. Ogilvie left the laager with an escort of four Boer marksmen mounted on ponies, and it was not long before they had the Tugela in sight from the summit of a hill overlooking Colenso, where the British regiments had fought and died only weeks earlier. After a careful examination of the terrain through field-glasses, the leader of the escort gave Ogilvie the All Clear.

'There's a drift over there,' he said, pointing. 'You'll use that. We'll be covering you with our rifles. To the British, if there are any around which I doubt, it will look as if we

258

are firing to prevent your escape. If that happens, we shall charge behind you—but we'll take care not to catch you. Good luck, Mr Bland, and may God go with you.'

Another handshake, another act of falsity to an honest man. 'Thank you,' Ogilvie said, 'and with you also.'

Leaving the pony with the escort, he scrambled down the hillside, taking from inside his jacket a white flag of truce on a short stick. There was a keen wind, and before he reached the river the rain started. It sliced down, chilling him, soaking him to the skin, a real downpour, turning everything to mud. Reaching the river and finding the drift, he waded across.

There was silence: no movement anywhere that he could see. Looking back, he saw no sign of the Boer escort. No doubt they were lying low till he was safely over, and after that it would all be up to him. Emerging from the Tugela on the farther bank, wet through and shivery with the intense cold of the South African night, he still found no hindrance. He felt a sense of dismay: surely Buller should have had patrols out, or even established outposts to watch for any Boer movement! It was turning into a curiouser and curiouser war. Roberts, with his North-West Frontier experience, would presumably alter that.

Using a compass which he was to say he had taken from the Boer whose clothing he was wearing, he advanced with his white flag prominently displayed. He advanced, he believed, for many miles, making a snail-like progress through thick mud. Dawn was not far off and he was feeling as if he must drop dead from the sheer exhaustion brought about by fighting through the mud and the downpour when he heard a sound from ahead: the snick of a rifle bolt.

He stopped dead and waved his flag urgently. He heard more snicks, though he saw nothing. Then, through the faintly lightening gloom of the dreadful night, he made out a low hill and began to see the heads kept low on its summit, the heads with the British military helmets, Wolseley pattern. The men were manning a schantze, a kind of nest of scrub and boulders.

He called out, 'Friend—hold your fire!'

There was a pause. Then—'Who are you, friend?'

He took a deep breath. 'A British officer. Captain James Ogilvie of the 114th Highlanders—'

There was a hard laugh and a very British voice called back, 'Ho, yes, bloody likely I don't think! Come on in, Brother bloody Boer, and show your ugly bloody brotherly mug, you bastard!'

Ogilvie had heard tales from the Boers of burghers who had been shot by the British even when under a flag of truce. He had never believed those stories, but when he heard the sound of bayonets being fixed he advanced across the bog-like veld with a loose feeling in his bowels.

CHAPTER FIFTEEN

The eyes were steady beneath the helmets; the rifles, six of them, were pointed at Ogilvie's breast as he went forward through the teeming rain. More men closed in from the flanks.

'Halt! That's far enough.'

Ogilvie stopped dead and kept his mouth shut. The British soldiers came on, surrounding him with a ring of bayonet-steel: the Boers, he remembered, never liked the bayonets! He heard heavy breathing from the rain-soaked men, then felt a sudden blow in his kidneys that made him gasp with pain, and a Scots voice said, 'That's for callin' yersel' a Hielander, ye dirty bastard—'

'Cut that out, Adie ! I won't stand for any ill-treatment of prisoners.'

A sergeant pushed through the ring of men, an Englishman from the West Country by his voice: looking at the man as he came close, peering through that first hint of a dirty dawn, Ogilvie saw the insignia of the Devons; the man who had butted him was a Gordon Highlander, a regiment whose recruiting area abutted on that of the Royal Strathspeys. Coolly, Ogilvie turned to the Scot. 'You're lucky I'm from the 114th and not from the Sheepshaggers,' he said. 'If I had been, I'd have cut your throat in return for a coward's blow!'

The man gaped: this was a highly personal piece of unofficial military history for a veld-bred Boer to know! Ogilvie looked at the sergeant from the Devons. 'Have I your permission to instruct this man a little more?' he asked.

'All right,' the sergeant said. 'You can go on.'

'Thank you, Sergeant. Tradition has it that a man of the Black Watch was once seen by a Gordon committing an act of sexual intercourse with a sheep—hence the highly libellous nickname! When the Gordons meet the Black Watch, any handy sheep are driven into the Black Watch lines with shouts of *'There ye are, Sheepshaggers, they're ready for ye, come on oot and do yer stuff.'* Am I right?'

The Scot spat on the ground. 'Aye, ye're right,' he said sourly. 'So ye're from the Royal Strathspey—so ye say! What's their war cry, can ye tell me that?'

'Craig Elachaidh ... Stand Fast, Craigellachie. It's the war-cry of my own clan, for we're linked with Grant through Sir Lewis Alexander Grant of Grant—and my regiment's closely linked with my clan. By tradition we salute inspecting officers with the tune, Riobain Gorm nan Granndach ... The Grants' Blue Ribbon.'

There was a pause. The sergeant looked at the Gordon Highlander. 'Well?' he asked.

'He knows a wee bit. He may be tellin' the truth.'

'He could be genuine?'

'Aye, he could.'

'If he is,' the sergeant said, 'you're going to be sorry for striking an officer—'

'No, no,' Ogilvie said. 'I'll make no charge—he was not to know.' He laughed. 'My own father wouldn't recognise me just now—'

'Your father? Did you say your name was Ogilvie, sir?'

'Yes.'

'And your father—'

'Is Sir Iain Ogilvie, commanding the Northern Army of India in Murree.'

The sergeant gave a long, low whistle. 'Private Adie,' he said, 'you're dead lucky it was a *gentleman* you butted in the rear! Now, sir, I'd better identify ourselves. We're a mixed patrol from the Seventh Brigade of the Fourth Division under Major-General Lyttleton—'

'Of Sir Redvers Buller's force, Sergeant?'

'Yes, sir. Where do you wish to be taken, sir?'

'Ultimately to Sir Redvers Buller, but first, I think, to my own Colonel, Lord Dornoch. I understand my regiment has already joined

General Buller—or is about to do so?'

'That I couldn't tell you, sir. General Buller's being reinforced by a good many battalions, but—'

'Perhaps you'd better take me to your own Brigade Headquarters, then, Sergeant.'

'Very good, sir.' The sergeant hesitated. 'Sir! I've no orders to return early from patrol, so I'll detach two men as guides and escort—'

'One's enough, Sergeant. I don't want to deplete you—in case there are any genuine Boers coming across the Tugela!'

*   *   *

At Brigade that morning, Ogilvie learned that the Royal Strathspeys had not yet joined from Modder River Station, but when they did so—and they were expected at any time—they would be brigaded with the Tenth, composed of the 2nd Dorsets, 2nd Middlesex, and 2nd Somerset Light Infantry under Major-General Coke, thus coming under the umbrella of Lieutenant-General Warren's Fifth Division arriving from Cape Town. The Fifth was a new division fresh from England, with as yet no battle experience as a force. Ogilvie had words with the Seventh Brigade Commander, Colonel Hamilton. When he had explained his position as fully as he was able, Hamilton telephoned to Division on his behalf; and while he was eating a hurried meal a message came back informing Hamilton that Sir Redvers Buller would see Captain Ogilvie at once.

On reaching Buller's forward base at Frere, Ogilvie found the General at breakfast outside his tent, beneath skies now clear of rain. Buller, a big-boned but well covered man with a number of double chins, was doing himself well. He continued with his breakfast after waving Ogilvie to a camp stool. In fascination Ogilvie watched the disappearance of porridge, steak, bacon, eggs, liver, toast and marmalade into Buller's thick-lipped, capacious mouth. Despite the rigours of recent campaigns, despite many days' rain and the resulting muddy conditions, Buller was immaculate; even his boots shone with polish. He looked strong, capable and confident: and well he might, even though little success had attended him to date. Colonel Hamilton at Brigade had told Ogilvie that Buller's force, including the troops at Chieveley and his other bases, would be brought to some 30,000 men once all the reinforcements had reported in.

Buller listened politely and carefully to all Ogilvie had to tell him, and seemed to understand perfectly when Ogilvie said with his tongue in his cheek that his mission had been undertaken in the general interests of intelligence on behalf of Lord Methuen—for Ogilvie, still mindful of Haig's and Allenby's instructions, felt it inadvisable to invoke the

265

name of Kitchener even to Buller.

Buller said ruminatively, 'It seems unlike Methuen—but I shall not press you, Captain Ogilvie. Your orders no doubt came *through* Lord Methuen at all events—no, I shall not press.'

'Thank you, sir.'

Buller drank coffee and told his servant to fill a cup for Captain Ogilvie: Ogilvie, having breakfasted at Brigade, had already declined the main repast. Buller said, 'Perhaps you'll be good enough to indicate the Boer dispositions, Captain Ogilvie. As you may have guessed, it's my intention to march on Ladysmith shortly— and intelligence would be most helpful, of course.'

'Yes, sir.' Ogilvie hesitated in great embarrassment. He had no wish to be hurtful to Sir Redvers Buller, revered throughout the army as a kindly and considerate man, nor to be impolite; but what he had been able to glean from the Boer command was to be delivered only to Lord Kitchener. He went on, 'Sir, my orders in fact state that I am to pass any information to one officer only. I'm sorry, sir.'

Buller nodded, looking away from Ogilvie across the veld, down towards the Tugela, the river itself invisible from where they sat. 'Well, well, never mind, my boy. You must stick to your orders. You've been away from our lines, of course, but you'll have heard that Lord

Roberts has been appointed in my place—though I still command overall in Natal. I cannot disguise that I am disappointed—but there it is. Sometimes I have the feeling they don't fully understand at home. But Lord Roberts is a fine general and much loved, and then of course there is Lord Kitchener. He is a forceful officer whom the Egyptians are doubtless most glad to lose—but he is our gain nevertheless! The Boer will quite soon now be in flight, Captain Ogilvie—and your regiment will be one of the pursuers.' He sat for a moment drumming his fingers absently on the breakfast table. 'No, I no longer have the high command, my boy. So I repeat, I cannot press, and shall not attempt to do so.'

'I'm very sorry, sir.'

'No need to apologise for keeping to your orders, Ogilvie—no need at all. I understand ... when you reach my age and position, you too will understand ... and I think you will reach high command one day. I knew your father, my boy—oh, years ago now. As majors, we were in neighbouring brigades in Zululand. A fine soldier, a fine officer, and a gentleman of the old sort. You're very like him.'

'Thank you, sir.'

Buller talked on for a while, rambling a little, seeming to appreciate his listener's attention. Ogilvie was in truth immensely sorry for the sixty-year-old General, a courageous fighter who had twice won the V.C. It must be a bitter experience indeed to be downgraded in the chain of command and to continue serving in a junior capacity under one's successor. Ogilvie had already fancied he had detected a similar sympathy in the attitudes of Buller's staff officers and in his servant, who had all seemed to lean over backwards to be nice to the old man. But, as Buller talked on, it became very evident that the few words of self-pity he had uttered were the fullest extent of that emotion in himself. His mind was projecting ahead, and his set determination to relieve the garrison at Ladysmith the moment he was ready to march shone out like a guiding star. The relief of Ladysmith was almost an obsession with him. As he drank coffee and munched toast, and talked, his rather protuberant eyes were alight. He gave Ogilvie a broad sketch of what would most probably be his plan of campaign. Once the weather improved—there had been too much rain recently, he said—he would break out across the Tugela, outflanking Louis Botha by making his crossing well west of Colenso towards the foothills of the Drakensberg, below Spearman's Heights, which had already been occupied by Lord Dundonald's mounted brigade. On the farther side of the Tugela lay a small mountain called Spion Kop. Beyond Spion Kop lay a twenty-mile stretch of plain that ran practically to Ladysmith. Buller's information was—and this Ogilvie in fact confirmed to him—that only some two thousand Boers were holding Colenso and this force represented virtually the whole Boer strength this side of Ladysmith.

'We shall make straight across the plain,' he said. 'Straight for Ladysmith, as soon as we're across the Tugela. I anticipate no great difficulty—' He broke off as a stag officer approached and saluted. 'Yes, Major Cummings?'

'A message by runner from one of the outposts, sir. A battalion is coming in from the south, from Estcourt. The Queen's Own Royal Strathspeys, with a field-battery, from Lord Methuen's column.'

Buffer gave a nod, and smiled at Ogilvie. 'Off you go, my boy,' he said. 'You'll want to meet them yourself, I have no doubt . . . but wait a moment. I shall come with you myself. Cummings, my horse if you please, and another for Captain Ogilvie.'

When the mounts were brought up, Buller and Ogilvie rode down together, with one of the General's A.D.C.s in attendance, to where the Scots and the gunners were coming into camp. Long before they saw the men, they heard from beyond rising ground the pipes and drums beating out 'The Old 93rd'. There was a lump in James Ogilvie's throat as the sound of the pipes grew louder, bringing back memories, as ever, of Scotland and the regimental depot at Invermore, and battle memories of the distant North-West Frontier; memories, too, of men who had gone, men who had done their duty to the Queen-Empress and the British Raj and whose bones had been left for all time under foreign skies, men who would never again march behind those time-worn pipes and drums through Speyside and never again pinch the bottoms of the rosy-cheeked lasses of Invermore ... He puffed himself up sharply: such thoughts were of no help at all in the present situation. Out here in South Africa there was another war to be fought and won, a war that to date had been going very far from well.

As the 114th Highlanders marched into sight Ogilvie scanned the ranks of men anxiously. Lord Dornoch was there, ahead of the column, behind his pipes and drums and the rolling limbers of the Royal Artillery with their sun-browned gunner crews, hard-looking men who would soon be dropping their shells on Louis Botha's burghers. Ogilvie thrilled to the sight of his regiment on the march, to the swing of the tartan, the skirl of the pipes sounding out far from their native mountain passes, the war-music of the clans of old. He saw Major Hay, second-in-command, and Captain Andrew Black; he heard the stentorian shouts that indicated the ubiquitous presence of Regimental Sergeant-Major Cunningham with his inevitable pace-stick. Rob MacKinlay, his friend of long standing, was there still, in front of D Company, his head heavily bandaged. From the corner of his eye Ogilvie looked at Sir Redvers Buller: Buller was beaming with simple pride in his newly joining guns and infantry, responding, as a soldier almost always did, to the stirring sound of the pipes and the thunder of the gun-limber wheels. Had Bloody Francis Fettleworth been here in Buller's place, there would have been emotion and moist eyes and much pompous talk about Her Majesty. But Buller was a much more practical, down-to-earth man, and he was seeing now a fine addition to his force and a further promise that he would soon be riding in to Ladysmith.

Buller returned the salutes punctiliously as the guns and infantry moved past. Ogilvie studied the Scots column more closely. Many men had fallen since he had left—that was all too obvious. There seemed to be some new colour-sergeants, obviously promoted in the field to replace casualties. Two at least of the subalterns were not to be seen. The Gods of War had, of course, to be fed with their sacrifices.

*   *   *

'Young Templeton's gone too,' Dornoch said, passing a hand wearily across his eyes. 'There'll be letters to be written to wives and mothers—I hate that job, James. I'm

271

particularly sorry about Templeton—his mother's only son, and she a widow!' He stood staring across Buller's camp, at the rows of tents being erected in the regimental lines. Ogilvie knew well how the Colonel regarded the men of his battalion: he was a kind of father to them, in the old clan way. He felt each loss keenly. Henry Templeton had been only a short time with the regiment, having joined by transfer from an English regiment serving at the Curragh in Ireland. He was himself an Englishman, something of a rarity for the 114th, and Lord Dornoch had tended to regard him as an honoured guest rather than as a blood-member of the clan; thus in a sense his responsibility was the greater. And Templeton had been a first-class soldier and officer, keen, competent and a splendid example to the men, foremost in action, the very epitome of the English gentleman and that military caste that for generations had woven its thread into English life as had the old clan chieftains into that of Scotland.

Dornoch turned from his contemplation of the settling-in scene. 'Now to the future,' he said briskly. 'I'll not ask for details of what you've achieved. That is for higher authority. But from what you've told me, James, I gather you're not exactly rejoining us yet—that is, your special mission's not complete, is it?'

'Not really, Colonel. I imagine I'll have to report to Major Haig again, or Major Allenby perhaps. I dare say I'll be informed ... and then there's Maisie Smith. That's important to me, Colonel.'

'Yes, indeed—you've given your word.' There was a smile lurking somewhere around Dornoch's mouth. 'Dangerous—you must be careful, James!'

'Oh, I'll manage, Colonel. The biggest difficulty will be *finding* her, I think—'

'My dear James, I wasn't referring to the physical dangers.'

Ogilvie's eyebrows went up. 'Colonel?'

'Matrimony, James! The dangers of being caught on a hook! You must beware. I understand this man Opperman is something of a moralist. If you should be taken prisoner, he'll send you to the altar with a gun in your back!' Dornoch laughed, and clapped Ogilvie on the shoulder. 'However, first things first. How are you to conduct this business—this sending back of information by heliograph? If you don't do so, then the girl will suffer—isn't that so?'

'Yes, Colonel, I'm afraid it is. It's essential I make some reports. I can always send back false information—with your permission, of course, Colonel.'

Dornoch shook his head. 'Not mine alone. That's for the General. I think Buller will have to be more closely informed, James, but you can leave that to me. I'll have a word with the Chief of Staff, and let you know what

273

happens.'

*   *   *

'Captain Ogilvie, sir!' Left-right, left-right, left. Stamp, bang, swing, salute. 'I'm glad to see you back. Sir!'

'Thank you, Sar'nt-Major. How's it been with you?'

'Very much on the go, sir.' Cunningham's waxed moustache gave a twitch. 'You missed something at Magersfontein Hill, Captain Ogilvie, sir. It was bitterly fought, was that! Bitterly fought, and I'm sorry to say the English regiments showed up some of the Scots, aye, and us included.'

'How was that, Sar'nt-Major?'

Cunningham said, 'Sir! I said to you once, this would be a different war. We've grown too accustomed to the Frontier fighting and the Frontier enemy. The regiments from home . . . they haven't to unlearn the past in the way we have, coming direct from India. Sir! There were sectors of the front at Magersfontein where the Boer marksmen made our lads run for it, and that I do not like to see. There was great bravery shown that day—but as God's my judge, sir, there was cowardice as well! The Guards were splendid—the Grenadiers and the Coldstream . . . so were the Lancers, and the English line regiments. But the Scots that day were in retreat, sir. Terrible! Poor Colonel

274

Kelham of the H.L.I. was trampled underfoot, and killed in the stampede—aye, and stampede it was!'

'But the bravery, Sar'nt-Major?'

Cunningham's bosom swelled. 'Piper Mackay, sir, of the Argylls, for one. When he played 'The Campbells Are Coming' . . . why, they became good soldiers once again.' He rose and fell on the balls of his feet. 'Ah, we're no' so bad! I dare say we'll survive the war, and even win it—maybe. And now if ye'll excuse me. Sir!'

Swing, salute, crash, about turn. Left . . . left . . . left, right, left. Ogilvie watched the swinging kilt vanish towards the lines of white tents, the pace-stick held rigid and exactly horizontal beneath the left arm while the right swung to the step. Bosom Cunningham had his own built-in pipe band, his own personal parade-ground in his massive head. Nothing would ever shake all that; Cunningham's military foundations were secure as the Rock of Ages. But, if such a man as R.S.M. Cunningham could speak of Scots turning tail and running away from action, then there must indeed have been sad sights at Magersfontein Hill and that didn't augur well for the future. Ogilvie sighed; the Colonel had said nothing of any cowardice and now he felt depressed by Bosom Cunningham's report. During the afternoon he prepared his own written report of his experiences; and that night, there was a

275

convivial party in the Officers' Mess tent, with guests present from other regiments in Buller's command. There was a plentiful supply of spirits and wine and Ogilvie had his share of both: so had Black, who indulged his liking for whisky to the extent that he staggered off to his tent a little after eleven p.m. a good deal the worse for wear. In the lines, after Lights Out, there was a good deal of uncharitable comment from the privates: it was fine for the gentlemen with their champagne and caviar, but for the poor bloody O.R.'s there was just one bottle of luke-warm beer, and tins of bully beef, and army soup, and a little, a very little, stale bread. And the gentlemen were not quiet, either: their laughter and their songs, and the pianos which some of the officers brought with them as part of their substantial and very heavy field equipment, chased the sleep right away from the suffering men until the party was over. The party would have kept going for a long while longer if the Colonel had not, somewhat pointedly, left fairly early with a quiet request to the Mess President that the guests be speeded on their way.

*　　　*　　　*

Next morning Ogilvie had a bad head, a head that threatened to burst asunder in protest at the pressure of his Wolseley helmet. Breakfast was no more than black coffee and a piece of dry bread. After breakfast a runner came to the Mess tent.

'Captain Ogilvie, sir. The Colonel's compliments, and General Buller wishes to see you immediately, sir, at Division.'

'Right—thank you.'

The man saluted and turned away smartly. Ogilvie, going out into more rain and clinging, sucking mud, made for his tent and found his servant. 'My horse, Garrett,' he said. 'I've to ride to Division. Have it brought round at once, please.'

'Sir!' Dropping bedding and blankets, Private Garrett slammed to attention and departed, at the double, splashing through the downpour. Within minutes the horse was ready, and Ogilvie, covered with a waterproof cape, mounted and rode out of the lines, bearing his aching head manfully, hoping the exercise would shake up his liver and bring him some comfort.

CHAPTER SIXTEEN

Division, out here at Buller's forward base, was not a spectacle of grandeur: Division was a mere tent, with the blazon of the Divisional insignia floating from the top of the tent-pole and a rain-drenched, miserable-looking sentry outside with a rifle which he would shortly have the task of cleaning and drying with many, many wads of four-by-two. But there was something indefinable in the air that morning, something that Ogilvie was not yet able to lay a finger on. There was expectancy amounting almost to a feeling of drama, of big decisions and big forward movements against the enemy. Grooms and orderlies stood about, holding horses while the steady rain soaked into them and the mud rose, as mud always seemed to, up their boots and puttees even when not in motion. Horrible, clinging, sticky mud, the mud of the South African veld— there could be no worse in all the world, surely!

Outside Division, Ogilvie dismounted into that mud. A man came forward to take his horse, an officer wearing the red tabs of the Staff detached from a group of damp-looking colonels, and lifted an eyebrow at Ogilvie.

'Captain Ogilvie, 114th Highlanders, with orders to report to General Buller.'

'Just follow me,' the red-tabbed officer said. Ogilvie advanced behind him, across a duckboard, and was duly announced. Buller's voice called, 'Send him in, if you please.'

Ogilvie went through the flap, bending his head. Buller was seated behind a monstrous desk, an article of furniture that must surely have impeded anybody's advance by its sheer size and awkwardness. Beside Buller sat Major Douglas Haig.

'So we meet again,' Haig said abruptly, giving Ogilvie a direct stare. 'I've been hearing good reports of you.'

'Thank you, Major.' Bidden by Buller to sit, Ogilvie took a folding camp-stool set before the great desk. 'I have my written report for Lord Kitchener—' He broke off, flushing at his indiscretion: Buller, presumably, was not intended to hear of Kitchener's involvement even now.

Douglas Haig, however, laughed and said, 'Oh, that's all right, I've been instructed to confide in General Buller. Lord Kitchener, by the way, is now in Cape Town with Lord Roberts, and I shall be going there immediately from here. I'll take your report, Ogilvie . . . and also—' He broke off, looking keenly at the Scots officer. 'The Red Daniel. You have it safe?'

'Yes—'

'Then I'll take that to Cape Town too, with your report.'

'If you don't mind, Major, I'd prefer to hand it to Miss Gilmour personally.'

Haig looked irritated. 'Don't be a damn fool, Ogilvie. You're liable to be in action shortly, and a battlefield's no place for a diamond of such value. If you've any sense at all, you'll give it to me and I'll hand it to Lord Kitchener for safe keeping.'

'But—'

'No buts,' Haig said crisply. 'You'll hand it

279

over.' His tone softened, and all at once there was the hint of a twinkle in his eye. 'I'll put it to Lord Kitchener that we aren't *all* such misogynists as he. I'm sure he'll be only too glad to leave you to give it personally to Miss Gilmour.'

'Then on that understanding, Major—'

'Yes, yes, you have my word.'

Ogilvie brought out the wash-leather bag from a pocket and handed it to Douglas Haig. 'Sensible fellow,' Haig said. 'Now: your full report, which we're all anxious to know about, of course, is for the eyes of Lord Kitchener alone in the first place. I'll not question you too closely on that. However, Lord Kitchener will approve if you'll give General Buller the gist of such strategical knowledge as you've gained—as I would presume you have—concerning this particular sector. Any such knowledge may affect his plans for the immediate future. Well?'

Ogilvie turned to Buller. He told the General of the Boers' plans to fall back on Greytown and Pietermaritzburg if they should be forced to abandon Ladysmith to the British; Buller, listening courteously, appeared confident enough that a small redisposition of his forces would meet any thrusts in that direction. If such should develop after he had relieved Ladysmith, he said with assurance, he would cope accordingly. Ogilvie went on to report that the Boers were ready to meet any attack on the siege line and that Christian de Wet in fact intended to mount a diversionary attack on General French.

Haig took him up on this. 'General French, as who should know better than I, is on the Central Front. Is this to be a feint?'

'Yes, Major. Botha hopes this attack will make us withdraw troops from this sector, and reduce the pressure on Ladysmith—even remove any threat to the siege lines until they've had time to recruit and train more of their burghers. They're suffering a good deal from leave-taking—from abstention on the part of quite large numbers of their available forces. At the same time, Botha intends to concentrate what forces he has, and they're not large, at Potgeiter's Drift on the Tugela, and at Trichard's Drift as well. He's also intending to position a strong force near Spion Kop.' Ogilvie hesitated. 'There's one more thing I should perhaps mention, sir, if I shall not seem to presume.'

'Go on,' Buller said.

'Sir, the Boer field craft. Their use of camouflage in particular ... because of this, because of their ability simply to melt away when they wish, their casualties are ridiculously smaller than ours. The Boers' forces, sir, may be comparatively small, but their use of the terrain has the effect of making them equal to our larger ones.'

'Yes, yes.' Haig paid close attention to this,

281

but Buller seemed scarcely to be listening; frowning, he drummed his fingers on the top of the desk and said in a rumbling voice, 'Potgeiter's, Trichard's, Spion Kop. Well, now. My intention's been to send my force straight across the Tugela, using in fact Trichard's, and then take the plain beyond Spion Kop. There's a crescent-moon shape of hills . . .' He opened a drawer and brought out a map, which he unrolled and laid flat. Douglas Haig got up and peered over his shoulder. Buller stabbed with a finger. 'There—beyond Mount Alice, d'you see, Major? The Rangeworthy Heights westward, Brakfontein and Spion Kop in front. The direct route to Ladysmith runs through there.' He frowned again, and pursed his thick lips. 'But, you know, if Spion Kop is to be at all *strongly* held—'

'The more Boers you shall kill, sir!' Haig gave a cold smile. Buller seemed uneasy: there was a curious driving force about Haig, an air of ruthless efficiency that showed little time for bumbledom. Haig went on, blatantly addressing his remarks now to Ogilvie: 'I believe you've already told General Buller that you've to pass back false information to Botha. You'll have to satisfy Botha's desire for news, misleading him all you can, of course, whenever there's any sun to make the use of the heliograph possible. General Buller will give you your orders in that direction, in the light of his own factual plans.' Haig paused.

'Anything you yourself want to ask, Ogilvie?'

'One thing, Major: Kimberley—and Mr Rhodes's false reports through me, that a surrender was likely.'

There was a gleam in Haig's eye. 'Yes?'

'Did this make any difference to the conduct of the campaign, Major?'

'Scarcely,' Haig answered with a harsh laugh. 'With the exception of . . . shall I say some alarm on Lord Methuen's part when certain rumours reached him before Magersfontein, no further attention was paid to the fulminations of Mr Rhodes. Under all the circumstances—you understand me, I think—I was able to say where these rumours originated. We all know Mr Rhodes rather too well, Ogilvie, and you may rely upon it, the sympathies of the high command are all with Colonel Kekewich. Be assured that Mr Rhodes will never be allowed to dictate our strategy—by rumour or any other means! Does that answer your question?'

'Very fully, Major,' Ogilvie said with a smile.

'Good! We shall relieve Kimberley without Rhodes's prodding. Now then: what's all this I hear about a woman?' Haig's eyes had narrowed. 'You'd better explain *that* rather more fully, I think—h'm?'

Ogilvie did so. 'I've promised to get her out when General Buller advances,' he ended.

Haig stared. 'My God, you damn fool!'

'Major?'

'I think you heard what I said. You'll have to break your promise—that's all!'

'But I've given my word—'

'Possibly. But let me speak for Lord Kitchener, my dear Ogilvie! He'll have no woman interfering with his plans, or holding up his officers in action with any damn fool ideas of chivalry—be quite assured of that!'

'Major,' Ogilvie said firmly, 'she's been of great help to me—'

'Help? I thought you said she'd blackmailed you—and nearly married you into the bargain!' Haig gave a harsh laugh. 'I wouldn't call that help! Is there anything further, Ogilvie?'

'Only that I wish to keep my word, Major Haig—that's all!'

Haig breathed hard down his nose, and his eyes held more than a hint of ice: there was the reflection of K himself about the man. He said, 'At your peril, Ogilvie, at your peril, you damn idiot!'

*   *   *

Later that morning, after the departure of Douglas Haig with his detailed report in writing, Ogilvie attended a long conference with Sir Redvers Buller and his staff. Agreement was reached on certain misleading items that could be passed back by heliograph to the Boer command across the Tugela

284

without danger to the British, even possibly with some advantage. As soon as this was settled, Ogilvie rode back to the Royal Strathspeys' lines through another downpour, and in no time his horse was coated with thick, slimy mud. The weather was appalling for an advance, but it had been obvious at the conference that the General considered he held all the cards in the pack. After all, had he not 24,000 infantry, plus almost 3,000 horses, with eight batteries of Field Artillery and ten guns of the Naval Brigade, with 700 wagons— and even a handful of traction-engines driven by steam? And the burghers of Louis Botha? Ogilvie recalled that his estimate that Botha could put little more than 2,000 of his burghers into the line appeared to be, supported by Buller's own information. It was natural therefore that Buller should feel impelled to take his opportunity. Although in point of fact cables from the Commander-in-Chief, whilst Roberts had been in transit from Southampton for the Cape, had urged him to remain on the defensive, it was his present intention to move out for Springfield and Trichard's Drift in two days' time. Orders, as Ogilvie made his way back, were already going out to the various Divisional Headquarters to prepare for the general advance. On arrival Ogilvie reported to Lord Dornoch and received the Colonel's formal approval of the heliographic communication with Botha's signallers. That afternoon, the rain stopped and the sun broke through. As the men in the regimental lines brought out clothing and bedding to dry, Ogilvie made his way alone with a heliograph to the far side of a hill from where he had a fine view across the river into Botha's territory. His signal was answered within minutes, just a short flash of acknowledgement which if spotted by the British could have been taken for no more than an accidental twist of a mirror. Botha's signallers were certainly alert enough. Ogilvie passed his fake message: the British were not expected to move for at least another week, and the gossip among the troops in the lines was that Buller intended obstinately to move east, crossing the Tugela, if cross it he could, in the region of Colenso itself, thus avenging his recent reverses in that sector, and striking where he considered the Boers would be the least likely to expect him. So far, so good; but Ogilvie had to face one bleak fact: when his heliograph deception stood revealed in the blinding light of the advance of Buller's divisions on a westerly thrust within the next forty-eight hours, the Boers would take their own revenge on Maisie Smith.

CHAPTER SEVENTEEN

On 16th January Buller's force moved out, slowly and ponderously, towards Springfield and Trichard's Drift on the Tugela. The cavalry, pushing on ahead of the infantry to Springfield, found it abandoned, and rode on towards Mount Alice a little to the south-east of Potgeiter's Drift. Here at Mount Alice Sir Redvers Buller decided to set up his headquarters; and here he received fresh reports of the Boer strength: the enemy had doubled their numbers on the other side of Potgeiter's Drift—and this notwithstanding the recent false signals across the Tugela, a fact that caused Ogilvie a good deal of concern in regard to Maisie Smith. He had words with the Colonel about this.

'I wouldn't assume the worst, James,' Dornoch said. 'We'll be across the Tugela shortly, in any case. When we are, I'll not be looking if you should detach to the young woman's assistance!'

'Thank you, Colonel—'

'But not too quickly—the fighting may be very fluid. You'd do better to wait till we make our position a little more stable.' Dornoch paused, and a glint of humour appeared in his eye. 'We'll see, too, that Lord Kitchener doesn't get to hear!'

'Thank you again, Colonel.'

Dornoch seemed about to say something further when a horseman galloped up and dismounted. Through the layers of mud Ogilvie recognised a staff officer from Brigade. The officer saluted Dornoch and held out an envelope. 'I have your movement orders, sir,' he said breathlessly.

Dornoch took the envelope and slit the flap. Quickly he read the message, and nodded at the staff officer. 'Understood,' he said. The officer saluted again, mounted and rode off; the Colonel tapped the message. 'James,' he said, 'tell the adjutant we're moving out immediately with General Warren. General Lyttelton's remaining behind to contain Spearman's, except that he'll make a feint across Potgeiter's Drift—which'll allow Warren to get through by Trichard's—'

'Is General Buller splitting his force, sir?'

Dornoch nodded. 'It seems so—there's been a change of plan, no doubt because of the current Boer dispositions across the river, James. By my guess, the whole force will join up again beyond the Rangeworthy Heights, for the final advance on Ladysmith—but meanwhile, yes, we're split. Our own orders are to cross the Tugela during tonight with the main body of men, then go north by way of Spion Kop.'

'Yes, Colonel. I'll tell Captain Black.' Saluting smartly, Ogilvie turned away to find the adjutant.

*   *   *

With the help of Lyttelton's diversionary attack on Potgeiter's Drift, Warren reached the river by Trichard's without interference from the enemy. There was plenty of optimism during the march to the Tugela, and it was fully expected by all ranks that Ladysmith would now be relieved within a matter of days. On reaching the river, Warren, himself a Sapper, personally supervised the bridging work of his engineers at Trichard's Driftwork that was superbly carried out under guard of the infantry brigades. When the bridging was complete, Lord Dundonald first took his cavalry across, to be followed by the infantry of the line; and after this, right through the night of the 17th, and all the following day, the baggage and supplies made their ponderous way across the river, with the oxen drawing the long lines of wagons over the pontoons. It was an apparently endless procession of supply wagons, ammunition carts, ambulances, and also guns, going heavily down to the bridges by way of channels cut from the river bank behind the advance troops, including the Royal Strathspeys, who occupied Tabanyama Hill north of the Tugela in face of very little opposition.

'Where the devil are the Boers?' Rob

MacKinlay asked as B Company fell out, sprawling on the wet ground of the lower slopes to light pipes and cigarettes and wait for the cooks to start the fires and brew up mugs of tea. 'I've only seen half-a-dozen heads to take pot shots at, James!'

Ogilvie stared around the hillside, so apparently empty of all life but for the British infantry. 'An ambush?'

'Of course! I don't like it. While we're hanging around here, waiting for that damn baggage train to cross, Brother Boer'll be bringing up his burgher marksmen—won't he?' Suddenly, he cocked his head in an attitude of listening. 'Hear that?'

Ogilvie said, 'Gunfire. Heavy stuff, to the west.'

'Right! Either it's Lyttelton shelling the Boers—or the Boers shelling Lyttelton.'

Ogilvie listened again to the thunder of the guns in the distance, slow, rumbling thunder that seemed to roll in echoes off the heights of Tabanyama above them. 'Doesn't sound like Creusots—or Long Toms. I dare say Lyttelton's giving the Boers a trouncing, Rob.'

'Let's hope so! They can do with it. They've had it too much their own way, right from the start—'

'Oh, rot! What about French at Colesberg, Colonel Pilcher at Douglas—and Talana—'

'All small stuff. The big stuff's all gone to the Boers.'

Ogilvie frowned, and squatted on the soggy earth beside his friend. 'You're not usually so pessimistic, Rob. What's the trouble?'

MacKinlay moved restlessly, pulling at his moustache, easing the neckband of his tunic with a finger. 'Oh, I don't know. Perhaps it's just that we all thought we'd go through these cowpat farmers in five minutes, and we haven't ... or maybe it's just a premonition.'

'Premonition—of what, Rob?'

'Oh, leave it, James, there's a good chap.'

Ogilvie opened his mouth to say something more, but thought better of it. He looked down at MacKinlay with concern: premonitions come fairly readily to some Scots, but up to now MacKinlay had never been that sort, and the doleful sound of the man distressed him. Later, however, MacKinlay cheered up: news came through that Lord Dundonald's cavalry brigade had been in action along the road running from Acton Homes to Ladysmith and, in company with some men of the 60th Rifles, had routed the enemy and taken a couple of dozen prisoners into the bargain. But these prisoners brought unwelcome news: the Boers were now, thanks to the British delay whilst all the baggage was brought across the river, fully alert to the dangers of Warren's massive crossing, backed up by the main part of Lyttelton's force still in reserve at Spearman's. The advantage of surprise, if any had indeed existed, was now quite gone.

On hearing about the prisoners, Ogilvie sought permission from his Colonel to speak to them, with Maisie Smith in mind. Just before the Boers were sent back under guard to the rear, permission came through to Dornoch from Dundonald for Ogilvie to interview them. At once he went across to where the burghers were being held, and found them being fiercely harangued by a firm-chinned but chubby-faced young officer wearing the uniform of the South African Light Horse. This officer broke off when Ogilvie came up, turning on him to ask, somewhat peremptorily, who he was.

'Captain Ogilvie of the 114th Highlanders. And you?'

'My name is Churchill and I am interviewing these men for my paper—'

'Your *paper*?'

The chubby officer smiled and waved a hand. 'I'm partly war correspondent, partly soldier, Captain Ogilvie. General Buller has commissioned me but is not paying me. The *Morning Post* is paying me very well indeed—so I am doing their work and interviewing prisoners for them.'

'Interviewing them, Mr Churchill? I rather thought you were making a speech to them!'

A laugh came from the captive Boers; Churchill looked peeved. Ogilvie followed up his advantage. 'I'm sorry, but the *Morning Post* must wait. I have more urgent matters to discuss, matters of life and death. And I'd be grateful if you'd be good enough to leave us while I speak to the prisoners, Mr Churchill.'

'Oh, really? I—'

'That's an order, Mr Churchill.' Ogilvie glanced with meaning at the officer's single pip, and the chubby young man, flushing darkly and murmuring a remark about insolent young puppies, which Ogilvie, though furious, disregarded, bounced angrily away out of earshot. The armed guards also withdrew a little way. Ogilvie scanned the faces of the Boers: he recalled none of them, but he might well be known to some, though they would not be expecting to see him in the uniform of a Captain of Highlanders. He said crisply, 'I've not much time before you're moved off to base, gentlemen, and I want your help. I know you Afrikaners . . . I know you have a sense of fair play and chivalry towards women. I'm going to ask you if any of you know of a young Englishwoman in General Botha's head laager—a friend of Commandant Opperman. If you do, I would like to know where she is at this moment. Will you help me?' He added, 'Her name is—Miss Maisie Smith, lately from Reitz.'

There was silence from the prisoners; but Ogilvie saw the curious stares, the nudges that passed between two or three of the unkempt farmers, the whispers; and then a man spoke

293

up. 'I recognise you, Captain,' he said in a harsh, ugly voice, a voice of scorn. 'You are Harry Bland ... Old Red Daniel's wonder-man from Kimberley! And you're a dirty traitor—or at best a dirty spy—'

'That's enough—'

'No, it's not enough, far from it!' The man who had spoken lifted big hands towards heaven. 'You've done a dirty thing, Mr Bland. Old Red Daniel was a splendid leader and a good man, and you have brought shame to him, for he trusted you, and made others trust you, and you have turned on him. I hope your treachery eats into your heart in the years to come! You deserve no peace nor happiness.' He paused, looking round at his fellow burghers. 'You ask about the woman, Maisie Smith. Louis Botha has taken care of her! When your army moved, Botha knew your heliographed signals were false, and he got the truth from the woman—'

'By force—by torture?' Ogilvie's fists clenched.

The man shrugged. 'Use your own imagination, Harry Bland! It may not be far from the truth.'

Sheer anger took over from discretion. Ogilvie moved forward, thrusting into the group of Boers, making for the speaker and confronting him squarely. He said, 'Tell me where she is, or I'll smash your teeth through the back of your throat.'

The Boer laughed insultingly. 'You're a pretty young man, Harry Bland, and it would be a shame to spoil your good looks, but if you make me, prisoner or no prisoner, I shall make sure your own mother never recognises you again.' He lifted one vast fist. 'Now, you see this? Do you know what it is called?'

'No, nor do I—'

'It is called Hospital.' He lifted the other. 'And this one, it is Sudden Death. Now, Mr Bland, I shall tell you where the Englishwoman is, for the knowledge will do you no good, and then I shall pay you back for your treachery. The woman is held under guard in a wagon in Louis Botha's head laager while Botha decides what is to be done with her. She'll not get away, you may be quite certain of that. Now.' He lifted a fist again, and lunged. Swift as lightning, Ogilvie dodged and caught the arm, holding it away from him. Laughing in his face, the big Boer lifted the arm, drawing Ogilvie's arm up with it, and at the same time struck him a vicious blow in the chest with his free fist. Ogilvie gasped and staggered. As another blow landed he heard a shout from behind. He let go of the Boer and lashed out, catching the man on the side of the head. Someone else struck Ogilvie from behind, and he went down in a melee of fists and boots before he heard the crack of rifles and saw the crowding, surrounding feet move aside. Bullets zipped overhead and a moment later Ogilvie was lifted by a bush-hatted trooper of the Imperial Light Horse, and his uniform was brushed down. A sergeant saluted, with apologies: the escort's attention had been diverted from the prisoners by gunfire to the east. As the Boers were once again rounded up, Ogilvie saw a wide grin on the pugnacious face of Mr Churchill, who was advancing to meet him.

'I trust I was of some service,' Churchill said in a booming voice, waving a cigar.

'You?'

Churchill grinned again. 'I gave the alarm.'

'Oh—thank you.'

'Don't mention it.' Churchill gave a mocking little bow, removing his head-dress and sweeping it across his body. 'Thank the *Morning Post*—were it not for them, I'd not be here at all! If you'll excuse me, I have work to do now, Captain.'

'Writing up your ... er ... interview, I take it?'

'Oh, no,' Churchill replied blandly, 'that can wait. I shall now assume my military responsibilities and give a little lecture to General Warren, who seems to me to be acting a trifle slowly—there is far too much delay in advancing. I shall call upon my experiences at Omdurman—which was a swift enough business to be sure! Good afternoon, Captain Ogilvie.' With a broad smile, Mr Churchill turned away. Ogilvie looked after him, shaking his head in wonder at the unmilitary figure and its cloak of total assurance. Winston Churchill was becoming quite a name: a brave but pompous young officer, formerly of the 4th Hussars but now, apparently, holding an unofficial kind of commission whilst carrying out his journalistic duties, he was said to be aiming for a political career and to have something about him that would one day lead him to high office, if he didn't make too many enemies along the line. Ogilvie in truth thought him a bit of a stinker, and reflected that General Warren, who had a reputation for acerbity, would be put into a fine rage if this newspaperman should attempt to instruct him in the conduct of his campaign.

Making his way back to where the Royal Strathspeys were bivouacked on the slopes, Ogilvie cast Churchill from his mind with ease: Maisie Smith loomed larger.

Somehow—and at present only God knew how—Maisie had to be cut out from under the nose of Brother Boer.

*　　　*　　　*

The word came down from General Warren's headquarters, which he had now set up at Fairview after deciding against the longer route implicit in any westward advance. It came via Division and via Brigade and it reached the Royal Strathspeys next day:

forward troops were being brought back to guard Warren's encampment, as also were Dundonald's cavalry. Upon their arrival, the heights above them would be attacked and the Boers swept from their entrenched positions along the summit.

The 114th Highlanders were part of this advance when it was mounted. With an excellently thunderous artillery barrage in support, the Scots moved up the slopes of Tabanyama in short rushes, using what cover they could find among the boulders and in the scrubby bushes and grassy tufts. With the Dorsets and Middlesex, and the Somerset Light Infantry, they gained the crest, ejecting the Boers as planned with surprisingly few British losses.

Taking a breather at the summit, Ogilvie looked down the glacis. The Boers were streaming to the rear—but only, it seemed, to occupy a second line of trenches.

Ogilvie turned to find MacKinlay behind him. 'I don't like the look of it,' MacKinlay said gloomily.

'The glacis? No more do I, Rob.'

'Any advance'll be cut to pieces, just simply cut to pieces.'

This opinion was borne out when the Boers sent up a withering fire, apparently to discourage any indiscretion on the part of the British. The whole glacis was swept with bullets, a hail in which no man would be able to advance so much as a yard. It was a fairly effective demonstration, and it was witnessed by General Warren in person. Word filtered through that he had turned pale and had expressed the view that he could not send his men to certain death; and that his glance had been seen to stray more than once towards his right, in the direction of the great eminence of Spion Kop itself, that vast top-rock of the ridge that stood across the route to Ladysmith.

'If he's thinking along those lines,' Lord Dornoch said that night, whilst chatting generally to his officers after a scratch meal in the bivouacs, 'then we're in for a hard task, gentlemen!'

Black asked, 'What do you suppose the plan's to be, Colonel?'

'Oh, it's not hard to guess,' Dornoch answered. He waved a hand towards the summit with the glacis beyond, and the Boer lines beyond that. 'If Warren can take Spion Kop and hold it, why, he should be able to enfilade those damn trenches below the glacis, shouldn't he? We're held in a vice of a sort, at present. Spion Kop could open that vice, couldn't it?'

'I dare say,' Black said. 'But the Boers'll have that in mind as well, Colonel.'

'You mean—?'

'Spion Kop will be well defended.'

'Of course it will! It'll be a bloody battle—I've already suggested as much. But if the order comes . . .' He said no more; a glance around the set faces of the officers was enough. There was no lack of stomach for a fight, no faint hearts. But Dornoch himself was troubled as a little later, under cover of the darkness, he made his way alone to the summit of the hill. They had all come through so much together, through so many years of comradeship, and Spion Kop would be a tough nut to crack. Yet it was a logical enough thing to do . . . to hold Spion Kop would be to free the approach from Fairview to Ladysmith, and allow Buller's army its relieving passage to Sir George White and his gallant force. Dornoch stood looking down the glacis, and then across towards Spion Kop. He had just turned away when he saw a figure coming up to join him.

'James?' he said.

'Yes, Colonel. May I have a word?'

'By all means. What is it?'

'Spion Kop, Colonel. Do you think that's the way General Warren is really thinking?'

Dornoch said, 'If I was in his shoes, it's the way I would be thinking. I can say no more than that. No orders have reached me as yet.'

'No, Colonel. But you believe yourself—'

'I believe the order will come, yes. I believe it will.' Dornoch gave an involuntary sigh. 'I have a feeling we'll not easily take that damned hill! And I detest losses—detest them!'

'Yes, Colonel.' Ogilvie hesitated. 'Colonel, I

have a request to make.'

'A request? Then let me hear it, James.'

'Colonel, if your assessment of General Warren's future planning is correct, we'll head straight for Ladysmith after taking Spion Kop. In that case, we'll not march anywhere near Botha's head laager.'

'No.'

'Colonel, Miss Smith is there—in Botha's laager, under heavy guard, and under threat too.'

'I see.' Dornoch's tone was grave and worried. 'What are you asking me, James? You must be precise now.'

'Yes, Colonel. This is not easy ... I don't want to seem to be asking to miss a fight. But I'd like permission to detach at once ... to go in and get Maisie Smith, and then rejoin. May I do that, Colonel?'

Dornoch shook his head, not as a negative, but in perplexity and an unusual indecision. He was about to speak when a runner was seen coming fast up the hillside. 'A moment, James. Yes, what is it?'

The runner halted and saluted. 'Orders from Brigade, sir. The General intends to split his column in two, sir—to be known as Right Attack and Left Attack—'

'On what, man, on what?' Dornoch's eyes met Ogilvie's.

'Sir, Spion Kop for the Right Attack, which includes the 114th under Major-General Coke, with Major-General Woodgate's brigade in the van.'

'I see. When do we advance?'

'At eleven p.m. on the 23rd, sir.'

'Tomorrow! Well—we shall be ready!' Dornoch's back stiffened and his mouth hardened. 'Thank you—my compliments to the adjutant, and I'd like all officers and N.C.O.s to assemble immediately. That's all.'

The runner saluted again, and withdrew down the hill, leaping from tussock to tussock to be soon lost in the darkness. Dornoch looked again towards Spion Kop, a dark shape rearing heavenward, a dark shape that seemed full of menace and bloodshed now. He put a hand on Ogilvie's arm. 'I'm sorry, James. We're going to need every man, and Miss Smith must wait. First the battle—and then you will have my permission to detach.'

CHAPTER EIGHTEEN

Obedience was all—once a direct order such as the Colonel's had been received. An army could not operate on less: that was an axiom of the military life. But James Ogilvie prepared for the assault on Spion Kop with a fair degree of sheer mutiny in his heart and soul. He was not sure, in fact, that his detachment to the Kitchener mission did not supersede his subordination to Dornoch's orders; on the other hand, it was always open to any officer in command of troops in the field, to require those close to him to obey emergency orders to assist: and any subsequent appeal to Kitchener should he deliberately disobey would fall upon the deafest of all possible ears, as had already been made quite clear by Douglas Haig.

Reconnaissance carried out next morning by Brigade indicated that in fact Spion Kop was but poorly guarded: little more than a picket, it was believed, garrisoned the hill. From the bivouacs on the Tabanyama slopes, Ogilvie listened to the increasing thunder of Warren's artillery as he softened up the ground for his advance. Shell after shell whined across, to explode in sound and flame behind the Boer lines or on the entrenchments all along the front. The very air above seemed speckled with bursts of shrapnel.

'It's the very hell of a barrage,' Ogilvie remarked to MacKinlay.

'More than two hundred guns, so I'm told. And no answer from Brother Boer—I wonder what *that* means, James!'

'All knocked out?'

MacKinlay shook his head, suddenly dour and sombre. 'Well, we'll be finding out soon.' He stared around the bivouacs; Ogilvie followed his gaze. More and more troops had moved into the area of the Tabanyama slopes:

men from the various Lancashire regiments mainly, together with some sappers and unmounted M.I. MacKinlay said, 'I'm not happy with the choice of password, James.'

'Waterloo?' Ogilvie lifted an eyebrow. 'Why not?'

'Whose Waterloo is it to be—that's why!'

'Oh, don't be so damn querulous—you're like an old woman this last day or two, with your premonitions!' Suddenly Ogilvie reached out a hand to his friend. 'Sorry, Rob. I didn't mean that. But we're going to take Spion Kop and you know it—*so cheer up!*'

MacKinlay shrugged but said no more. During what remained of the day the artillery bombardment was kept up, kept up on a still increasing scale as daylight faded. At eleven p.m., in a pitch dark night with a light drizzle falling, the order for Woodgate's brigade to advance came through. The men got to their feet, headed up for the mist-shrouded summit of Spion Kop by way of Three Tree Hill. The Royal Strathspeys, held for the present in reserve, watched them fade away through the night. For some four hours, nothing was heard. At the end of that time, there was distant rifle-fire which brought the Scots sentries to the alert, and the officers were woken. Within minutes of this rifle-fire, the artillery opened again and shells started dropping between Spion Kop and Tabanyama Hill.

There was no further news until well into

the next forenoon. When it came, it was a cruel deception.

*   *   *

There had been wild cheering from the ranks, right along the line: General Woodgate had taken the summit at four a.m., chasing off the picket and causing the rest of the Boers in the vicinity to run for the rear, and his troops were now digging trenches. But three hours after this apparent taking of Spion Kop, the mists had cleared from along the summit, and another crest was seen to the north: Woodgate had in fact occupied only part of the summit plus the southern crest, and quickly the Boers began to pour men on to the summit to the north. And the troops on Spion Kop found themselves wide open to fire from every direction: Botha had driven his men back to the attack, fearing that if Spion Kop went then the whole of the Tugela defence line would go with it: and he was determined to re-take what he had lost. Thus Woodgate's brigade came under intense attack from every kind of gun, light and heavy, from Green Hill and Conical Hill and Aloe Knoll, whilst a heavy enfilading fire swept them and cut them through from the easterly Twin Peaks. At eight-thirty a.m. Woodgate fell dead, mortally wounded in the eye: Colonel Crofton of the Royal Lancasters, taking over the command, reported back to

General Warren that if reinforcements were not sent immediately, all would be lost. In response to this, Warren ordered Major-General Coke to send up more men from his Right Attack force; and the Middlesex, the Imperial Light Infantry, and the 114th Highlanders received orders to advance and engage. Before they moved out they had the horrifying report that the Lancashire Fusiliers had been mown down in heaps, that they were lying in three-deep rows of corpses with every officer killed or wounded. Spion Kop was a scene of death and carnage that day, with demoralisation beginning to set in below the terrible thunder of the guns.

*   *   *

The Royal Strathspeys advanced up the slope with Bosom Cunningham's loud voice swearing at them. *'Dinna bunch, ye bastards, dinna bunch! Remember the Maxims!'* Hearing the R.S.M.'s bellow, the Scots separated, foregoing the comforting comradeship of a shoulder-to-shoulder advance. Reaching the top they found appalling confusion and heap upon heap of dead. Gazing around with a degree of helplessness at first, Dornoch took the battalion, with the pipes wailing, to the assistance of a large officer wearing the insignia of a lieutenant-colonel who was rushing vigorously hither and thither exhorting, encouraging and swearing. From then on, the 114th were in the thick of an intense fight. Ogilvie found himself in hand-to-hand combat with a huge Boer wielding a rifle-butt like a club. Whistling past his head, the weapon was within an eighth of an inch of smashing his skull. Ogilvie hurled himself at the man, seizing his throat and bringing him to the ground, but the Boer fought like a cat, twisting and turning and lashing out with big fists that took Ogilvie a number of heavy blows on the face. He was saved from certain death by a lance-corporal of the Middlesex Regiment, who held a bayonet to the Boer's throat and, when the man refused to surrender, deftly slid the shining steel into the gullet.

Spattered with blood, Ogilvie got to his feet, feeling groggy. As another Boer came for him, he collected his senses and dived for his revolver, which had fallen to the ground when he had been evading the first swipe of the rifle-butt. Taking quick aim, he fired: the Boer gaped, looking totally surprised, then slid to the ground in a heap. With the fresh arrivals the fighting was now going better for the British in the sector: under the impact of the bayonets the Boers were starting to scatter down the north side of the hill. Within a comparatively short time, the defenders were left in possession, somewhat to their surprise, and a ragged cheer from the ranks sent the

307

Boers scurrying the faster.

Lord Dornoch approached the officer to whose assistance he had gone. This officer came forward with his hand outstretched, and wrung Dornoch's hard. 'Thank you,' he said. 'Your men were splendid. I don't know who you are, but I'm damn grateful! I'm Thorneycroft, by the way. What news from the rear—what's Warren up to, does *anybody* know?'

'I'm afraid I don't, other than that he's sent us to reinforce.' Dornoch brought out a handkerchief and mopped the streaming sweat from his face. 'Who's in command, now poor Woodgate's gone?'

'Damned if I know,' Thorneycroft answered. 'It could be Hill of the Middlesex— he's the senior—it could be Crofton, or it could even be me I suppose. I dare say we shall be told in due course!'

'A little confusing, Colonel.'

'So's the damn fighting.' Thorneycroft shaded his eyes and scanned the slopes below. 'They've reinforced well and fast—those Boers! Must have had men sent down from Ladysmith.'

'How many have we against us?'

Thorneycroft shrugged. 'Ask me another, my dear chap! I haven't the faintest idea, but it's a damn sight more than Buller ever bargained for, I'll be bound!' He added, 'Those Boers are a curious bunch, though—so often they fail to press home their advantage, don't you know. A lack of real tenacity— they're not keen on close-quarter fighting and they run like sheep from the bare steel. But there's one old demon . . . feller with flaming red hair, Commandant Opperman according to our prisoners—he's been chivvying up the burghers no end, putting the fighting spirit into 'em as though he were God in person— it's uncanny! Wouldn't mind him on our side— I can tell you!'

Looking up, Dornoch caught Ogilvie's attentive eye. Casually he asked Thorneycroft, 'Is Opperman still in this sector, d'you know?'

'He's just down there.' Thorneycroft pointed down the northern glacis. 'Down there—with his damn commandos from Carolina and Reitz. They're the strongest opposition we have to face, rot 'em!'

*   *   *

It was not long before Ogilvie became convinced it was a case of now or never. Things were again going badly: the Boers' gunnery was far too good, the British position far too exposed to their heavy concentration of artillery and rifle-fire. The casualties were appalling and the groans and cries of the wounded and dying jagged cruelly at the nerves of those as yet untouched. Water was so short as to be virtually non-existent, and raging thirsts added to the troops' misery. There was the feeling of imminent retreat in the air: and if that order should come through from Warren or Buller, then it might well be too late to cut Maisie Smith out from under the Boers' noses. During the day word filtered through that General Lyttelton was moving the 60th Rifles from Potgeiter's Drift, to head westerly and cross the Tugela by a pontoon thrown across by Kaffir's Drift; later intelligence indicated that the 60th had taken Twin Peaks, and for a while the enfilading fire from the Boers was reduced. Ogilvie took advantage of the lull to talk to Rob MacKinlay. In him, and in him alone, he confided.

'I'm not in a position to tell you much, Rob,' he said, 'so you'll just have to take my word. There's an English girl in the Boer lines, and I've promised to get her out.' He gave MacKinlay as much of the story as he felt able, and added, 'It's not fair, I know, to ask for help, but—'

'You don't think you can manage on your own, James. I don't think so either!'

'You'll come, then?'

'Yes, I'll come. *Look out!*' They both flattened as the scream of a shell came at them: the projectile flew over their heads to burst on the trench farther along. Bodies hurtled into the air and fell back, shattered. Medical orderlies moved up. 'By God, James, this begins to look like another of our good old

British blunders, doesn't it!'

'It may not be, Rob. The Boers aren't having it all their own way. Our gunners are pretty hot too! If only we can hold out till we're reinforced by more infantry . . . that's the thing.'

MacKinlay laughed. 'I doubt if Brother Boer knows just how badly we need reinforcements, James!' He held up his face in an attempt to catch an evening breeze: his skin, like that of all of them, was painfully burned from a day's blazing sun, a day in which the unwounded among the officers and men had seen no water at all to help cool their insides and take the dust from dry throats. 'Well—what's your plan of campaign to be?'

'Simple and straightforward. When the light's gone tonight, we just slip away, down the hillside—'

'*Do* we? And what of the Colonel?'

Ogilvie said, 'I'm saying nothing to the Colonel.' He remembered the way Dornoch had caught his eye that day, and the way he had drawn Thorneycroft out about Opperman for his benefit. 'I'm pretty sure he's given me tacit consent, which of course is not to say *permission*—I mean, he won't want to know, but I do know he'll turn a blind eye.'

'A little foolish, isn't it—on your part and his?'

'I don't think so. As I said, I can't tell you everything. But does it make any difference to

311

you? Naturally, I'd understand—'

'No, no—no difference. I said I'll come, and come I will. But when we're down the hillside, what then?'

'We cut Opperman out from his commando, and make him ride with us to where Maisie Smith's being held. There's Boer dead on the hillside—we'll take their clothing. Opperman's bound to have access to ponies. When we've got Maisie Smith, we rejoin with her.'

MacKinlay raised an eyebrow, grinning. 'Simple—is it?'

'Perhaps a little exaggeration, Rob!'

*   *   *

It had been an appalling day, a day of blood and slaughter on both sides, and a day of complete misapprehension on the part of both Boers and British as to the remaining fighting potential of each other. Louis Botha's burghers had grown despondent that all their gunfire, all the brilliance of their marksmen, had so far failed to dislodge the defenders of Spion Kop; and many of those burghers were slipping away to the rear, going off on their ponies as they had so often done before when the victory did not come fast, rather than face the overwhelming numbers of men that they knew Buller had at his disposal and which they had no reason to imagine he would not commit. On the heights of Spion Kop itself, where these numbers had not in fact been deployed at all, indecision nagged like a cancer at the British command, indecision as bitter as the rain of shells sent down so continually and accurately by the Boer gunners. Those shells were crunching everywhere, wrecking the trenches, shattering even the piles of dead. The air was choked with dust and explosive fumes, and the survivors cried out for the water that never came. The firing-line was approaching utter panic and confusion as the rifle bullets, adding to the shellfire, snicked between the boulders. Sir Redvers Buller had apparently no idea of how badly events were going for his advanced force, and still he sent no reinforcements. By dusk Thorneycroft, gallantly holding on with dwindling numbers, watched helplessly as weary, frightened soldiers began slipping away down the hillside to the rear. He felt a galling sense of having been let down, of having been left by his seniors to defend an impossible position. He saw nothing but defeat looming, though Buller had enough troops at his disposal to send the enemy flying back if he would only order them in.

Worse was to come when Colonel Crofton ran up through the fading light, dodging the shell-bursts. Crofton called out, 'Buller's withdrawn the 60th from Twin Peaks.' He pointed down towards the south, where across the Tugela a bonfire was blazing. 'He's lit that

313

fire down by Spearman's, to guide them in!'

'But ... they took Twin Peaks...' Thorneycroft's voice held the tone of a broken man. *They took them!*'

'Yes, indeed. But against Buller's orders— so he's ordered them back. I'm sorry. It's dreadful news.'

Thorneycroft's fists clenched hard. 'In my view,' he said, 'it's better to save what men we can now, rather than be sent to blazes in the morning, Crofton.'

'I agree, Colonel. I hate to say it, but I do agree.'

*   *   *

Ogilvie and MacKinlay had already detached themselves and were making their way down the hillside when Thorneycroft, in complete ignorance of the fact that the Boers below him were now in open defiance of their leaders, gave the order to withdraw from the heights. At eight-fifteen p.m. the regiments were fallen in and, carrying their wounded but leaving their dead unburied, began to retire. No indication of a withdrawal reached the two British officers in their descent towards the Boer lines. They went down fast, running from rock to rock, wondering when they would be spotted by the Boer outposts, chancing bullets. In fact, they advanced into peace and quiet: no bullets assailed them. They had their choice of

314

clothing on the way down: any number of Boer dead lay around the slope, bodies that had had to be left on account of fire from the British on the heights. Chivalry, at Spion Kop, had with a few exceptions run a little thinner than usual. The Scots officers, after their corpse-robbing, continued their journey in the guise of good, solid burghers. In Ogilvie's mind there was a strong sense of his having come full circle: Kimberley, the Tugela, and now, once again, back to the Boers and Old Red Daniel Opperman. That circle might well remain tight closed . . . Not far to go now, and they had not been spotted. In fact, though they were almost at the foot of the hill, they had seen nothing moving anywhere; no live Boers in sight, but plenty of evidence of the battle in shell-holes and smashed wagons and the horribly dismembered bodies lying in grotesque attitudes; and over all the very smell of death and war.

They came to a trench, approaching it with caution: it was, however, empty of all but the piled dead awaiting burial. Jumping down, they crossed the corpses and climbed out on the far side, and went on into the night. It was a long walk to nowhere. 'They've all gone,' MacKinlay said in awe, a noticeable shake in his voice. 'They've all gone! D'you know, James, I think we ought to go back and report this.'

'Report what? They'll realise at daybreak,

Rob! There's not much point in reporting a vacuum—poor old Buller wouldn't advance, he'd order a Bank Holiday! Besides, it could be just a feint.'

MacKinlay nodded. 'I suppose you're right. But where the devil do we go?'

'Straight ahead—until we meet someone. It's all we can do.' They walked on through the darkness, not seeing even any campfires ahead. It was the eeriest walk of Ogilvie's life. Nothing stirred but for the aasvogels, seeking their meals, finding them, tearing with great beaks revoltingly. It was a long while seemingly before they heard another sound in the night: a sound of sobbing—heartrending, chilling. It was right ahead of them on their track, and a moment later, through the night's gloom, they made out the bowed shape of a man, bending over something on the ground. The man didn't even hear them come: Ogilvie, halting by his side, asked what the trouble was, using the Afrikaans he had picked up whilst with Opperman.

'My son,' the man said.

'I'm sorry. Is he—is he dead?'

'Yes. Torn ... torn to pieces by shrapnel from a British shell.' The man bent to the shattered remains, racked again by deep sobs. 'Would that God would strike down all the British murderers before our whole land and all our sons are gone!'

'I'm sorry,' Ogilvie said again. 'I must

316

disturb you further, I'm afraid.' His Afrikaans had run out now, and he spoke in English, relying on this man having the language, as most of the Boers had.

The man looked up incredulously, and got to his feet. He seemed fortunately to be unarmed. 'What's this? You're British, you—'

'Yes, we're British.' Ogilvie and MacKinlay both had their revolvers levelled now. 'We've come on certain business with Commandant Opperman. Can you tell us where we can find him?'

The man said something in Afrikaans, a sound as of swearing.

'You must help us,' Ogilvie said, 'or I shall shoot you—'

'Then shoot. I wish only to join my son, killed by your guns, killed fighting for his country and his way of life when only seventeen years of age!'

It was a cold night: but Ogilvie felt the sweat start out all over his body. *How did one threaten effectively a man who wished, at any rate in this moment of shock, to die?* With a touch of sheer desperation, he improvised. He said, 'Listen to me. I'm sorry about your son. He died for his country, and I am sorry. But my friend and I . . . we come with terms from General Buller. We want to talk to General Botha—but first there is our business with Commandant Opperman. Many fathers' sons among us British have died too, fighting for

317

what *they* believed to be right. Perhaps I sound pompous, even unfeeling ... but will you not now help your son's cause by putting us in touch with your leaders—so that more of your men may not die? Would this not be what your son wanted? Or is he, by your act, to die uselessly? The choice is yours, my friend!'

Feeling his fingers trembling on his revolver-butt, he waited. The man bent his head, shaking it slowly, then once again got down on his knees as if communing with his son's spirit. After some minutes, long minutes, he climbed slowly to his feet.

'This war will end in defeat for your people,' he said in a broken voice, 'but if I can save some lives on both sides, that I will do. Yes, I will take you to Commandant Opperman, if he is where I believe him to be.'

'Thank you,' Ogilvie said with full sincerity.

* * *

In the laager there was utter confusion: the wagons were being made ready for departure. Trek was in the air—trek back towards Ladysmith or the Drakensberg. It was fantastic and unbelievable. With victory in their very grasp, the Boers were simply melting away, even now entirely unaware of the havoc they had caused in the British trenches. Old Red Daniel himself was a broken man, alone and unguarded in his tent, an easy prey to the guns

318

of the two British officers. He stared with bitter hatred at Ogilvie.

'Mr Bland—or whatever your real name is! You dare to show your face to me! I spit at you.'

He did so.

Ogilvie said, 'Believe me, Commandant, I'm sorry. I've hated my job all along—'

'You are a most despicable person. I trusted you. I treated you as a guest, an honoured guest. I am deeply grieved. You have proved a bad omen for me.'

'I repeat, I'm sorry. But this is war, Commandant—'

'Yes, it is war!' Opperman shouted, getting to his feet and brandishing his fists helplessly. His face was suffused, veins stood out like ropes in forehead and neck. 'Oh, it is war, all right!' Shaking, he sank back again on the chair and put his head in his hands. 'It was terrible. I could not stop my burghers running. *I could not stop them*—even I, even Old Red Daniel! They went, and they went in ever-increasing numbers ... like an ebbing tide along the sea-shore, and I was powerless—powerless! To think I should have lived to see this ... I would have rather been sliced by the British steel, or fallen victim to your own traitorous bullet, Mr Bland—or that of the man who tried in Reitz to kill me—'

'Remember I saved you from that, Commandant—'

'You did—you did. I know not whether to thank you now. My Boers defied me to my face. Oh, things were bad, I know! There were terrible mutilations from the British field-batteries on Three Tree Hill, also from Mount Alice—the guns of your Naval Brigade—the heaviest barrage yet seen. That was early in the battle.' Opperman lifted his head from his hands and stared almost unseeingly. 'What have you come to do now? To gloat? To kill me?'

Ogilvie shook his head. 'Neither. I shall not gloat, Commandant—rather, I would ask your forgiveness if I thought you could give it. We come in peace. All I want is—Miss Smith.'

'I know—now—about Miss Maisie Smith,' Opperman said bitterly. 'To think that I could have allowed myself to be so deluded! What do you want with her?'

'To take her back to our lines. Where is she, Commandant?'

'She is here, of course.'

'Safe—and well?'

'Safe and well. It was necessary to be a little hard—'

'If you—'

'Yes, yes.' Opperman held up a hand, with a curious dignity in the gesture. 'We, also, are chivalrous towards women, Mr Bland. There was no real violence used, I promise you. Go to her and see for yourself. Go to her—and take her out of my sight!'

'You're prepared to let her go, without hindrance?' Ogilvie glanced sideways at MacKinlay, with a warning in his eyes.

Opperman shrugged wearily. 'We don't want her. She is another mouth to feed, another prisoner to be guarded, and she can do us no harm by going back with you. Besides, I've no wish to involve a woman in war when the need is past.'

'I think you're a good man, Commandant—'

'No compliments from you, please. Take the woman, and go. You'll not even need those revolvers you are pointing at me.' He got to his feet again, stumbling a little with the effort. 'Come with me. I'll take you to her, and then bid you goodbye, or good riddance, for ever.'

Ogilvie kept close behind Opperman as he and MacKinlay followed the Boer from his tent and made across the disintegrating laager towards one of the wagons, where a solitary Boer stood leaning against a wheel, smoking a pipe and holding a rifle in his arms.

'Off you go now, Deneys,' Opperman called out. 'Back to your farm if you've a mind to! There's no more need of you now, go away from here before the British come!'

The voice was bitter: it was in truth an unnecessary defeat-feeling that crawled worm-like through Opperman's mind. If his visitors had told him the true state of the British on Spion Kop, that worm would have turned into a ramping lion, Ogilvie thought. Meanwhile

Opperman's voice had disturbed the occupant of the wagon. The canvas at the back parted, and Maisie Smith looked out, in some surprise. As Ogilvie came forward she recognised him, and there was a cry of incredulous relief and joy. 'James! Oh, James love, you've come for me! Oh, James!' She came out like a cannon-ball and flung herself into his arms. 'James, they made me talk, the dirty bastards, but I didn't tell them anything worth while, I swear I didn't, I'm still bloody British and able to hold me head up. Hooray for the Queen, I say, and the good old Union Jack!'

As she clung to him, Ogilvie, looking across her hair, saw in the flickering light of a guard-lantern the look on Old Red Daniel's face. Opperman was regarding him as if he were carrying the plague, as if he could not wait for uncleanness to leave the remnants of his laager. Grasping Maisie Smith, with Rob MacKinlay at his side, Ogilvie turned and walked away, back towards the retreating British Army, his spirits right down in his boots. War was war, but never had it been as dirty as this.

*   *   *

'It's a bloody long way, James.'

'It's further to Hounslow.'

'Don't I know it! Oh God, I hope my baby's all right—'

322

'There's no war in Hounslow,' Ogilvie said impatiently. 'I doubt if baby Alexandra's under any attack—'

'Oh, don't be stupid, you know what I mean! How much bloody further? I tell you, I'm *sore*. This bloody pony's all jog and me bloomers are sticking to me—'

'We're doing our best,' Ogilvie cut in. 'Don't you want to reach the British lines?'

'Yes, of course—'

'Then be quiet, save your breath, and ride.'

There was an indignant gasp. 'You've changed, haven't you, eh? I s'pose I'm not good enough for you now—now you've joined up with the dear old regiment again.' There was silence for a while. Then, complainingly: 'You could have chosen a less bony pony, couldn't you? The one I rode down from Reitz was like a sofa compared to this!'

Ogilvie said, 'I'm sorry. There wasn't time to pick and choose. There seldom is—when you're horse-stealing.' That had been the final bitter act against Opperman: war engendered a need for haste, and three ponies were probably fair enough game. They rode on towards the upward slopes that would lead to Spion Kop, moving as fast as they could through the night. As so many times before, Ogilvie noted the absence of the indigenous black population. Naturally, the native tribes would have quickly cleared the actual battle areas faster than they had cleared the other

323

areas, the areas under a general threat of operations as the opposing armies made their dispositions; but it still felt odd to be traversing an Africa devoid of Africans, innocent refugees from a White-made nightmare. Thinking about the Blacks' plight, Ogilvie felt the sudden pressure of MacKinlay's restraining hand as his friend pulled up his pony, short and sharp. Ogilvie pulled up likewise. 'What's up, Rob?'

'A sound ahead there.'

'I don't hear anything, or see anything either—'

'Be quiet and listen.' MacKinlay cupped a hand over his ear. 'Horses. Or ponies—look, let's dismount and get into cover—over there!'

'Now what is it?' Maisie Smith asked. 'I—'

'Get down quickly—here, I'll give you a hand.' Ogilvie dismounted himself and reached up, taking the girl's waist. She flopped down into his arms, gasping. Ogilvie looked around: there were some handy boulders and scrub, leading to a cleft in rising ground to his left. They led the ponies into cover and had hardly vanished from sight themselves before the hooves of horses were heard clearly, horses moving at a gallop: from the cleft they saw fast-moving men storm past and disappear.

MacKinlay gave a whistle. 'Someone in a hell of a hurry!'

'I caught a sight of one of them,' Ogilvie said. 'I'm pretty certain it was Louis Botha—

324

probably riding to stop the rot!'

'With a report of the true state of affairs?'

Ogilvie nodded. 'Very likely. I suppose we should have tried to take him, but—'

'We wouldn't have had a dog's chance. Come on, James, let's rejoin the battalion before Botha brings his burghers up! At least we can warn the Colonel.'

There was a cry from Maisie. 'What if there's any more?'

'Any more what?'

'Any more Boers, of course—'

Ogilvie gave a short laugh. 'That,' he said, 'is something you'll have to chance, if ever you want to see Hounslow again! Come on, Maisie—mount and ride. It's not all that far now.'

They mounted and rode out, going fast but keeping an extra watchful eye ahead. Soon after this they made out the distant loom of Spion Kop, rearing upwards through the African night. Told what it was, Maisie breathed a deep sigh of relief and said, 'Well, thank God, James, I couldn't have lasted much bloody longer.' When they reached the start of the slope they dismounted finally, leaving the ponies loose, and began the climb, moving as fast as possible for the heights, with Ogilvie giving Maisie Smith a hand up in the early stages and carrying her bodily in the later ones. Above them there was silence: total, eerie silence—no patrols out, no outposts, no sentries, no anything. Ogilvie was gripped by a strong and terrible sense of apprehension: the lack of any activity was uncanny, weird, unnerving. Almost in a whisper he said, 'Rob, it's as though they've all left . . .'

'Yes. God, this is a ruddy mess, isn't it? Of course, Thorneycroft wouldn't know Brother Boer's packing up and going home, but . . .' He hissed out air, through set teeth. 'James, I'll take any money we've pulled out and cleared the summit. Things weren't happy when we left . . . and now the whole place has the smell of retreat. Anyway—we'll find out soon enough!' He reached out a hand. 'Come on, James, let's get on.'

They climbed again. When they reached the summit they found how true MacKinlay's foreboding had been. Spion Kop was totally deserted and abandoned, and there was every sign of a hasty and disorderly withdrawal. Ammunition, empty water-bottles, pieces of useless equipment—and the dead. The dead in hundreds, piled three deep along the trenches, shattered by shell-fire, cut to fragments by the enfilading rifles of the Boer marksmen.

It was an appalling sight, and a most tremendous tragedy: there had been so much individual heroism, and it had been all in vain. The three Britons looked around in awe, scarcely daring to speak in the presence of so many abandoned, unburied dead. Ogilvie walked about dazedly, seeing here and there

326

the tartan and badges of the 114th, still clinging to bodies that were hardly recognisable. Scots and English and Irish, all together—regiments whose rivalries, sometimes bitter, sometimes friendly, had all ended in the one line of trenches on Spion Kop.

It was Maisie Smith who put the situation into words: 'Each side believed the other was winning,' she said in a high, strained voice, 'and each side beat it. Oh, my God, when will the world stop being so bloody stupid, when will it stop making bloody war?'

CHAPTER NINETEEN

Louis Botha's rallying ride had had its effect some of the burghers rode back, among them Old Red Daniel and the remnant of his commandos. Opperman waited with his ponies at the foot of Spion Kop while a few men climbed to the heights. After they had scaled that bloody summit, the men waiting below heard two shots fired, one a rifle, the second a revolver. Then silence. Silence, and a long wait, and then the creeping dawn, dawn that showed Opperman two men upon the summit, waving hats and rifles. At first the significance of this escaped Old Red Daniel: then, as with a blinding light, he realised the truth; and at once sent word to Louis Botha. On the far side of Spion Kop Ogilvie, unknown to Opperman, was making his way down with Maisie Smith and the body of Rob MacKinlay, killed by that last Boer shot to be fired in an extraordinary series of engagements for the possession of the summit. Stumbling along down the hillside, passing unused dumps of sandbags and water-containers sent up earlier by General Warren and which, as it turned out, had never been reported to Thorneycroft, Ogilvie and Maisie Smith began to catch up with the straggling files of the retreating army as it made towards the Tugela. They came upon Warren himself— Warren, amazed and aghast at the turn of events: Warren, whose one wish was to reoccupy Spion Kop—Warren, who was about to send off a battalion of the Royals to carry out a reconnaissance when, at the same time as Ogilvie reported, Sir Redvers Buller arrived from his base camp. Buller would have none of it: he was amazingly still buoyant for the future, but had decided to cut his losses for the present.

'We shall live to fight another day,' he said from horseback. 'This is not disaster, General Warren. I myself shall take over for the withdrawal, and I shall march the men back in good order. First we must build bridges.' His eye lit on Ogilvie: there was a spark of recognition. 'Who are you, sir? I believe we have met, have we not?'

328

'Yes, sir. Captain Ogilvie of the Royal Strathspeys—'

'Ah, yes. And the lady is—?'

'Miss Smith, from Reitz, sir.'

'The one who helped you—yes, yes. Well, I'm glad you managed to bring her out. Well done indeed—well done!' Buller paused, frowning. 'Now I think of it—a despatch has come from Cape Town. You're to have an audience—I believe that is a fitting word— with Lord Kitchener, as soon as you can be spared. My compliments to your Colonel, Ogilvie. I'd be much obliged if he would give you leave of absence to make the journey.'

'Thank you, sir.'

With a nod of dismissal, Buller turned back to Warren. Ogilvie, marvelling at Buller's extraordinary composure, made his way through the mass of men, searching for his regiment. He encountered Andrew Black looking dishevelled and with a bloodied shoulder from which his tunic-sleeve hung in strips.

'So you've rejoined at last.'

'I have.' Ogilvie's face was stony.

'And where's Captain MacKinlay, may I ask?'

'He's dead.' Ogilvie turned away, but before doing so had seen the accusation in Black's face: that accusation would linger, might be reflected in other faces. Ogilvie was uncaring about such accusations: he had lost a friend,

329

and that was enough. The accusation that mattered was the one in his own mind. He had a word with Lord Dornoch, who understood and gave no blame. Ogilvie passed on Buller's message, and was granted the required leave of absence; before starting for the Cape with Maisie, he took part in the march back across the Tugela. On the 27th January, two days after the retreat from Spion Kop, in a teeming downpour, the British infantry of the line made the crossing over Buller's bridges, marching in good order as Buller had promised, and with no Boer attack. The Royal Strathspeys marched behind their pipes and drums, a brave beat of tunes of war that echoed off the slopes of the hills as the regiments and the guns withdrew, the kilted, bonneted pipers stepping ghost-like through the misting rain, the tartan plaids of the Royal Strathspeys drooping from their shoulders. In the sound of those highland pipes there was the promise, and a savage one, of a return across the Tugela in the not far distant future. The men who had fallen were going to be avenged, their sacrifice honoured in victory. Ladysmith, Kimberley, Mafeking would never be left in Boer hands. Lord Roberts of Kandahar and Lord Kitchener of Khartoum were the guarantors of that! In the fierce strains of the 114th's pipers and the strong beat of the drummers, in the tramp of the marching feet of all the regiments, Ogilvie heard that earnest for the future, and was able to find comfort. Buller's simple words had been right: Spion Kop, though terrible enough in its loss of nearly two thousand British lives, was not disaster.

*   *   *

'It's goodbye, I suppose.' Maisie sounded glum, even though she was standing beside the gangway of the ship that was about to take her back to baby Alexandra. 'God, I'll miss you, James. Oh, it's daft—but it's true!' She seemed close to tears. 'P'raps we'll meet again in London when all this is over.'

'Perhaps,' he agreed.

'Kiss me.'

He removed his helmet, and took her gently in his arms. It was to be a brotherly sort of kiss, but she wasn't having any of that. She engulfed him, swamped him; she did begin to cry, and he felt her tears on his cheek. With difficulty he disengaged himself, and patted her on the shoulder. 'There, there,' he said in embarrassment. 'You're going home to your baby, after all.'

She brightened: she was a curious mixture of emotions with everything on the surface, mainly. 'Well, that's true. Thanks for all you've done, James love.'

'Don't mention it—'

There was the blast of a ship's whistle. It

came from another vessel in fact, but it galvanised Maisie Smith, who started up the gangway quickly, then turned to wave. 'Well, ta-ta,' she said.

'Goodbye . . . Dolly Gray!'

She laughed and blew him a kiss. Stiffly, he saluted. He watched her go aboard and vanish into the steamer's interior. It was a transport, and was carrying back a large number of wounded soldiers to Portsmouth and the military clearing hospital at Gosport. A band was waiting on the quay to play them out, and soon the England-bound troops in their sick berths and wheelchairs would be singing 'Dolly Gray' and 'Soldiers of the Queen'. Before the band struck up, Ogilvie had turned away and was marching from the quay, as smartly as Bosom Cunningham, in his clean, starched khaki-drill tunic and his kilt swinging. He had to get back to the war; but he had first to have that audience with Lord Kitchener, and recover the Red Daniel from him, and hand it over to Katharine Gilmour. He went, in fact, straight to that meeting, in a hired brougham from the docks. Kitchener, he had been informed, had virtually occupied Government House, and it was here that the brougham took Captain James Ogilvie. He was punctiliously saluted by an armed sentry, met by an orderly, handed over to a Staff Sergeant of Kitchener's retinue, and thence to an A.D.C. who conducted him ceremoniously over acres of carpet and through magnificent apartments to the presence of the Chief of Staff, whom one might well have thought was the Commander-in-Chief himself, if not the Prince of Wales. Lord Kitchener was sitting at the head of a long, well-polished mahogany table set before a cluster of tall windows at the end of a high-ceilinged and most splendid chamber. Even had Ogilvie not known whom he was approaching, the moustache and the compelling eyes would have been identification enough. Those glittering, piercing eyes, the frown bringing the brows together over them, the heavy moustache failing to conceal the hard mouth, the firmly set jaw—the determined character of Lord Kitchener of Khartoum. And Lord Kitchener, like Queen Victoria, did not that day appear to be amused.

He was, in fact, in the instant that Ogilvie first saw him, engaged in throwing a seemingly heavy book at an officer wearing the uniform of a major-general. 'Take it away!' he was shouting. 'I will not consent to follow their damned printed rot!' Ogilvie never discovered which set of instructions and regulations was being referred to: the major-general vanished as if in a puff of smoke, and Ogilvie was alone, once the A.D.C. had withdrawn backwards as though from royalty, in the electric presence of K. He was rigid with apprehension as he came directly within the target area of the eyes and

333

felt the hard gaze boring into his very guts.

'Well?'

Ogilvie cleared his throat, grasped the hilt of his claymore tightly with his left hand as if to gain courage. 'Sir, I—'

'Silence, sir!' Lord Kitchener seemed to swell behind the polished table, whose top reflected his uniform with its medal ribbons on the left breast. 'Captain Ogilvie, you are a damn disgrace to the British Army—d'you hear me, a damn disgrace!'

'Sir—'

Kitchener's fist slammed into the table-top and made a line of candles dance in their silver sticks. 'You left your trenches to go to the aid of a damn woman, a woman of the damn servant class who didn't matter a tinker's curse to me or England! Worse than that—you were so determined to reach this wretched woman that you failed in your duty, which was to return to your Colonel with word that the stinking enemy was in retreat! Had you done that, Captain Ogilvie, do you know what would have been the result?'

'Yes, sir.'

'Oh, you do, do you?' Kitchener seemed taken aback. 'What, then?'

'Sir, I would have broken my word to a lady—'

'Lady! Lady my damn bottom!' Kitchener, scarlet in the face, waved his arms violently in the air. 'I've told you what she is, and that's that. I will not have damn females *of any class* interfering with my campaigns,' he shouted, in total disregard of the fact that it had been Buller's campaign and not his. 'War's war, Captain Ogilvie, and the army is the army. Now let me tell you what would have happened: had Colonel Thorneycroft known the facts, he would not have abandoned Spion Kop. General Warren would have followed up the obvious advantage. General Buller would have remained north of the Tugela and would have marched upon Ladysmith with his relieving army.' Kitchener lifted his right hand and pointed the forefinger at Ogilvie's face. 'You, sir, and you alone, sir, are responsible for leaving Sir George White unrelieved in Ladysmith. What have you to say to that, sir?'

'Sir, I deny the charge absolutely.'

'*Do* you?' Kitchener's eyes bulged. 'Do you indeed?'

'Yes, sir.' Ogilvie was white-faced but composed. 'At that time I didn't know the Boers were pulling out—it could have been a strategic diversion, a feint. Any information I might have given Colonel Thorneycroft could have been misleading. And in the event, sir, it was seen that the Boers were still present in some force further to the rear. If they hadn't been, they wouldn't have been there to be rallied by General Botha, sir.'

'You are impertinent, Captain Ogilvie.'

'With respect, sir, I don't mean to be. I am

335

simply defending myself.'

'I've had officers cashiered for less!'

Ogilvie said nothing to this; he remained rigidly at attention, hating Kitchener's guts. But Kitchener seemed to have spent the worst of his rage now. He was silent for a full two minutes, two interminable minutes during which he remained staring into Ogilvie's eyes. Then at last he said grudgingly, 'Well, you're no coward, that's one thing in your favour. You didn't run from the enemy, you went to meet them. I like that about you. But all for a damn woman! If I allow you to remain in the army, Captain Ogilvie, you'll have to mend your ways—and not detach yourself from your regiment in action to go off on a whore-hunt! Now to other matters. I've studied your report, of course. Another time, make it more concise—I can't stand *wordy* people. That apart, I find it interesting.'

'Thank you, sir—'

'Don't interrupt me, Captain Ogilvie. You made reference to the Boers' possible political gambits with Germany and France. In reporting that, you may have averted a disaster for your country. Your report has strengthened my hand with Whitehall and I've seen to it that Count Bülow's devilish machinations won't succeed—spokes have already been put in certain wheels and that damned Kaiser's going to feel a draught where he doesn't expect it and won't like it. Detestable fellow, whether or not he's the Queen's grandson, poor woman. He'll not be using South Africa as a testing ground for his damned Uhlan Guards at all events! You've given me what I wanted, Captain Ogilvie. I'm grateful.'

'Thank you, sir—'

'And there's another thing that will have even further reaching results in the long run. In your report you wrote of the Boer field craft, their brilliant use of the natural features of their country, their use of camouflage. I referred to your report as wordy, but on this point I would like more and from your own mouth, Captain Ogilvie.'

'Yes, sir. I spoke of this to General Buller—'

'General Buller has a rigid mind. I have not. Do as I say.'

'Very good, sir.' Ogilvie gave Kitchener a full report of all he had seen of the Boers at exercise and in action, of the remarkable manner in which they could materialise almost from nowhere and cut down a force before that force had realised that a single Boer was hidden in the scrub. He spoke of their very different tactics from the British, of how, in his conversations with Opperman, he had learned the lesson that the Boers never showed their force in the field in the British manner, how they did not march as regiments—and how the British, who maintained their traditional formations no matter what the terrain, could be so easily cut to pieces with comparatively

337

light casualties to the attacker.

'A concept of war, different from Waterloo?' Kitchener asked with a cold, rather contemptuous smile.

'Yes, sir—'

'And it is on the lessons of Waterloo and the Crimea that we seem, in your view, to have been relying so far?'

'I think so, sir. To some extent at all events.' Ogilvie hesitated, feeling keenly his lack of years, rank and experience when confronted by the former Sirdar. 'I . . .'

'Come on!'

'Sir, I was merely going to say, the Boers naturally know their own territory better than we ever can. In that respect, perhaps, it's not possible to adopt—'

'Nonsense—we can learn. We can abandon rigidity of thought and movement. Agile-minded officers such as Baden-Powell . . . a very great deal can be done. I was not unaware of a degree of *senility* in our tactics, of much more flexibility on the part of the Boer—and I am delighted to have your observations made at first hand. I am grateful again, Captain Ogilvie—you have done well. I promise many changes in our strategy and tactics—and soon! For a start you shall talk to my staff officers and thus begin the process of change. Things will not be the same again in the field.' Kitchener smiled once more; the smile was still cold, but somehow, this time, friendlier. 'By the time this war is over, Captain Ogilvie, the British Army will have changed almost out of recognition. I shall see to it. You—and Commandant Opperman—may consider yourselves to have had some hand in that! And now I believe there is something *you* want from me—is there not?'

'Sir?'

Lord Kitchener reached into a pocket and brought out a package: the small bag that contained the Red Daniel. He sent it sliding along the polished table-top towards Ogilvie. 'Take it and deliver it—to another of your confounded women! Not that I'm ungrateful to the lady. That stone has done well enough for the Empire, Ogilvie. It shall now have its place in history.'

'Yes, sir. I—'

'The Boers,' Kitchener interrupted, getting suddenly to his feet. 'The damn Boers . . . they meant to break the Empire! They meant to bring in against us all those who want to see us beaten, while we were facing difficulties. In that, you may take it from me, they've failed. And on their own they're not going to win this war. There have been reverses and Spion Kop's better not spoken of—except for the heroism of General Buller's regiments. But we're going to win, Captain Ogilvie, and I know it, and our soldiers know it, the damn civilians know it, and so do the Boers themselves. Now I'm here, there will be much more despatch towards victory. Do you ever read poetry, Captain Ogilvie?'

Ogilvie gaped. 'Sir?'

'I don't myself usually—still less do I care for recitations. Nevertheless, I'm going to quote you something I read in a Cape newspaper the other day. It impressed me with its basic truth. It's supposed to be the thoughts of an old Boer rifleman . . . lamenting the fact of the British Army being deep in his damn territory.'

He began reciting from memory, never moving his gaze from Ogilvie's face.

'The old, old faiths must falter, the old, old creeds must fail,
I hear it in that distant murmur low,
The old, old order changes, and 'tis vain for us to rail;
The great world does not want us—we must go.
The veld and spruit and kopje to the stranger will belong,
No more to trek before him we shall load;
Too well, too well I know it, for I hear it in the song
Of the *roi-baatje* singing on the road.'

There was little melody in Kitchener's harsh voice, little feeling for poetry; but it was simply said and movingly, and with much sincerity. Ogilvie, long after he had left the Chief of Staff's presence and was making in the brougham for Katharine Gilmour's house,

340

found the sad words haunting his mind. At the same time he found his thoughts going back again to Maisie Smith, and their rumbustious love-making in those secret, dried out dongas on the veld. No doubt he would be passing across that same territory again before long, once Bobs got into his stride—always assuming that the womanising iniquities of a mere Captain of Infantry soon faded from the mind of Lord Kitchener, which it behoved that Captain of Infantry to hope would happen! Here in Cape Town there was undoubtedly optimism, possibly largely Kitchener inspired. Ogilvie could feel it in the very air: the Boers were going to get it hot and strong when the British advanced to seek revenge for Spion Kop.

*   *   *

'It's come to you the long way round, I'm afraid,' Ogilvie said, smiling down at Katharine. 'I was waylaid . . . in the Ladysmith direction.' He shook the Red Daniel out from the wash-leather bag, from the surrounding tissue paper. As he had seen it in old Mrs Gilmour's bedroom at Kimberley, as he had seen it under examination by Wessels and Opperman and Maisie Smith, so now he saw the diamond shine and gleam again, this time in Cape Town's sun. 'It's beautiful, Katharine.'
'It is, truly.'

'Worth all the trouble.'

She looked up into his eyes. 'Do you mean that, James?'

'Of course I do.'

'*Was* it a great deal of trouble?'

He grinned. 'We won't go into that. I brought it back—and that's all that matters.'

'No,' she said in a low voice. 'That's not all. Oh, I'm so relieved you're safe, James ... so happy. If anything had happened to you—I would never, never have forgiven myself. It seems so dull of me just to say thank you ... but I do thank you, from the bottom of my heart!'

Smiling, he touched her cheek with his hand. 'It was nothing,' he said. Suddenly into his mind came an image of old Mrs Gilmour, sitting up in her bedroom in Kimberley. 'It was a privilege to meet your grandmother,' he said. 'And she'll be glad to see the Red Daniel again, once Kimberley's relieved—and that won't be so long now, Katharine. Keep it safe—the diamond, I mean.'

Her eyes were shining. 'I shall keep it very safe, James, for it means more to me than ever now. When the time comes that we have to sell it ... then it'll be like—'

'Don't think about that,' he said, and held out an arm. 'I have a brougham waiting. You know Cape Town better than I. I'll leave it to you to choose where we shall have luncheon, Katharine. But first ...'

'Yes, James?'

He laughed. 'Don't tell me I'm too forward,' he said, 'but I'm claiming my reward,' and he bent towards her. There was a faint blush on her cheeks at his words, but she turned her face up to his, and her lips parted a little. Gently, he took her in his arms.

We hope you have enjoyed this Large Print book. Other Chivers Press or Thorndike Press Large Print books are available at your library or directly from the publishers.

For more information about current and forthcoming titles, please call or write, without obligation, to:

Chivers Press Limited
Windsor Bridge Road
Bath BA2 3AX
England
Tel. (01225) 335336

OR

Thorndike Press
P.O. Box 159
Thorndike, Maine 04986
USA
Tel. (800) 223-2336

All our Large Print titles are designed for easy reading, and all our books are made to last.